AF

MARC E. FITCH

BOY IN THE BOX

This is a **FLAME TREE PRESS** book

Text copyright © 2020 Marc E. Fitch

FLAME TREE PRESS
6 Melbray Mews, London, SW6 3NS, UK
flametreepress.com

Distribution and warehouse:
Baker & Taylor Publisher Services (BTPS)
30 Amberwood Parkway, Ashland, OH 44805
btpubservices.com

Publisher's Note: This is a work of fiction. Names, characters, places, and incidents are a product of the author's imagination. Locales and public names are sometimes used for atmospheric purposes. Any resemblance to actual people, living or dead, or to businesses, companies, events, institutions, or locales is completely coincidental.

Thanks to the Flame Tree Press team, including:
Taylor Bentley, Frances Bodiam, Federica Ciaravella, Don D'Auria,
Chris Herbert, Josie Karani, Molly Rosevear, Will Rough, Mike Spender,
Cat Taylor, Maria Tissot, Nick Wells, Gillian Whitaker.

The cover is created by Flame Tree Studio with
thanks to Nik Keevil and Shutterstock.com.
The font families used are Avenir and Bembo.

Flame Tree Press is an imprint of Flame Tree Publishing Ltd
flametreepublishing.com

A copy of the CIP data for this book is available from the British Library
and the Library of Congress.

HB ISBN: 978-1-78758-384-9
PB ISBN: 978-1-78758-382-5
ebook ISBN: 978-1-78758-385-6

Printed in the UK at Clays, Suffolk

MARC E. FITCH

BOY IN THE BOX

FLAME TREE PRESS
London & New York

'How does one kill fear, I wonder? How do you shoot a spectre through the heart, slash off its spectral head, take it by its spectral throat? It is an enterprise you rush into while you dream, and are glad to make your escape with wet hair and every limb shaking.'
Joseph Conrad

'I shall then suppose, not that God who is supremely good and the fountain of truth, but some evil genius not less powerful than deceitful, has employed his whole energies in deceiving me; I shall consider that the heavens, the earth, the colours, figures, sound, and all other external things are nought but the illusions and dreams of which this evil genius has availed himself, in order to lay traps for my credulity.'

René Descartes

CHAPTER ONE

Gene Hendrickson was not a good man.

That singular thought pierced Jonathan Hollis through the heart as he stood in line and waited to kneel before the closed casket of his former friend. The term 'good man' is generally bestowed upon any male who has reached adulthood without being documented to be awful. It is used far too often to describe the dead, to hide the reality of their true lives, and Gene's somber, muted wake at Marshall's Funeral Home was no exception. Only Jonathan Hollis and the Braddick brothers knew the truth.

Family, friends, co-workers and acquaintances stood in the big, melancholy room and whispered quietly about how much fun Gene was at parties, that he always had a big smile and loved to laugh. But in truth, he was a drunk trying to hide from his past – a past Jonathan shared with him. The mourners milled about like they were lost and trying to find their way home. Some of them assumed Gene's propensity for booze and smiling meant he contained some kind of inner goodness – a light snuffed out when he put the barrel of a rifle beneath his jaw and pulled the trigger. But Gene's death wasn't the tragedy. The tragedy was much bigger.

His obituary gave the usual platitudes, but left out the cause of death, saying only that he was found deceased in his home at 41 Crestwood Terrace. In lieu of flowers, mourners could donate to a charity, but a jungle of flowers surrounded the cheap coffin anyway.

Jonathan understood why others would think well of Gene; he had tried to be a good man, but the burden was overwhelming. They had all grappled with it, trying to live with this secret for the past ten years. Jonathan tried his best to be a good father and husband despite the singular, brutal and unalterable fact that comprised his existence. He wondered how the scorecard might stack up at the end of his life. If no one knew, did it count?

Jonathan stood in the procession line against the wall. Folding chairs arranged in square patterns checkered the center of the room, and mourners – some of whom he recognized, but most he didn't – sat in them, forming small semicircles of quiet conversation. Gene's mother was still alive and seated in a wheelchair beside the coffin, heart so broken her legs couldn't or wouldn't work enough to hold her upright. It was a closed casket. A .30-06 will do to a face what no mortician can piece back together.

Jonathan reached the casket, knelt and, feeling the eyes of the room on him, did his best to say a Catholic prayer to a god he wasn't sure existed. He crossed himself – north, south, east, west – and moved to his right. Gene's mother was receiving condolences, the life gone from her, like a puppet whose strings had snapped. He bent down and kissed her cheek. Her skin was like paper. He had known Mrs. Hendrickson since he was a young boy, when he and Gene would play together on summer days, riding bikes, eating lunch in her home, having sleepovers together with Conner and Michael Braddick. But in this moment Jonathan felt he had betrayed her. He'd let Gene slip away and never raised a hand or uttered a word to stop him. Perhaps, having reached this point in their lives, it was almost a relief. No one wanted to talk about the last few years of Gene's life when the pressure – the guilt and remorse – had truly broken him down, left him a drunken, rambling mess. He was without a wife or children, his friends came and went with the seasons of his insanity, and his job with the town Public Works Department was tenuous at best. Gene had been Jonathan's best friend since they were eight years old, and Jonathan had just watched him wander away into the darkness.

Perhaps he had secretly wanted it.

"He missed you," Mrs. Hendrickson said.

Jonathan didn't know what to say. He couldn't say he missed Gene, but he did miss something, and he wondered if this might have been the best outcome. Was it then the best outcome for himself and the Braddick brothers, as well? Perhaps one less rogue, living reminder of their shared guilt was better for each of them. It was a horrible thing to think, but horrid thoughts had a way of sneaking into the mind.

Jonathan imagined the feeling was mutual between the remaining three of them. Conner and Michael probably wouldn't be upset if Jonathan took the same way out. If he was honest with himself, he was heading down the same path as Gene. His guilt over that night drove him to drink, alienated his wife and seven-year-old son, drove away friends. Sure, he wasn't as bad as Gene. He was at least able to keep the appearance of respectability – a wife, child, house, car. He didn't live like he was raging against life. But still, in the quiet hours at home, the times when he should have been nurturing his small family, he was losing himself down a well of alcohol and remorse. In the end, his demise and subsequent wake would probably not be much different from Gene's. It felt inevitable, as if he'd been suddenly transported to an unfamiliar world and had no idea where he was or what he was doing. Everyone was a stranger and he was completely and utterly alone. Decisions and consequences had a way of doing that.

He wished it was different. He wished he was valued, a positive force in people's lives, a good man who would truly be missed by his oldest friends, but in the end, he was unsure.

All Jonathan could offer to this frail woman he'd known for thirty years was "I'm sorry for your loss." Then he moved down the line of aunts and uncles to mutter the same tired, meaningless phrase while weakly touching strange hands. Mrs. Hendrickson watched him as he went, her eyes wide with rage.

Jonathan spotted Conner and Michael in the adjoining room. The brothers had arrived together and stood together, both wearing similar suits. They had always been like that – a little too similar, too close. They were like two arms of the same body, controlled by the same mind. Conner politely nodded in conversation with an elderly, bald man whose body seemed to shrink from its own skin. Michael kept his hands in his pockets, staring at nothing in particular, barely acknowledging the old man's existence. Conner was good with people – he always had been. Good-looking, charming, with a trendy, close-trimmed beard and well-kept hair, he could feign interest and make conversation with nearly anyone if a situation required it. He was now a manager at one of the major insurance companies in Hartford, cajoling with other executives, entertaining his bosses with sports statistics and the ability to hold his alcohol, taking frequent trips to Boston to discuss God knew what in relation to insurance dealings. He was always destined for that kind of social climbing; his confidence and competence was etched in his genetic code. Conner's chameleonlike ability made people comfortable around him. He conformed to their desires so easily that even he was unaware of it. So he nodded and shrugged and looked at the floor and gave all the physical signals of a man completely aware of where he was and why he was there and how he should act to assure others of the solemnity of the moment, to show the appropriate amount of remorse, whether he felt it or not.

Michael just stared and said little. He was bigger built than his younger brother, but was of such a mind that he could not be bothered with the little inanities that made humans so boring. He was the smarter of the two, perhaps to a fault. Michael was an engineer with multiple degrees, his days spent stress-testing military aircraft to the point they broke in order to find the weakness and fix it. He looked at the world the same way, seeing how it worked, finding the weaknesses and then despising them because, unlike aircraft, human weakness couldn't be fixed. Michael looked uncomfortable in most social situations but seemed especially uneasy at the wake for his old friend. Jonathan could almost sense Michael's thoughts: *Gene broke, Gene took his own life, Gene was weak.* Right now, Michael was probably calculating the statistical chances of people in the room driving home tonight and killing themselves.

Gene had certainly been the most boisterous and fun-loving of their small group. He had been one of those naturally happy people, those who are content with minor lots in life, getting joy from easy, simple things like Patriots football, beer, and a job guaranteed to go nowhere but that paid enough to keep him fishing and hunting with his buddies. Who his buddies were these days, Jonathan was unsure. Gene had married once and then divorced, but even that did not deter him from being the kind of guy who was only looking for a good time and nothing more. Luckily, there were no children from that marriage, and Diana wasn't at the wake. Gene wore his heart on his sleeve, so to speak. Couldn't play poker to save his life because he had the type of face that constantly betrayed his emotions, his thoughts.

That had all changed ten years ago. Jonathan, Michael and Conner were the only ones who knew why, but everyone else saw it. His mood changed. He wasn't a good time at the bar anymore. Instead he became that drunken oaf who would either cry into his beer or start a fight. But, of course, no one would acknowledge the change. They preferred to remember Gene as he had been before and ignore the downward spiral. There were a couple of the bartenders from the East Side Tavern in attendance. They had probably seen it coming a mile away.

Jonathan watched Conner and Michael at a distance and then looked away to the rest of the crowd. He didn't feel he could leave yet, so he waited, shifting back and forth on his feet, hands in pockets, then out, staring momentarily at a generic painting on the wall as if contemplating its meaning, and then staring down at the carpet, tracing geometric shapes in its pattern. He stayed for the penance. He at least owed Gene an hour of his day. Jonathan was comfortable being alone. More and more he found himself alone these days, on the outside looking in and wondering, *What the hell happened?* Usually, the answer to that question was quiet, sad, and inconsequential – something that could only be expressed with a resigned shake of the head, the way one might react upon hearing news that a child was shot and killed in some far-off place. Jonathan caught a glimpse of himself in a large, gilded mirror. He looked tired and old.

He turned and drifted purposefully nearer to the exit. The outer room had couches, rarely sat upon, which looked as if they were purchased at an estate sale. More suits and dark dresses mulling about, people shaking hands, exchanging the same greetings used at other social events, which in reality are totally inappropriate for a funeral. Guests would shake each other's hands and say, "How are you?" and respond with "Good" or whatever they automatically say every other day of the year. Mere inanities, yet uttering it always came with a twinge of guilt or shame. He was sure there was probably some culture in some other country that had a more appropriate way of socializing during funerals. Here, though, death was ignored through vagaries and social convention.

In the corner of this anteroom was an easel holding a large cardboard mosaic with pictures of Gene from childhood through his adult years. Jonathan stood before it momentarily and felt the years slip behind him. There he was as a child. All of them together, smiling at a birthday party or standing on the roads with their bikes. All of them so young, their faces grainy on old Kodak film, their clothes from another era. Certainly, something more than just a friend had been lost. Age. Jonathan felt it. It was more than just growing older; it was a shift from one world to another, leaving behind people and moments – the beauty and value of those moments preserved in two-dimensional still shots of fading, corruptible memories. The past was gone, seemingly eaten up by the mundane horrors of life.

Jonathan leaned close and stared at a picture of himself, Gene, Conner and Michael standing with their bikes on the road, arms and legs nothing but joints and awkward angles. He stared into Gene's young eyes and wondered if he somehow knew back then these dark days were ahead.

He turned to leave and found Conner and Michael standing before him, each a head taller, each mumbling a 'hey'. They all shook hands in the strange way old friends do who know so much about each other it breeds boredom and resentment.

Conner leaned down close to Jonathan's ear. "We have to talk," he said quietly and then stood straight again.

Jonathan looked around and then waited, arching his eyebrows, waiting for Conner to begin, doing his best to be a prick.

"Not here. Can you meet us tonight? East Side Tavern around seven?"

Jonathan said nothing, but nodded. It was an excuse to get out of the house and get a drink away from his wife and son, whose presence during his drinking binges just made him feel more desperate and alone. The brothers walked away and Jonathan watched them go. He then made his exit and walked outside into the deep light of an autumn evening.

Conner's tone was serious, worried even, which was odd for him – a man who seemed unshakeable most of the time. The fact that they wouldn't or couldn't discuss it at the wake made him uneasy. Gene, the poor bastard. He'd become such a drunk in the past few years it was entirely possible he'd broken down and told someone, spilled his guts. He was always the weakest of them in that way.

Perhaps he was the weakest in every way. He had been like a big, dumb, injured animal and every year he became worse. Jonathan had at least been able to discipline himself enough to live with the guilt. He could be a good little actor, go about the stage of life, go through the motions of kissing the wife and kid goodbye and going to work and pretending he was a good little battery in the great machine. It was an entirely manufactured persona, he knew. But it was also his only survival mechanism. Time doesn't heal wounds, he thought, it just hides them in the little, everyday treacheries until you can't tell the difference anymore.

But there were still those times when his heart and mind spun out of control. When the guilt overwhelmed and consumed him. When he would drink himself to sleep and hope to wake in the morning to find the past ten years were nothing but a misstep in a waking nightmare. But it never happened like that. He was trapped, trying to be the best man he could be, while that noxious memory grew tendrils reaching out for the light of day, killing him from the inside out.

Jonathan drove home in the soft light of September dusk. Theirs was a home situated in a small enclave of his hometown. The house was a small but fairly new Colonial on an acre of land that dipped into trees and a surrounding lowland area of swamp and streams. The forest had been carved out of those trees, and the house was surrounded on three sides by remaining tributaries of wet, woody land.

Technically, the forested backyard was considered wetlands and they had to obtain special permission to build. In reality, their property was the lowest point on the street, a dip in the landscape, and all the runoff water flowed into their patch of land, muddied the forest and settled into a marshy swamp between two long, low ridges. In the summer, with the leaves in full bloom, Jonathan could barely see his neighbors to the right and left through all the thin trees with their leafy branches. They had a yard that seemed forever choked with clover and crabgrass, a small patio with a firepit in the back, and a two-car garage that was barely large enough to actually house two cars. He and Mary purchased the property after learning she was pregnant, and, shortly after Jacob was born, they moved into a newly constructed house. The neighborhood was set off from Route 4 – which had the distinction of actually bringing people to shopping centers – and shaped like a horseshoe with a few cross streets. The only cars that traveled the neighborhood roads belonged to those who lived in its confines – blue-collar people who were striving for middle class and almost pulling it off, men who wore work boots and women who were teachers, and combined they were able to make a small family and maintain a small, respectable life.

A small, respectable life – Jonathan Hollis felt he had the small part down, but he was falling further and further from respectability. He tried, he pretended, but in the end he always saw himself as far, far short of that. He felt polluted, forever guilty and small. He had never moved out and away, had never shed the clutches of that small, quiet place that hung like low clouds over his life.

Harwinton was a place of rolling hills and one traffic light. Too small to have its own high school, patrolled by state police because the population of 5,000 didn't require more than one officer at any given time. Jonathan had lived here his whole life. Gene, the Braddick brothers and himself had all attended the tiny elementary school together. They rode their bikes through these small neighborhoods where everything seemed perpetually uphill and made bike riding an arduous task with occasional downhill thrills. Gene had skipped college and gone right to work for the town. Conner and Michael attended the state university, their parents always a bit more well-off than everyone else, and Jonathan attended community college for journalism.

Now, he wrote for the *Gazette*, which was lying on death's door and barely able to pay the bills. Jonathan didn't make a lot of money, and he would probably end up jobless in the next year, forced to join the unwashed hordes of professional internet writers. Mary worked weekends as a nurse at the local hospital. She made more money in a weekend than he did in a week. Perhaps he should just give up the writing completely and get something more respectable, where one works with his hands all day and all week and in the end has something to show for it – a new deck, a house, a building, something more than a five-hundred-word article that disappears into the annals of forgotten history.

Seeing his house, something he and Mary had worked and saved for, brought all of it back. He should have been proud of this place, despite the desperation they both shared in trying to pay for it. But it

was built after that night in the Adirondacks; it was built during this
fever dream of remorse, and, because of all that, it seemed to sag in
under the weight of the past, sinking slowly into the wet soil. Every
time he set foot inside, he felt it sink deeper.

He pulled into the driveway, and something in the trees behind
the house drew his attention. He looked but saw nothing in particular,
as if his animal brain had registered something important but his
civilized, human mind could not put the pieces together. He stared
into the trees that led to that marshland farther back. The leaves
hadn't changed yet. It was a warm autumn, everything hanging on,
living out their last days to the fullest and brightest. No. He didn't
see anything. It was nerves, imagination, ghosts of the past. Jonathan
wandered into those trees occasionally with Jacob, helping the boy
explore the woods the way Jonathan had done when he was young. It
was always muddy, even when there were weeks without rain. Jacob
liked it, but he wasn't the only one. About an acre back, at the edge
of the marsh, they found a clearing in the trees with a small circle of
rocks for a fire and benches made of carved-out deadwood. Liquor
bottles and old beer cans littered the forest floor here. Jonathan
hoped it was teenagers and not some wayward vagrants. He didn't
like the thought of strange men loitering in the woods so near the
home where his boy played and his wife stayed home alone much
of the day. Teenagers being stupid was one thing, but bums using
the clearing as some sort of camp downright disturbed him. Since
making that discovery, Jacob couldn't go into the woods alone. He
always had to be within sight of the back porch and either Jonathan
or Mary would be there watching him. It wasn't enough having to
worry about the bears and coyotes that frequented the area during
the summer; now he had to be concerned about whatever weirdos
could be hanging around in the woods near his home.

He stepped inside, shut the front door, and felt the house sink a bit
more. It seemed strangely quiet. Images flashed into Jonathan's brain
from old, forgotten television programs and commercials that showed
a father arriving home and his family running to greet him happily at
the door. But that was not the case. He found Mary at the kitchen
table, poring over her computer, her thick brown hair resting on her
shoulders, glasses perched on a small nose.

She looked up and smiled with quiet, wet eyes and said, "Are you okay?" He wasn't sure if she asked because of Gene's wake or if it was a more generalized question. Either way the answer was no. How many times had she begged him to come clean? To fess up to whatever was lingering inside him, but he couldn't – he wouldn't. It would destroy everything in one fell swoop. Although, maybe this slow destruction was worse. He couldn't tell and he hadn't the courage to test it.

"Where's Jacob?" he said.

"In his room, playing. How was the wake?"

"About as you'd expect it to be. Lot of people, though. So that's good, I suppose. I'm meeting Conner and Michael tonight. Talk about things."

"That's good," she said. "You all should get together and talk this through. It's been too long, and I'm sure this is hard on each of you."

"Right," he said and nodded appreciatively. He tried to look her in the eyes, but she turned away and that hurt most of all. She hadn't touched him in a couple of weeks now. They hadn't made love for two months. They were less husband and wife now than roommates with a shared responsibility.

"You need to get out more," she said. "You know I worry about you. You need to reconnect with your friends or make new ones or something. Do something you love again. You always just work. It's not a way to live your life."

When they were first together, every weekend, every day, seemed a celebration. Jonathan did things he loved with the people he loved – hunting, fishing, camping with thirty packs and fires and the sweet smell of marijuana lifting into the darkness. They began their relationship under those circumstances – laughter and joy and good times with good friends. But that dissolved away. Friends fall away, children and responsibilities take up time and drive wedges into relationships. The good times give way to those long, gray days of blandness. He supposed it was just life, the way things were meant to be, and accepted it as best he could. Mary felt differently. She tried to jog him out of his despair and laziness. She was probably the only wife in the world who was actively trying to push her husband out of the house to go mingle with his old buddies and hopefully rejuvenate that old spark of life in him. She had married a young, dynamic man who dreamed of being a writer someday, a Hemingway-like creature, who took the world as his hallowed hunting ground. What she had now was a thirty-eight-year-old man who seemed broken, and, unlike her patients at the hospital, there was no way to tell what was wrong or how to fix him. Instead, she could only watch as he descended further into whatever dark depression grew from within.

Jonathan knew all this. He knew what he had been and he knew what he'd become. None of this was what he'd intended when they first wed, but he was so far down this hole he didn't know where to start, how to get back on track. He couldn't give up on this life, this family – it was all he had. He knew it had all started that one night ten years ago, but the past remains unchangeable and so too, it seemed, did his future.

Something had to break eventually. Something would have to give.

Jonathan heard a pair of feet hit the floor at the bottom of the stairs, and Jacob appeared around the corner. The boy smiled, happily yelled, "Daddy!", then ran and jumped into Jonathan's arms. He caught the boy with a *whoompf* of exhalation and twisted his body in such a way to keep the boy's knees from landing squarely in his crotch. Jonathan held his son for a moment, then patted him on the bottom and asked him how his day had been. Jacob was the spitting image of Jonathan as a seven-year-old boy – light brown hair, blue eyes, baby fat melting away, his face radiating innocence that tragically would be lost in time. Jacob was a quiet boy. An only child at this point, and, as far as Jonathan could tell, he would remain an only child for the foreseeable future.

When Mary first announced she was pregnant, he had feigned excitement as much as possible, but inside, he was afraid. Afraid that somehow the sins of his past would be transferred to his unborn son.

Jonathan ran his fingers through Jacob's thick hair, feeling the contours of his scalp, thinking of how easily everything can be broken and praying to whatever god he could find that his one and only son be spared. There was still love inside him; his love raged at times, made him feel strong and even insane with it. But those surges of emotion did not last for long – they couldn't. He looked in Jacob's eyes for a moment before he placed the boy back on his feet and made for the television room.

"Try not to drink too much while you're out," Mary said.

He looked at her. She was still sitting at the table, her face resting in her hand as if she were bored, but looking up at him. "I still love you, you know," she said. "I don't want anything bad to happen to you. Jacob and I need you here."

"Yeah," he said, looking back down at her. "I know."

CHAPTER TWO

Jonathan hadn't been to the East Side Tavern in years. It was their old hangout, but he, Conner and Michael had put it behind them. Gene never had. He remained their regular, their best customer, even when he became increasingly pathetic. Jonathan stopped and bought a pack of cigarettes at a gas station. He didn't normally smoke but wanted an excuse to step outside the bar, take in the night air and escape the Braddick brothers, if necessary. He wasn't sure what they wanted or what they had in store for him, but he remained concerned. The more history people share, the more likely they are to do horrible things to each other.

The East Side Tavern was a single, stand-alone brick building beside a busy road that served draught beer to lonely men and women working through multiple divorces, and underage kids who could fake a decent enough ID to get a shrug from the bartender. Most people drove by and didn't realize it was there. There were a couple of cars out front and more in the back when Jonathan arrived. He recognized Conner's and Michael's cars in the rear parking lot. It was dark now, and the only neon in the bar windows was the open sign, which occasionally shut off early on dull weekday nights like tonight. Inside was a dark hovel with old wooden tables and shadowy booths. The walls sparkled with liquor bottles. The televisions played endless loops of ESPN – old Red Sox games that seemed broadcast from the other side of time. Jonathan saw the bartender – a middle-aged woman with large, dyed blonde hair and a shirt revealing her flabby midriff – serving pitchers of cheap beer with red plastic cups, part of Gene's sad memorial special for the evening. Behind the bar was a large picture of Gene, trimmed with smaller pictures of him in various stages of drunken exploits and a small sign that read, 'We Will Miss You'. He was well known here, and, Jonathan imagined, so were his former friends who had left him to wither in his last years. The bartender eyed him as he walked inside. Five or six bleary-eyed mourners seated at the bar turned, stared hard at him for a moment and then went back to watching colors and figures move across television screens, whispering into their drinks, leaning left and right to converse in muted tones. Everyone seemed strangely familiar, as if they were people he actually knew wearing skin masks, staring at him with an eerie intimacy.

He feared for a moment that Gene had told them stories of his old friends who weren't there for him anymore, who had run off, started families and left Gene behind with his dark and terrible secret. Perhaps those men at the bar were plotting his demise.

He saw Conner and Michael seated beside each other in a booth. A yellow pitcher of beer and several cups sat on the table. They were playing some kind of game like drunken frat boys, trying to flip one cup placed upside down at the edge of the table and have it land inside a second empty cup placed right-side up. It was one of those small competitions that drive brothers, and Jonathan watched as they kept trying over and over in rapid succession. Even after landing one inside the other, they kept going. Conner trying to gently and accurately hit his target with soft and subtle flips of his fingers, only forcing the cup into the air enough to clear the white lip and slide into position. Michael, much more forceful, flipping the plastic container higher into the air, causing it to spin end over end several times before either bouncing off the Formica-topped table or rumbling into its intended position like a nesting doll. They kept going and going at it like obsessives.

As kids, the Braddick brothers were better than nearly everyone else at small feats of accuracy and skill. Not athletes in the usual sense of the word, but rather savants at things most other people thought unworthy of practice. It made them great fun at parties. Conner would perform a card trick and Michael would dominate a drinking game. They were masters – not of games but of parlor tricks. Their funny little skills helped them slide into social circles, made them popular and well liked. Jonathan had tagged along for most of his life, ridden their coattails into adulthood. Personally, he never saw the point of these ridiculous little games.

But watching their cup-flipping at the booth reminded him of when they began to hunt together with Conner's and Michael's uncle when they were all in high school. Conner would fell a buck from two hundred yards with a light and fast bullet; Michael would put a shotgun slug in its heart from fifty feet away because he had baited the deer in with female scent and whistled so it perked its head, exposing its flank. They were good hunters. Jonathan was lucky if he got a doe the entire season, and Gene was largely along for the beer and camaraderie. But Conner and Michael took it seriously, as if it were the ultimate parlor trick – touch the trigger and *poof!* the deer has disappeared.

Even after all this time and all they had been through, Michael still hunted. He was the only one. For what reason he continued, Jonathan couldn't understand. Maybe it was Michael's ability to rationalize and compartmentalize life into little boxes and equations. For him it always seemed so simple, so *mechanical*. Fix the problem; no need to let the defective part affect the rest of the machine. With Conner, he was less sure. Conner had the ability to put something out of his mind enough to pretend it never happened in the first place. His ability to adjust and adapt meant that he was equally talented at covering things up that would impact his life and ambitions. Indeed, the whole cover-up was his idea. He had pushed it harder than anyone, supposedly in order to save their lives.

The Braddick brothers looked up as Jonathan sidled into the booth like a third wheel imposing on an exquisite date. They shook hands and nodded to each other like old business partners. The waitress brought another pitcher and Jonathan poured a cup. He glanced back at the bar and caught some latent stares. The owner of East Side was now behind the bar with arms crossed, watching them. No longer in their suits from the wake earlier in the evening, Jonathan and the Braddick brothers were dressed like every other man in the bar – heavy fabrics, denim and flannel, and old jackets that seemed stitched from burlap, worn when raking leaves on weekends or working on the car. They blended in perfectly, but still the others stared as if an aura of guilt hung over their heads – or maybe targets on their backs.

They quietly toasted their beers. The brothers were a bit drunker than they let on – Michael had a wet glaze over his eyes and Conner was slightly flushed. Jonathan sensed the opportunity to tie one on without judgmental eyes. He drank his beer fast and poured another. He looked at the brothers from across the table. "So. Is this some kind of tribute? A commiseration?"

"Something like that," Michael said. Conner was busy tapping on his phone.

"How's Annie doing?"

"She's fine. Same old thing. New job, heading up HR. We stay busy." Michael and Annie had married three years ago and had been trying to have children ever since. It was a small town and people talked. Although the men rarely spoke, all their respective wives stayed in touch, unaware and unaffected by the wedge that drove their husbands apart. They had all been friends years ago, and despite the busy lives of children and jobs, the women remained friends enough to know what was happening in each other's lives. Mary occasionally told him of Annie's troubles. Jonathan couldn't help but see some kind of cosmic connection.

Jonathan looked to Conner. "It's been a while. How's Madison and the kids?" Conner had a son one year younger than Jacob, a daughter and another on the way.

"I coached T-ball this past spring," he said. "Fourteen little kids trying to run around the bases. It was a bit of a nightmare. Aria is starting school next year."

"Madison make up your mind for you to do that?" Jonathan caught himself being an asshole for no reason.

Conner smiled slyly and drank his beer. He was the most successful of them all, which made sense. He lived in a large house atop a hill in town with isolated and sweeping views. Madison was the archetypal suburban mother and wife, a woman from a moneyed family, who left her nursing job to raise the children, creating a life that was by the book, directly out of a magazine or a made-for-television movie. She determined life should be as proscribed by *Redbook* and planned accordingly. She stayed attractive enough to put on a black dress and wow businessmen at company dinners and fierce enough to run the Parent Teacher Association. Even when they were dating the world could see where Conner's life was leading.

"When's the last time you went out?" Michael said.

Jonathan stared long and hard at Michael. "I haven't hunted in ten years, Mike."

"Yeah, me neither," Conner said.

"I didn't stop," Michael said. "It wouldn't make a difference either way." He shifted in his seat, rocking back and forth slightly like a child grown excited. "Got an eight-pointer last year up at the Gunderson property."

Jonathan and Conner grunted an approval. It wasn't the hunting he missed; it was the way things were before. It soured in his stomach.

Jonathan said, "So what the fuck are we doing here, anyway?" He looked from brother to brother. "This can't just be to catch up. 'Cause, honestly, it's been a long day and we could do this anytime – if we actually wanted to."

Conner and Michael went silent and solemn. They touched their beers with light, pensive fingers, eyes cast downward.

"We need to make a trip," Conner said. "To the Adirondacks. Coombs' Gulch. Opening day of this year."

Jonathan looked from one to the other and then back to Conner, incredulous and growing angry.

"No, and get the fuck out of here." Jonathan moved to get up out of the booth, but Michael reached out and grabbed his arm. It was a hard grip, filled with desperate energy and perhaps rage. Jonathan stared down at Michael for a moment, hoping the larger man wouldn't stand up and make it official. He looked up to the bar. The dying, pale eyes were staring again, watching this little drama unfold. The owner crossed his arms, waiting to see what happened.

Jonathan looked back at Conner, whose eyes were now pleading. "Just hear me out," he said. "It's important. I wouldn't have asked you here if it wasn't."

Jonathan waited and then slowly eased back into the booth. Michael's grip on his arm loosened.

Jonathan poured another beer and Conner looked like he'd just come from the grave.

"There's a road being built," he said, and Jonathan knew what was coming next.

"The state is building a new route off the interstate, trying to connect the towns. They've sold off ten thousand acres of state forest to private developers for motels, gas stations, stores – all that shit. My company is underwriting the insurance plans. That's how I found out. The project starts this spring and it's going right through Coombs' Gulch."

CHAPTER THREE

Jonathan's bachelor party ten years ago was a small affair – just the four of them heading deep into the Adirondack Mountains. They were searching for someplace 'real', a place where they weren't bagging juvenile whitetail with only two nubs protruding from the top of their heads, like they had in the small, heavily hunted forests around Harwinton. They couldn't afford a trip out west to Montana or Wyoming, but the upstate mountains offered thousands of square miles of pure, untouched forested mountains. A place where they could truly be men, communing with nature, hunting, killing together like a pack of wolves. A place where a hunter could lose himself. The long, toothy mountain range was like a rip in time, a place where the past could be glimpsed, where it would seem wholly reasonable for a T. rex to wander out from the tree cover. It was perfect to them – big deer, moose, bear and mountain lions; no need for passports; no trying to pack rifles on a plane. They rented a cabin far outside the small village of Pasternak, a town built in shadow, at the edge of a massive swath of state forest and valley known as Coombs' Gulch.

Jonathan didn't know the trip was coming. He and Mary had rented a hall for their wedding, which was scheduled for the fifteenth of November. It was one of those places that provide a classy-looking venue to churn out two weddings a day, but was really just a money-making machine. It didn't matter to Jonathan. These were things that had to be done. Mary was happy with it, and once all the requisite hoops were jumped through they could finally settle into their life together and let the rest of the world slowly fall away. They were the first of the group to get married, and it became an affair of friends, a celebration of that first leap into true adulthood. Seemingly everyone was involved on some level. Madison and Annie were bridesmaids, Michael and Conner groomsmen. Gene, in all his bumbling around town hall, had managed to become a justice of the peace and would perform the ceremony. It was all funny and joyous at the time, but now seemed quaint and sad.

Conner, Michael and Gene surprised Jonathan on a Wednesday morning as he was leaving for work and dumped him into the back of an SUV and set out for the mountains. They had arranged everything ahead of time with Jonathan's editor and, naturally, with Mary. Mary had let them into their shared apartment at the time and helped them pack up all his gear. They were popping beers in the back seat before they even hit the interstate.

They didn't make it to Pasternak that first night. Too eager to get on with the drinking and partying, they stopped in the small city of Allentown, three hours south of Pasternak. The town's entire economy relied on a strip club owned and operated by the Hell's Angels and attached to a seedy motel in a hidden enclave just outside the town proper. The club was a two-story industrial-looking monstrosity set below hills with a wide parking lot bathed in the neon glow of a nude woman with horns and a tail. It was a Wednesday night, but the lot was half-full of cars and trucks. Gene, Jonathan and Michael were already drunk. Conner took a long pull from a bottle of whiskey in the parking lot.

The doors opened to a purple haze of colored lights. Women danced on stage like snakes rising out of the grass, hypnotizing and deadly. Mirrors lined the walls; dark rooms were set off from the main stage. Big, hard men lurched over the bar, beers in one hand, cash in the other. The four of them joked with the bartenders, bought drinks for the locals, waved cash at the girls, who then came over and sat on their laps and draped thin, strong arms over their necks. Their asses soft and warm; their skin smelled of perfume and sweat and sparkled with glitter. The girls all laughed with them, sold them lies, pretended to enjoy this life and their company. For all their willingness to expose their naked bodies to the world, the girls dancing on stage were the biggest mystery and the boys – each and every one of them – perfectly played their role of the willing and eternal sucker.

Then it was as if something shifted. Jonathan was unsure how long they were there, but suddenly he noticed a strange, new intensity, as if everyone were suddenly plunged into a thrashing, living version of hell. The music grew louder. The whole world seemed lost in an LSD haze. The women danced with renewed vigor; they began doing things to themselves and each other – touching, kissing, fingers reaching into flesh. The club itself seemed to undulate with the hips and legs of living ghosts. Men laughed and fought, cash spilled onto glossy stages, lights shifted. A tight quadricep brushed just beneath Jonathan's nose, and suddenly he thought of splitting a deer open from stern to stern, spilling out the guts, stripping the meat from the bone.

A sweet-smelling, doe-eyed girl took Jonathan's hand and led him from his barstool through a mirrored corridor of violet light. The club suddenly seemed as large as all the world – a maze in which he was now lost and she his only guide. Everywhere he looked there was a distorted image of himself reflected back, superficial and flat and glass. Even now, Jonathan remembered that moment with shame and regret, realizing how he'd never truly known himself. He saw in those mirrors a dopey kid, ugly with flesh and drunkenness, lost in some kind of vague illusion. The entire world was nothing more than a strip club filled with lies of coming pleasures meant to rob you of your very essence. When he saw himself in that moment, hand in hand with this dark-haired, beautiful girl, stumbling along like a diseased cur, it was the second worst moment of his life. He stared into the mirror and something awful stared back.

She took him into a small room behind a curtain. She wrapped her arms around his neck. He stared into those dark eyes. He felt pure rot. He buried his face into her chest. He plunged into her and she raked her fingernails across his back, leaving bloodied streaks across his spine. He knew that he was infecting her with some spreading, moral disease, a genetic mutation that had infected all men since the dawn of time and left the world a horrid place. In the strange light, as Jonathan plunged in and out of her, he looked into her eyes and she seemed utterly different – inhuman, an animal. For a moment in his drunken, debauched haze, he saw her as a buck, a crown of antlers reaching out from her dark, luminous hair. He was terrified. He fucked harder and harder until he finally came and her body stiffened under his melted weight, and he lay on top of her – near dead – while she stroked his hair like a long-lost mother.

Jonathan woke in terror the following day. He was in a bare, cheap motel room and had no recollection of how he'd got there. Gene was on the other bed. Jonathan was in nothing but his boxers. His head lost in a fog; missing memories from the night before came to him but seemed nothing more than flashes of forgotten dreams. Gray light glowed behind the curtains of the lone window of their motel room. Jonathan walked over and peeked out. The strip club was next door, quiet and dark, the hills beyond trapped in a dull shadow. The neon was gone, the multicolored light. Now there was only the pale grayness and cold. In that moment he remembered the girl, the nails raking across his back, her body under his, and he wished he could go back in time and erase it all. That was the worst part of guilt, he thought – the inability to make it right no matter how hard you try. He had done exactly what was expected of him, behaved like an absolute boor, cheated on the woman he loved with a girl who was undoubtedly worse off for having spent time with him. He felt less human for having done exactly what every movie and television show about a bachelor party said he should do, what every woman feared her fiancé would do, for having left an indelible mark on the life of a beautiful dark-haired girl.

He remembered that girl for a moment, and a strange, terrifying image crept into his mind, the flash of a nightmare.

"Jesus, she did a number on you or what?" Gene was awake, lying on his bed with his belly spilling out onto the mattress, staring at his back.

"What do you mean?"

"Take a look at your back in the mirror."

Jonathan walked to the mirror and twisted his body so he could view his back. Five bloodied streaks went across his spine.

Gene walked over to examine the scratches more closely. "Those will heal up in a week. Just keep Mary away." Then Gene shoved him. "Last piece of strange you're ever gonna taste, huh?"

They met Conner and Michael in the parking lot, both bleary-eyed and largely silent. "How 'bout we never do that again?" Conner said, attempting to break the silence.

"That's what we always say after a night out," Gene said. He cracked a beer. "Hair of the dog, boys!" He handed a Budweiser to Jonathan. His head was starting to hurt with the onset of a hangover.

"Fuck it," Jonathan said and took a drink.

They pulled into Pasternak that afternoon. There was a dull, blue gloom hanging over the town as if snow was about to fall. Pasternak was a brief Main Street of brick facades, each a couple of stories high with window shops that advertised power equipment and handmade dresses. The main strip was surrounded by cheap bungalows, originally built to house factory workers during the 1940s war manufacturing boom. Now, it was one of those dying places where children moved out, eager to escape the boredom and the impending sense of doom, and the remaining residents were willing to embrace their oncoming death, easing the disquiet with booze and cheap television. The nearest supermarket was a town away and accessible only by interstate. There was a Sam's Club that doubled as a liquor store, grocery and pharmacy. They stopped and loaded up on beer and liquor, food for sandwiches and snacks with the idea they'd be eating strips of meat from their kills and fish caught in the creek that flowed through the center of Coombs' Gulch. Bill Flood owned the cabin at the edge of the Gulch and had an apartment above a small diner on Main Street.

Bill Flood was one of those guys who aged but never died. His skin sagged heavy off his face, and his eyes seemed to look past whoever he was talking to, out into the oncoming future. He didn't even say hello when they arrived at his front door, but just nodded and said, "I'll get my things." His big frame stooped at the neck, his arms flapped back and forth with his stride, his hands were like the tips of wings. He drove his pickup truck, and Jonathan and the brothers followed him as they dipped into the mountains, the way a boat might drop below the surface of the sea during a storm. They drove north for forty-five minutes on broken back roads that wound snakelike through the mountains. Finally, they turned down a dirt road at a small opening between the silent rock bluffs. They bounced and jostled in Conner's SUV, beer bottles crashing together. It was another twenty minutes down the dirt path.

"Are we sure there's even a cabin out here or has the old guy just lost it?" Gene said.

"Middle of nowhere, boys," Conner said. "You can forget about civilization out here. No grocery stores, phones, nothing but trees and hills." And that was the point: true hunters living off what they caught, away from all the bullshit of modern life. Conner gloried in it.

The cabin was larger than they had expected, a welcome surprise. It was more of a house with two floors, dormer windows looking out into the trees like a pair of eyes, three bedrooms, a front porch with wicker furniture and a barn in the back with a massive firepit.

Bill got out of his truck and flapped his arms to the front door on pure autopilot, his mind a million miles away.

Jonathan looked at the forest surrounding them. The trees were truly dense here, black-and-white slash marks that built up layer on layer until fifty feet out was just a solid wall of wood. The air was cold and thin, making Jonathan feel as if he were trying to breathe in space.

"This is a big place," Conner said to Bill. "You don't live here instead of in town?"

Bill didn't even stop walking to and fro, doing whatever he felt was necessary for their stay. "Too far from town for my age," he said. "I can't be hauling food and everything out here." He stopped for a moment and looked at the four of them. "You boys be careful out here. One of you gets hurt and there ain't no one else can help you. Nearest hospital is about a two-hour drive from here. Your nearest neighbor is over that ridge of mountains." He pointed to some peaks that marked the eastern ridgeline of Coombs' Gulch. "Had a couple guys up here once; one of 'em fell out of his tree stand, broke his leg. Damn near had gangrene by the time they got him to the hospital."

The inside of the cabin glowed dull with wood. Dust swirled in sunlight that streaked through old, drafty windows. The furniture was circa 1970s, old couches that itched your skin, a table and chairs probably picked up at a garage sale and single beds that looked built for children rather than full-grown men. Bill waved them over to a map encased in glass and hanging on the wall. The Gulch was a five-mile valley running north to south between two ridges of mountains, a deep scar through the Adirondack range. "You can hunt or fish or do whatever you want in the Gulch," he said. The cabin was at the southernmost edge. "The creek is good for trout. A couple years back I had a guy bag a moose up here. Be careful around them, though. They're angry animals, not like your whitetail that'll just turn and run."

"Any other hunters up here?" Michael asked.

"No. No other hunters. Nobody hunts these parts. Most people usually go south of Pasternak. Good hunting down there and not so far away."

"The hunting is good up here, though, right?," Gene asked with a nervous laugh, hoping their money hadn't been wasted.

"Better hunting up here," Bill said. "But I'm the only one that has any property, and I keep 'em off. The first thousand acres going north is mine; the rest is state land."

"Moose, huh?" Gene said.

Bill looked them up and down, clearly eyeing them as a group of weekend warriors who had little business in such a place. "If you didn't bring enough firepower, just let them walk on by. Otherwise you're gonna get hurt."

"Would a .30-06 do the trick?"

Bill turned toward Michael for a moment and then back as if he'd heard a familiar sound. He looked out into the trees through a window. "Yeah. That'll do it."

There was a two-way radio in the house with two channels – one to Bill's apartment and one to the nearest state police barracks.

"They probably couldn't get out here if they had to," he said.

Bill finally left, his old pickup rumbling down the road and suddenly buried by the trees. The silence was overwhelming.

"Don't even hear any birds up here," Michael said.

"That's 'cause they're terrified of the big, bad hunters!" Gene said, slapping him on the back.

The first night, they drank beer and liquor and lit a bonfire in the back. Together, they sat at the edge of Coombs' Gulch, getting drunk and laughing, the flicker of orange fire dancing in the darkness.

The fears of ancient man crept into the back of their minds, and, looking out at the immense darkness of Coombs' Gulch, they all felt a little uncomfortable. That first night, while the others kept their eyes on the fire to avoid staring out at the forest, Jonathan snuck glimpses into the blackness. He felt it cloister around him, reaching dangerous tendrils of cold over his shoulders. He felt that ancient presence in the primordial world that forced men into caves with fires just like the one dancing before him. In those endless trees of Coombs' Gulch were the sounds of rustling dead leaves and footfalls in the night, slight affairs, barely audible above the sound of the crackling fire. For a moment, Jonathan thought he saw something look back at him. He straightened his spine and nerves sparked needles throughout his body. It may have been a trick of light, but he was sure he saw something inhuman exhale a puff of hot breath that rose out of the darkness into the cold night air.

Jonathan told himself it was just his imagination. But he remembered that moment for years to come. He was sure they all felt it. He was sure they drank and joked and laughed to keep that frightening darkness at bay. That first night, he wondered if they were in over their heads – they were not great hunters but still-frightened children wandering and lost in a cold world.

The first morning out they traveled up the west side of the valley. It was early and cold, and their breath formed clouds that dissipated into the miasma of trees. The black spruce was thick, the lower branches like sharpened spikes of some medieval torture device. They could barely get through it without impaling themselves and began to wonder aloud if they'd been had, if old Bill Flood had rented out his cabin with tales of deer and moose when it was just a dead, forgotten wood. But because of the density of the trees they couldn't help but find the deer trails – they were practically the only way to get through the area. They followed the pellet droppings and spruce trees with the bark scraped off where the bucks sharpened their antlers, down to the vein of water at the base of the Gulch that flowed through an open field of tall brown grass bordered by the thick forest. Jonathan was the man of the hour, so when they finally spotted a large herd at the river's edge, he lined up the shot first while Conner zeroed in on a second. Jonathan had a good-sized buck in his sights – the biggest he'd ever taken – but for some reason, when he squeezed the trigger, he could only think of that girl from the strip club, Mary, and his suddenly tainted future. Somehow, it all felt like a giant kill shot.

The impact of the bullet rippled the buck's thick skin, and he took off bounding toward tree cover, disappearing in the brush. Conner put down a doe. It was a vital, precision shot. She dropped like a sack of rocks. Gene accompanied Jonathan into the woods, following the flow of blood that grew heavier and heavier and puddled on the dead leaves until they found the buck panting and moaning beside a massive uprooted tree, whose root system resembled a cave festooned with dirt and moss. The buck panted heavy and hard with its small tongue protruding slightly from its nimble mouth. He was the biggest whitetail Jonathan had ever bagged. Easily two hundred and fifty pounds with twelve points on him. Gene clapped him on the back and said, "Now we gotta drag this son of a bitch all the way back." Jonathan put a nine-millimeter handgun round in the buck's head to finish him off. They gutted him right then and there beneath the cavernous root system, the dark blood and intestines spilling out onto the dead leaves and cold ground, steam rising up from the buck's body cavity. The smell was always the same, raw and sickly sweet. Jonathan stared into the guts of the beast and thought he saw something. Like an ancient shaman who saw the future in the innards of a tribal kill, Jonathan saw a face staring back at him – a moment that left him with a feeling of dread, of being watched by the dead.

Jonathan and Gene took turns dragging the carcass back a couple of miles to the cabin.

Conner and Michael were already there, the doe strung up in the barn, the meat settling and cooling in the cold air, their clothes spattered with blood.

"Red in tooth and claw?" Jonathan said.

"We'll cut her up," Michael said. "Eat good tonight."

That was what the first two days were. Hunting during the day, eating and drinking at night, trying to reclaim a heritage lost on American men. They were living at the edge of civilization, raging against the darkness and the loss of existing in the modern world.

Those couple of days were the last good memories Jonathan – or any of them – had from that trip. Perhaps even from life itself in the ten years since.

It was the fourth and final day of the trip when the world came to a sudden halt. The week had gone spectacularly – Jonathan, Conner and Michael had all bagged deer. The fishing had been solid, and the nights around the fire were full and true, with the fire keeping their collective fears at bay. Gene remained at a loss for a trophy. After a morning in which they all came up empty-handed, they decided to put down the rifles and go on a day-long bender.

But as night grew heavy, they fell into that state of mind in which one drunken idea builds off another and another until they were challenging each other to do something dumb. They teased Gene for coming up short, and by night he was growing angry, saying that he would go out into the night with one of the hand-held spotlights and bag a night kill. The deer see the light and stand up straight and tall, eyes shining yellow in the dark, the same way they do in the headlights of an oncoming vehicle. Despite spending the entire week hiding from the overwhelming darkness of Coombs' Gulch at night, they suddenly thought it was a fantastic idea. They already had a freezer full of meat and fish. If they took another deer, they'd have to strap it to the roof of the SUV. But then they could drive it victoriously back into Pasternak and drop it off to Bill Flood as a thank-you for letting them rent the cabin.

Gene grabbed his bolt-action rifle and Jonathan took the mini-spotlight from the SUV. But as they donned their gear, their spirits changed; it wasn't about getting Gene a deer or showing off for the locals. It was something deeper, something more challenging. They had spent the entire week staring out at that darkness in the forest with a brooding, nibbling fear in their guts. It wasn't about hunting now; it was about proving themselves, about venturing out into that darkness to show they were unafraid of that ancient terror. The joviality became more somber. They all sensed it; like ancient man, they all knew there was something *other* out there, and now, in their drunkenness, they prepared to face it.

Michael took a bottle of whiskey to keep their blood and courage flowing, and, together, the four of them stepped away from the light of the cabin and the drone of the gas-powered generator and into the dark silence. They found the nearest deer path and made their way to a small ridge, using only their flashlights. They knew that just a hundred yards away the creek that bifurcated Coombs' Gulch lazily rolled over rocks and between grassy tuffets. The four of them settled down behind a hillock rimmed with shrubs, and Gene put the butt of the rifle into his shoulder, sighting down the scope but seeing nothing in the night.

Jonathan switched on the spotlight, and the world was suddenly cast in shadow and light, the long grass around the creek bed seemingly inter-dimensional, waving slightly as if in a breeze, an entire universe hiding just behind each individual stalk. The light reached out and showed the immense cold and darkness beyond its reach. They were all stunned for a moment, staring out at that strange, inverted world, until Gene spotted two glowing animal eyes at the edge of the darkness. They were high off the ground, too high for a deer. Gene sighted in; the others saw the eyes shine for a brief second – so quickly that ten years on they would each wonder to themselves if they saw anything at all. Jonathan didn't recall seeing the body of what could only be a moose, or the largest stag in history, but he remembered the eyes lighting up and glaring at them for that brief second. Jonathan tried to say something – he couldn't remember now what he meant to say – when Gene fired and the deafening crack echoed over all of Coombs' Gulch. Gene was always a sporadic, impulsive man. He fired and the eyes blinked out of existence.

Gene was up and over the hillock before the rest of them, whooping it up. "I know I got him! I know it! A perfect shot, center mass! I know it! Did you see the size?"

Gene was running, stumbling through the underbrush toward the creek, the image of his big, burly body charging out through the corona of the spotlight toward his kill forever etched in their memories.

Then suddenly he stopped his joyous yelling and there was nothing but silence. Jonathan, Conner and Michael saw the cone of his flashlight stop beside a massive wild raisin bush. Then came the most god-awful wail any of them had ever heard from a human. It didn't sound like Gene's voice but like an animal. It wasn't loud; it wasn't born of pain, but rather it was a slow, mournful cry – a fading terror, as if he were falling off a cliff – a cry against life itself and all the coincidences, machinations and riddles.

When they reached Gene he was on his knees sobbing, grabbing at the ground as if he were trying to dig into the cold dirt with his clawed hands. Before him was the body of a boy. Scrubby jeans, dark jacket now sprayed with blood and brain matter. His hands and neck were pale white, his hair black and slicked down. His face was broken like a porcelain doll. The bullet moving at 3,000 feet per second entered his skull, fragmented and released all its energy. Where his left eye had been was a star-shaped hole the size of an orange that reached arms and cracks across the rest of his face.

He couldn't have been more than ten years old.

Steam rose from the red-and-black opening in his head, twirling in the light of their electric torches, and all around them the Gulch came alive with the sound of movement as if a stampede had suddenly been loosed. Dead leaves crunched under hooves, saplings bent and snapped, the ground itself seemed to shake, the air electric as seemingly every living thing in Coombs' Gulch stirred to life and ran.

Their attention shifted from the boy to the swirling maelstrom throughout the surrounding forest. The force was overwhelming. They clutched their rifles.

Jonathan turned the spotlight out toward the tree line, but there was only darkness.

CHAPTER FOUR

Two weeks later, Gene pronounced Jonathan and Mary husband and wife as Conner and Michael, dressed in tuxedos, watched on, standing beside him like sentries. Mary's eyes lit up when Jonathan said, "I do." His heart was consumed with guilt when she slid the ring on his finger.

They panicked the night Gene shot that boy. They were drunk. It was pitch black – not even a moon – and they were in the middle of nowhere, living out every hunter's worst nightmare. The whole Gulch was filled with movement and they were terrified. Looking back, Jonathan wasn't sure what he'd been more terrified of – the fact they'd just killed a child or that someone might be there in the woods who'd witnessed it. But the sound was too great to be any one person – it was like a fast-moving river and the four of them a small rock in the middle.

Gene was still crying, pulling at the boy, trying to revive him, trying to check him for a pulse until Michael decided to end the lunacy and dragged him away from the body like a man handling a small dog.

"Where did he even come from? What the hell is he doing out here?" Michael was screaming, raising his voice over the din of Gene's breakdown.

Conner was talking about calling 911 and what to tell them. "It was an accident! We saw the eyes!"

"Those eyes were eight feet off the ground! A kid's eyes don't light up! It was a moose or something, it had to be!" Gene sat on bloody grass, rocking back and forth, his voice trembling "I didn't do it. I didn't do it. It's not right. It can't be…"

Jonathan stood staring down at the boy with a star-shaped crater where his eye should be. Michael searched the tree line and the creek bed with the spotlight, trying to find where the boy had come from and what he was doing there. Conner weighed the possibilities, how this might all turn out.

The boy was dead. There was no one else in Coombs' Gulch.

Michael searched high and low that night, but there were no other people, campers, hunters – nothing.

And there was nothing that would bring the boy back from the dead. Involving the authorities, at this point, would be futile. Decisions had to be made. There was no life to save other than their own. It would be irrational and unreasonable to ruin their lives and futures by going public with the accident. No good could come of it.

"We would be on the hook for murder, manslaughter, whatever it might be, but it would certainly mean careers ending, relationships ending, public shame and prison." Conner was exasperated, his voice growing louder with each breath. "And why should we have to face that? Where are this kid's parents? What the fuck is he doing out here in the freezing night miles and miles from the nearest town? We saw the eyes in the spotlight! It was a clean shot! Where the fuck is the goddamned deer?"

The world would have no sympathy for them. It isn't just hunters who shoot to kill; courts and newspapers can sometimes do worse than a gun. Gene was still too distraught to think, but Jonathan, Conner and Michael stood in the night staring at each other and knew beyond a shadow of a doubt that this accident would ruin their lives. There was no one else for miles around. It was the middle of the night and they were alone. It seemed the best thing for everybody.

"This is the only way we'll still get to live our lives," Conner said.

"It's not our fault," Michael said.

"What would Mary say?" Jonathan said.

"Mary isn't going to know. Two weeks from now, you'll get married and go on to live your life the way you're supposed to. This is a fucking fluke. It's not our fault. What is he even doing out here?"

"Don't they always say the cover-up is worse than the crime?"

"Not this time," Michael said. "And only if you get caught."

Michael and Conner hiked back to the cabin while Jonathan waited with Gene, who had now gone silent, sitting in the tall grass, wet with the boy's blood and cold condensation. They returned with a thick, airtight plastic trunk from Conner's truck, a military-grade storage container meant to keep gear outdoors for long periods of time, immune to water, rot or rust. They brought shovels and a pickaxe from Bill Flood's barn. It was two in the morning and freezing, but they were sweating, digging, chopping through the stony soil, digging deep enough that it wouldn't be found. The sealed trunk ensured bears couldn't smell the body or that a wayward hunting dog wouldn't bring a boy's desiccated hand back to his owner instead of a turkey. They laid the boy in the trunk, bending him into a fetal position so he fit. Conner locked and sealed it, and together they dropped the trunk into the ground beside the massive wild raisin bush where they found him.

The work took all night and by the end they were dead tired, dazed and no less guilty.

It was all for nothing, Jonathan thought. Here he was now, sitting before Conner and Michael in the East Side Tavern, his childhood friend dead, his own life in shambles under the burden of that one night, and now he was being told he had to go back and relive it – to dig it all back up.

A tree falling in the forest may or may not make a sound, but the death of a child reverberates the world over with or without a witness.

Jonathan felt the world drop out from beneath him. "I can't," he said. "It's too much. I don't think I can do this."

"They're going to be clearing out the forest and digging up the ground," Michael said. "It's only a matter of time."

"I can't, it won't matter."

"It will matter," Conner said. "Everything we have now, our families, our lives, will be gone. It's still out there, and they will find it, and it will be all too easy for the cops to figure out who it was."

For years afterward, Jonathan had scanned missing person reports, news sites, online databases, anything he could find for a sign of the boy they buried in a box in the woods. He was sure the others had as well, trying to see if and when the axe would fall. He combed through the seemingly inexhaustible lists of the missing, the vanished, the ones who had been given up on by all but their parents, and even the parents – grown so weary of the search and not knowing – were relegated out of news reports to poor webpages where their child was nothing more than a needle in a haystack of other special and forgotten children. He looked through them for years. He pictured each boy with a giant star-shaped cavity in his face, and each time that horror anchored his guilt. There were plenty of boys who resembled the boy in the woods, but the details were all wrong; a kid who goes missing in Colorado probably has little chance of showing up in the middle of Coombs' Gulch near the Canadian border. Not impossible, but not likely.

But even more convincing than the lack of any picture, and without any bit of rationality, was that none of them felt right; there was not that blazing moment of recognition where the ancient, evolutionary part of the brain that puts faces together cries out and says, "That's him." Even though Jonathan couldn't quite be sure of his features, there was something inside him that screamed he would know the boy when he saw him. It was the same something that made him shake his head when he gazed upon some other black-haired boy who wandered away from home never to be seen again.

Despite years of searching, there was no record of a similar-looking boy missing in that area. No reports of pleading and terrified parents. No news stories of a body being uncovered in a remote part of the Adirondacks. It was as if he'd never existed, and in one way it was a relief, but in another, more tragic way, it was worse. Had no one cared enough to look for him? Was he a tortured creature totally alone in the wilderness? Jonathan eventually gave up the search. After this long, if there was no sign of him in the world, there probably never would be.

It made him question his sanity, whether the incident that night had even occurred, whether they had somehow all just imagined it together – one drunken, shared hallucination.

But no. That was impossible. The gunshot was deafening. The eyes in the night were bright yellow. The steam rose from the bloodied hole in his eye socket and curled in the night air. He could remember the goddamned smell of it. Jonathan's life was a spent shell of what it should have been, and Gene was dead by his own hand – a rifle shot under the chin. It was all too real to have been imagined.

"There's never been any report," Jonathan said.

"You think we don't know that?" Conner said.

"It won't matter once they find it," Michael said. "We don't know for sure there hasn't been a report, and it won't matter. Once they find it they'll have to investigate. They'll figure out cause and approximate time of death, and the first goddamned person they're going to ask is Bill Flood. It will probably take them a week before they're knocking on our doors."

"I just don't think I can go back there," Jonathan said.

Michael turned his head away, sighing with frustration, perhaps disgust.

"This is not about us," Conner said. "It's about Mary and Jacob. It's about Madison and Aria." Conner looked at Michael. "It's about Annie and the family you're trying to have. This blows open and our lives are over. Maybe we were wrong with what we did, but admitting to it now would just be worse. We owe it to the people we love to make sure this is gone forever."

Conner was speaking in platitudes, Jonathan thought. Ripping lines he'd heard countless times in made-for-television movies or paperback thrillers. It made the whole notion of it more unreal, as if it were all scripted and they were just reading their lines. He had no choice but to continue. *The show must go on.*

Michael's eyes were dead serious with a glaze of ice over them. "You don't have to convince me."

Jonathan said nothing but stood and went to the bar for another pitcher of beer. He slugged down a rocks glassful of Canadian Club while he was there.

The bartender eyed him. "You okay?"

"No." He took the beer and sat back down at the table. He looked at Conner and Michael. "So what are you suggesting?"

Conner, realizing that he was finally reeling Jonathan toward this terrible shore of reality, held his hands up in a calm, stabilizing manner – likely taught to him by Human Resources. "We just have to go up and move the trunk," he said. "I've already arranged to rent the cabin again from Bill Flood."

"Jesus. He's still alive?" Jonathan said.

"Yes. And that's part of the problem. Any records he has will have us on them at the same time that kid went missing. Plus, he's got a mind like a steel trap. Remembered everything about us when I called. One of those old guys who can't find his way home, but remembers everything about you. He's selling his land to the developers. This is the last shot we have at this before they break ground and start digging in the spring. We just go up there like we're going hunting again, dig up the box and move it somewhere no one will ever find it."

"What makes you think we can even find it once we're up there?" Jonathan said.

"Have *you* forgotten where it is?" Michael said.

Jonathan looked down at his drink. "No, no, I haven't." Then, "Where do we move it?"

"There's a lake on the other side of the western ridge," Conner said. "Part of the deal for the roadway and the developers was that section of forest would be preserved indefinitely. The lake there is deep, two hundred feet, easy. Made from an old glacier back in the ice age. It's even more remote than Coombs' Gulch."

"How far?"

"Seven miles."

"Seven miles? Are you kidding me? Hauling that thing through that terrain?"

"We put some holes in the trunk, load it with rocks, take it out to the center of the lake and sink it. It'll never be found."

"It," Jonathan said.

"That's the best I can do. I don't know what to call...whatever. That's the plan. It would probably be a two-day hike, considering the gear. We'll need a raft to get the trunk to the deepest part of the lake. After that we haul ass back to the cabin and just...just forget about it."

"This is so wrong," Jonathan said.

"It's been wrong since the beginning," Michael said. "Wrong would be letting it ruin everyone else's life besides our own. This is the best we've got."

There it was, Jonathan thought, the same excuse used around the world for centuries to justify every lying, cheating and murderous man of means or politician to cover up his crime after the fact. But they weren't even men of means; they were just three losers sitting in a bar, trying to eke out a middle-class existence. Their downfall would ruin the lives of the people they loved. For everyone else it would be a quick headline in the newspaper.

But still, the thought of Mary or Jacob knowing what he did – and subsequently who he truly was – meant he had to do it. Exposing his soul terrified him more than any prison sentence and more than any seven-mile hike, hauling the remains of his life over a mountain so it could sink to the bottom of a lake. Jonathan realized just then that *he* was the most frightening thing he'd ever encountered. He thought suddenly of that night in the strip club, of stumbling hand in hand with a dancer and catching a glimpse of a pathetic and evil creature in the mirror. Since that night in Coombs' Gulch, he had lived with that mirror image; it was horrible and twisted and inescapable. He was no longer sure which version of himself was true, but he didn't want to gaze upon it anymore and never wanted his wife and child to see it – ever.

"No one else will be up there?" he asked.

"According to Bill, no one has been up there for years. Hunting went to shit. Place is all dried up. He even tried to convince me not to waste the money because the animals had all cleared out. I told him we just wanted to get away, old times' sake."

Jonathan looked at the Braddick brothers across the table, both of them staring back in unison like a pair of snakes, entrancing him with their eyes.

"How long have you been planning this?"

"I found out six months ago," Conner said.

"And you're just telling me now?"

"We didn't think you'd say yes until now."

Jonathan slowly moved his finger around the rim of his beer. "Did Gene know?" He already knew the answer, but he wanted to hear them say it. He looked back and forth between the two brothers.

Conner sighed. "We told him last week. We thought he could help convince you."

Jonathan stared at them. "You're the reason he's dead. The two of you. You fucking killed him."

"No," Conner said. "Gene killed himself when he pulled the trigger and if we don't fix this it will kill the rest of us, too."

Jonathan drove the short distance home that night drunk, the heavy, impenetrable darkness of a moonless night surrounding his car – the lone beacon of light on the roads. There were no streetlights in their small town; the setting sun plunged the area into darkness. He turned into his wooded neighborhood and it seemed abandoned, every house light off, everyone unconscious in their sleep, a whole world slumbering away, blinked out of existence. Up ahead – just beyond the cone of his headlights – some animal trundled across the street and looked up at his encroaching vehicle. Its eyes shone two spectral, glowing circles in the night before it scurried into the underbrush. The truncated lope told him it was a large raccoon, but in his dreamlike state of fear and drunkenness, he pictured it as a skinny, naked child demonically galloping across the roadway in a horrifying animal pantomime. Jonathan wondered, deep in the reaches of his most delusional suspicions, what had truly happened that night in Coombs' Gulch. All of it – the terror, the fear, the shame, the years of searching – made him question the very facts of the night that ruined his life.

Jonathan unlocked the door and walked into a silent house, both Mary and Jacob asleep. He walked upstairs to change and pass out in bed. He saw Mary breathing lightly beneath the sheets. Beside her a smaller figure, curled into a ball and tucked back into her belly. Seeing them there together in a symbiotic-like unity made him feel achingly alone, as if he had no part in Jacob's creation. No. He was meant only for destruction. *Perhaps that is all men are good for*, he thought, *tearing down, blood, death*. Perhaps that served a purpose, but it was not the purpose he glimpsed while watching Mary and Jacob curled together, breathing in unison.

He took some blankets from a wicker bin in the living room and fell asleep on the couch.

CHAPTER FIVE

He told Mary they were all taking a trip – a final send-off for Gene and a chance to rebuild their friendship. It was a lie, but it seemed to give her hope and relief, as if she might finally be unburdened of the tension that radiated within her husband and darkened the nice home she was struggling to build. Mary was, of course, supportive. She always said the *right* things to him, but that was all she said, and the words rang empty. For the past several years she spoke to him the way a stranger with a modicum of social awareness would converse with a new acquaintance. But he could see the relief in her eyes, the way her body somehow relaxed upon hearing the news that he would be gone for a few days, that he would be gathering with his old friends. He saw her hope that maybe a piece of the man she fell in love with would be revitalized. More than once, Jonathan had thought of divorcing Mary so she would no longer be infected by the sins of his past, and he was sure the thought had crossed her mind at some point, that she had wondered how her life had gone from such hope and joy to a morass of quiet desperation. But then he would look at Jacob and know he couldn't actually do it. He was responsible for Jacob. His boy was the only chance he had at redemption. He may have buried one boy in the mountains, but he could endure anything to be sure Jacob survived, was loved and cared for.

Jacob's birth was not an easy one. He became stuck in the birth canal, sending the doctor and the nurses scrambling to be sure he didn't suffocate. They tried forceps at first, plunging this crude metal device into Mary's soft, fleshy body in an attempt to pull the boy by his face into the world. It all seemed very medieval at the time, the wonders of medicine given way to harsh instruments. Then they attempted a suction tube. As there was only one doctor and two nurses, Jonathan was co-opted to hold one of Mary's heavy, swollen legs on his shoulder while they attempted to extract Jacob from his mother. The vacuum inserted inside his wife could not keep hold of Jacob's head. It pulled loose and sprayed them all with blood and afterbirth. It spotted his shirt and face. It was a messy affair, filled with images and smells he associated more with hunting and gutting a deer than with the miraculous beauty of birth. But even hunting was cleaner than the day his son was born. Cleaning a kill was not rushed. There was no scramble to save the animal. It all went smooth as clockwork. Jacob's birth was entirely different. Life was messier and more traumatic than death.

But when the boy was actually birthed, in the open air, trembling with his mouth open, eyes shut as he screamed for comfort, Jonathan felt something so much bigger. He couldn't get his head around it, couldn't fathom it. It was like standing before God, and he cried for hours afterward, Mary having to soothe him. It just kept coming – pieces of unthinkable realization, little births in his soul that testified to the terrifying reality of life and death and whatever lay between.

Since Jacob's birth, Jonathan worried over him like an old grandmother. Mary would tell him to let the boy be, let him grow up and learn the hard way on occasion. "You have to let him explore and get hurt," she said. "You have to let him be a boy on his own." Part of him wondered whether it was that exact line of reasoning that allowed a ten-year-old boy to end up in Coombs' Gulch in the middle of the night. The thought of any tragedy befalling Jacob was enough to send Jonathan's mind spiraling back to that moment of birth, that massive, overwhelming power he'd felt that day. He did his best to suppress it, but it stayed with him all the same. Mary, on the other hand, seemed to accept that tragedy was a part of life, at peace with the prospect of cancer and car crashes, kidnappers and boys accidentally shot by hunters in the dead of night. But, of course, it was easy to be at peace with the prospect when you had never experienced the reality. Her peace was built on innocence and, for that, he resented her.

"Are you okay?" she asked. "You seem so distant and..." She paused for a moment, like she was considering her words. "Angry."

"I'm not angry," Jonathan said. "I just have a lot on my mind." He anticipated her follow-up question and answered it before she could ask. "You know, just with Gene and everything."

"I don't think that's it," she said.

"Well, then I don't know what to tell you," he said.

"You're using Gene to hide something else. It's like a ghost haunting this place. Or maybe it's just haunting you. There are only three people in this family, Jonathan, but I swear the house feels crowded."

She was right. The house was crowded and they were haunted. It was suffocating. Mary could take Jacob and leave, but he had to live with it. He hoped that if they could all just tough it out for a few more weeks, it could finally be over. That somehow returning to Coombs' Gulch and confronting the past, burying it forever, would stop the decay because it was seeping poison into the rest of them. It was infecting Jacob.

It began with the night terrors. The doctors said it was normal for children, but there was nothing that could convince Jonathan that what he saw and heard when his son was in the throes of this nightmare was normal. He and Mary would be seated on the couch, watching a television program, and suddenly a scream would burst forth from his son's bedroom. A scream in the dark and then more screaming and crying, and by the time they reached his room he was up wandering around his room, completely unconscious, but his eyes looking everywhere as if he were lost. Jacob never actually saw his parents standing in front of him. Instead, he looked through them, seeing whatever terrors existed in his mind. No amount of consoling and hugging and petting made the crying and trembling stop. Nothing about that seemed normal to Jonathan. What could a child possibly dream that would cause such terror? Jacob's life was devoid of anything frightening. He knew only his small, sheltered life, his parents and his school.

Perhaps some vestigial memories from his time in the womb, Jonathan thought. Or maybe his memories were even older.

One night Jonathan yelled at the boy more than he should have, more than would otherwise be acceptable. Mary wasn't home. She was out with one of her girlfriends. They went to a gym together at night sometimes, after the friend's children had gone to bed, though he believed she was just trying to escape him for a time, to limit the one-on-one time they spent together between Jacob falling asleep and him retiring to bed after a couple of tumblers of scotch. Mary had always been in fair shape, although she never exercised much. But she found solace in this new friend and Jonathan pretended he was unaware of her true motives.

Jacob woke screaming and crying earlier than usual, but Jonathan was exhausted after the day and just wanted some quiet time to himself. Jonathan dragged himself up the stairs toward Jacob's room, cursing that he couldn't have a single moment of peace.

By the time he reached Jacob's room, the boy had already sleepwalked into his closet and peed all over his clothes and shoes.

Jonathan snapped. He screamed and cursed at the small, terrified boy and threw the wet clothes out of his closet into the center of the room. Jonathan's initial roar shocked Jacob from his sleep, and suddenly he was looking at his father – truly looking at him – his eyes wet in sheer terror, his small body trembling, newly awoken to a raging, giant figure in his room.

Jonathan saw it all happening. Somewhere in his mind, in another part of his consciousness that makes calm, compassionate decisions, he saw Jacob's fear and terror and knew it was an accident, that it wasn't the boy's fault, that he had been sleepwalking, and Jonathan felt so desperately sorry for his son, that this awful moment should become one of those earliest memories of his father, never forgotten.

Jonathan knew all this. But still some other part of himself – a more violent and frightening part – moved forward with his verbal abuse until he had run himself hoarse and breathless. Jonathan turned around in the room, now strewn with urine-soaked clothes, and looked down at Jacob, who was still trembling in shock. He took Jacob, put him back to bed and shut off the light. Jonathan went downstairs and took a long, long pull from a bottle of scotch. He hoped with all his heart that his son would not remember any of it in the morning. He took another drink, hoping it would erase the memory from his own mind. It was another terrible moment of his life, the number of which kept racking up, but he felt it inextricably tied to the other mortal guilt on his soul.

It was all a darkness, raging, reaching fingers out to affect his boy, his wife, everything he saw or felt or touched or thought. He would do anything and everything to end it. Somewhere in his mind he suspected that returning to Coombs' Gulch and sending the boy's body to the bottom of a lost lake would not ease his soul. But any chance, no matter how slim, was worth it to avoid this blooming disaster in his small family. He would move forward, just like Conner and Michael. It was worth the risk.

"I'm sorry," he said to Mary, but he was fresh out of ideas and there was a wall that would never let the truth out. "I'll work on it. I'm trying to be a good person, I really am."

She touched the side of his face. "You are a good person, Jonathan. I don't know why you would ever think otherwise."

"Yeah," he said and buried his face into her hand, "we're all good people."

"I hope you find what you're looking for up there," she said.

Late that night, under the guise of preparing for his trip, Jonathan went to the basement, moved aside an old, cheap room divider and unlocked a dull green metal safe with a key. His rifles and a shotgun stood upright and dusty in the dark of that thin locker; the top shelf held two handguns. He hadn't opened the safe in more than a year, and the smell of old oil and steel touched his nostrils. Staring at them after so long a time, Jonathan thought the firearms looked dull, inert, like a hammer forgotten at the bottom of a toolbox. For all the political mileage guns made for politicians, for all the anger and sorrow that surrounded them, they were underwhelming – pieces of metal and wood, narrow and devoid of the life given them. They leaned dumbly against the side of the safe and looked like toys. He took out his Remington .30-06 and felt its quiet heft. He slid open the bolt and checked the breach. Dust clung to oily remnants. The last time he'd held this rifle they'd buried a boy in the woods.

Jonathan took a long drink from a glass of whiskey and waited until the liquor dulled his brain. In the dim light of his concrete basement, he wiped down the barrel with an oil cloth. He shined the wood stock, wiped out the interior of the breech and ran a long, snakelike brush through the spiraled rifling of the bore. He sprayed new oil onto the bolt and action. He ran a couple of dry fires, the firing pin clicking home with each cycle. He took another drink and thought about Gene.

He took down the nine-millimeter handgun he carried for finishing off deer who were not yet dead but unable to run any farther. It happened more often than not. Even with a solidly placed kill shot, the deer still takes off running. They're dead but still going, running deeper and deeper into the woods. Then you find it still hanging on, curled up in a bed of leaves, blood pumping from a hole in its side, tongue peeking from its black snout as the breath comes shorter and shallower. The nine millimeter puts them out of their misery.

Unlike humans – unlike Gene – an animal never admits death; they never quit. A deer could have its organs blown to bits and a hole the size of a human head in its side, excruciating pain strangling every breath, and still it would never conceive of ending its own existence. It was up to the hunter to ensure the animal ceased to live. It was the hunter who set it all in motion and who had to see it through to the end. Once the shot was fired the hunter and deer were wed, bound to each other until the end. Sometimes that marriage between hunter and hunted resembled a child's game of hide-and-seek after the deer bounded into the forest; other times it was a quick, silent process. Once the shot is fired the game is set. You see yourself in their dark eyes and die just a little with the final shot.

It was a strange facet of human existence, he thought. Human consciousness is like a curse – a dull, never-ending pain that finally kills its host. An animal can endure any amount of physical pain and never conceive of death as the answer. People, on the other hand, look to it, seek it out. What physical pain cannot do – namely, drive a creature to desire its own death – human rationale can do over mere feelings spurred by memory, morality and society. It was not pain that pushed Gene toward death but anguish coupled with pure rationality. He just did an easy equation: *history plus growing day-to-day misery with no chance of change equals death as the best option.*

Gene had run like a gut-shot buck. They all had. Their injury wasn't physical; the pain wasn't from severed nerves or blunt-force trauma. The pain, the *anguish,* was invisible. The shot was fired; their lives and their minds were the exit wounds. Gene was both hunter and hunted – wed to his own death from the moment he squeezed the trigger. Like a decent hunter, he did the right thing and put himself out of his misery.

The liquor swirled in Jonathan's mind. He turned the nine millimeter over in his hand. Somewhere upstairs Jacob screamed; his mind saw terrors the world couldn't imagine.

CHAPTER SIX

The days shortened and nights grew longer in the weeks between Gene's wake and the trip. Time flew in a blur and crawled with maddening torpidity. The weather turned like leaves before a storm. Nights came early, and Jonathan found himself avoiding the dark, making sure he was indoors with the lights on and the curtains drawn. A strange, childlike fear drove him – some unknown chaos out there in the dark, in the trees. It was in the forest of the night that his life took its most chaotic lurch, and now he tried to hide from it – for now. He would be back in that place soon enough.

The boy in the box had festered in the back of Jonathan's mind, but he hadn't actively searched for answers for at least five years. Now he felt the need to search through the online lists of missing children again to find the answer, to place a name with that broken face, that ghost that haunted his life. He scrolled through the lists of names, the grainy, pixilated photos of lives that disappeared like a pair of yellow eyes blinking into nothingness. He began in the Adirondack area, Upstate New York and Vermont. One boy went missing four years ago, still unaccounted for, last seen playing outside his home in the town of Malta. He was only four years old, his glistening eyes and tiny-toothed grin glimpsing out from the computer screen. Far too young.

Another boy, aged fifteen, disappeared from Alexandria on the northern edge of Lake Champlain. He was believed to be a runaway, but no one was sure. Still, he was too old and disappeared several months after their night in Coombs' Gulch. Most of the missing were adolescents. Most had been found at some point. There were a number of missing black children from cities like Albany or Buffalo who seemed to disappear with little media attention and even less police interest. But there was nothing, no one like the boy they buried in the box that night, no one missing from anywhere near Coombs' Gulch or the town of Pasternak.

The month of October birthed Halloween-themed ghost stories, spooky accounts of eerie, unexplained incidents and folklore that fueled the morbid imagination of autumn. It was happenstance that he found a faux-news article out of Texas with the clickbait headline 'Mysterious Ghost Girl Captured on Hunting Camera'. The image was of a girl, dressed in a jacket, knitted wool hat and boots, kicking her leg up in the darkness of the forest as if she were in the middle of a childish game with her friends. It was captured on a motion-activated camera a hunter attached to a tree in Upstate New York. It was in the Catskills, far south of Coombs' Gulch, but, still, Jonathan saw something in it, sensed a similarity. That the girl was captured on this camera was especially strange because the hunting area was so far away from any town or home where the child – who looked about nine or ten – could have wandered from. Also, the picture was snapped in the middle of the night, her image blue and ghostly, bordered by tree trunks glowing like Roman pillars in the background. Some speculated she was a ghost – it was the reason the story became popular. Others said that it was clearly a living child and police were investigating, trying to find out who she was and what she was doing in the forest at that time of night. Most believed it to be a clever hoax.

But something caught Jonathan's eye: a few paragraphs down, it noted the girl resembled a child who disappeared from the area nearly forty years ago. It was, of course, impossible, but the image on the hunter's camera did truly resemble the missing girl from 1975. She was even dressed the same – third-hand clothes, probably from Goodwill, outdated by decades. The resemblance fueled the ghost speculations. The parents were long lost to history and couldn't be found for the article, probably old and senile, lost to the tangling complexity of life.

Why had no one ever searched for that boy they buried in Coombs' Gulch? Why was there no record of anyone remotely resembling him posted? Where were the news articles, the school pictures, the haunted, weary parents pleading for help and mercy? It was all too mysterious to ignore. For lack of anything better, he started a new search.

He found images, some clearly staged or faked, others with tales to accompany them, a few with tabloid or blog articles published online. The ghost child of Cannock Chase woods was a video that purported to show the ghost of a child walking through a dark British forest. It was filmed for one of those ghost-hunting programs where a bunch of idiots wander around in the night, yelling, asking questions into the silence, pointing their fingers at nothing and scaring themselves. The image was blurry, barely visible, but the ghost hunters seemed pleased with themselves. Another video from Cannock Chase was shot with a drone in the middle of the day. It showed a girl – clear as the day itself – standing in a night dress at the shadowed edge between the rolling moor and dense trees.

He found other images captured on camera from around the world, sometimes by unsuspecting campers or vacationers who only realized what their photos contained after they'd returned home and scrolled through their digital pictures. An overweight husband and wife smiling for the camera; in the background a child peeked out from behind a tree, his face blurry but recognizable, eyes shadowed and dark. Still others showed a child's face buried in the foliage or underbrush so deep it was difficult to tell if it was an actual child or the human brain piecing together a recognizable form out of disparate parts. But the faces, real or imagined – or perhaps a little of both – were there in the background, a part of the landscape, watching, as if drawn to people, seeking them out or, perhaps, trying to be found.

Many held their mouths open to impossible dark lengths, as if screaming louder than any living thing could possibly scream.

Then there were still other photographs taken from hunting cameras. Pictures that made shivers run down his spine and caused his stomach to drop – the pallid night vision coloring, the wrongness of the scene, the *misplacement*. It was the most terrifying aspect of those photos, and now, it occurred to him, it was the most terrifying aspect of that night in Coombs' Gulch. Those children didn't belong there. Their presence in those photos meant something was intrinsically wrong. Whether they had been misplaced by God, man or computer graphics, Jonathan couldn't tell and didn't care. It caused him to recoil. A young girl wearing a nightgown caught in a photograph of two deer in the night, her eyes glowing from the camera shot. A boy of four or five years old at the periphery of a night-vision shot, frightening off a large buck. A figure standing at the edge of the camera's range, whose eyes were deep holes, mouth open in a scream, a pale, white face like the one they had buried ten years ago. Jonathan stared at that photo for a long time, wondering, debating himself, fighting credulity, conceding points about everything that could not be known and trying to hold on to his sanity.

This last image came from a game camera in East Texas. Jonathan followed the digital trail of links back to the original source: an online video with the poster's contact information. He said he posted the video because he thought the child might be in trouble and the local authorities had come up with nothing. He was looking for anyone who might have information. Jonathan looked up his profile on different sites. He wasn't a ghost hunter; he was just a regular guy, a mechanic during the week, a hunter on the weekends – someone not unlike himself before the incident in Coombs' Gulch. His name was Daniel Degan of East Amarillo.

When Jonathan called, Degan's voice was packed with southern twang and an ethos of 'leave me the fuck alone'. Jonathan told him briefly that he was a fellow hunter in the Northeast so Degan wouldn't hang up the phone on him too quickly.

"I wanted to ask you about the video and photo you posted online. The one that shows the boy in it? At the very edge of the camera's range?"

Degan sighed, and, for a moment, he seemed defeated, as if he were about to beg and plead to be left alone. "Look. I know y'all interested in that picture. I can't tell you how many nutjobs have called me up and wanted me to take them out to that hunting ground to look for some 'ghost kid' or whatever, but I ain't doing it. All you fuckers are just wasting my time. I searched those woods myself; got nothing. I contacted the police; they got nothing. So I finally posted it online to see if someone out there knew something and got a whole lotta shit for it. You know what? Now, I don't even know what it is in that picture. Maybe it *is* just a fucked-up lens on the camera or something like all these online camera wizards say. I don't know. Camera don't fuck up any other times I use it. Even that same night, got plenty of other photos that are just fine. But it damn sure looked to me like some kid lost in the woods in the middle of the night, and I wanted to figure it out, and all I got was grief for my trouble. So no thanks. I just want to let it alone."

"I'm not looking for anything like that," Jonathan said. "I guess, I'm just… I think maybe I've had a similar experience and I just wanted to talk to you, to see if your picture is real – if you were real – and not one of these made-up internet pictures that are all over the place."

"As real as your mother," he said. "I don't just go around putting this shit up 'cause I think it's fun. It was fucking weird, you know? Spooked me out! Let me tell you, that hunting area was way out there. Can't no kid just accidentally wander out there, especially at night. And no kid *should* be out there! Place is filled with razorbacks that would tear him up something awful. Nah. That picture's real. What it's a picture of, I'm not sure anymore."

Jonathan kept his explanation vague, that he'd been hunting at night and thought he saw a kid running around and so he started researching it. Degan's voice rolled off the phone: "Fuck. If I'd been out there that night I damn well coulda put a bullet in him; then I'd be on the hook for murder or somethin'."

Jonathan hung up the phone, and waited in the silence of the evening. He tried to listen. He tried to find a voice inside himself – the voice that sits on the periphery of self-made illusion and whispers the truth, but all he could hear was the blood pumping through his heart, and all he could think of was a question he'd once asked a fellow hunter.

Richard was an old neighbor who'd lived two doors down when Jonathan was growing up. He was an avid hunter – bow, single-shot, black powder. It didn't matter what part of the hunting season it was, Rich was out there in the early-morning hours. He was an older man with skin leathered by the elements, a thick mustache and sandy hair. He had always been quiet, but when he saw Jonathan and the boys unloading their gear from the truck one Saturday afternoon, he wandered over and struck up a conversation. After that, Jonathan, Gene, Michael and Conner looked up to him as a kind of hunting guru. He knew literally everything about it, no matter the species, no matter the location, no matter the tool. They would bring him beer sometimes and pick his brain. Rich drank Coors Lite and sat on the porch in the evening, talking with them. He wasn't married. He had no kids they knew of; it was just him in this small ranch-style house with a small arsenal and a seemingly endless supply of hunting knowledge born out of past military experience in the Arctic Circle. During the Eighties he became a guide for various hunting safari networks throughout the world, tracking and locating top game for wealthy clients who showered wildlife preserves with six-figure donations in exchange for a hunting trip – guaranteed by Rich, of course.

"Why'd you stop doing it?" they'd once asked him, but he just shook his head and drank his beer like they would never understand.

"It ain't what it seems," he finally said. "It's not true. I don't think there is much that's true anymore."

His last few years before coming to this quiet hamlet were spent back in the Arctic Circle, working for an oil company and doing side work tracking wildlife movements for the Environmental Protection Agency.

Jonathan once asked him which animal was the most dangerous to hunt. Naturally, Jonathan's mind drifted to the Big Five – lions, elephants, those exotic, dangerous and massive African animals – but Rich's answer was instantaneous: polar bears.

"Everything is white up there. So white it can blind you. And they're white. They're like ghosts, just appear out of nothing. You don't see them coming, but they can see you. You're out there and you think you're hunting them, but you're not. You're just trying to catch sight of them before they kill you. The truth of it is they're hunting you as soon as you step on the ice. If you're lucky, you get a shot off before they take you down. There's a story I can tell you about that someday. 'Bout work I did in Alaska. But that'll have to wait for another time, another place. I can't tell you about it today."

Jonathan hadn't seen Rich in years, but he suddenly wanted to find him and ask him to tell that story. For some reason, it seemed important right then, the idea of being stalked by something sinister that blends in so well with the world around that it's invisible. It follows, it waits, it watches every day, and by the time most people notice, it's too late.

CHAPTER SEVEN

On the eve of Halloween, just one week before he would leave, Jonathan and Mary took Jacob to the traditional Halloween parade down the streets of neighbouring Collinsville. Originally begun as a small event for Collinsville residents only, with a smattering of children and adults feigning celebrity as they marched down the center of town, it became such a draw that the board of selectmen finally opened the parade to kids from all over, knowing full well their parents would spend money like fiends getting liquored up in the trendy, little outdoor cafés that lined the parade route. Now it was an event that drew easily two thousand people each year. Collinsville was the perfect town square for a Halloween event. It was set beneath a cemetery on the slopes of a hill so steep it boggled the mind as to how the corpses and coffins remained in place and didn't slide down the mountain and break open on Main Street. Abandoned factories with broken windows and brick facades lined a slow, dark river, which became deep just before a subsurface dam, and then gracefully gushed over, flowing beneath a walking bridge connecting the town to a paved river-walk path that stretched miles downstream. Collinsville had previously specialized in blade-making – axes, saws, knives and any sort of industrial cutting tool. The new restaurants and cafés decorated their walls with old Collinsville creations – crude, bladed steel instruments that seemed vaguely menacing but quaint at the same time. The factories were slowly being converted to apartments, antique shops and art galleries in a small-town version of gentrification.

Jacob, like any boy his age, was excited to dress up, to run through the night, to collect candy from neighbors. He was dressed as a mad scientist, an easy enough costume, which, thankfully, cost very little to create – a simple white jacket, some iron-on lettering, blood spatter, gloves and goggles. His naturally messy hair was trussed up into spikes, jutting out in different directions. Some fake glasses gave him the look of intelligence gone awry. He was picture-worthy even for people who didn't consider him the center of their world.

Jonathan and Mary were never desperate or organized enough to arrive at Collinsville ridiculously early in order to park in the center of town. Conner and Madison would probably have the finest parking spot available. They also attended every year, parading their children, taking pictures, telling everyone that everything was wonderful. Jonathan recognized he was here to do the same thing, and somehow it seemed a bigger lie.

They parked along the river walk outside of town and joined other families who walked beneath the looming trees beside the river. It was dusk and quickly growing dark. The warmth of the sun faded off, and a mist rose from the black waters and drifted through the trees. As they approached the town, Jonathan could hear the laughter, the voices of revelry just beyond the walking bridge and behind the old brick buildings. The other families shuffled along, their children jumped and ran, and their parents called them back. Jacob walked quietly and calmly and Jonathan wondered to himself if something was wrong. The fear every parent secretly harbors that their son or daughter is somehow *different* – that they were not playing properly with other kids, not behaving like *normal* kids – crept into his mind. Jacob, at times, seemed morose and isolated. He had no brothers or sisters, and there was no best friend up the street with whom he played. And with that concern came guilt. How could any child come out 'normal' with a father like him?

But it wasn't just Jacob's quiet manner at a time when he should be a bounding barrel of excitement and joy; the whole evening seemed off. Jonathan knew he had been avoiding the night, hiding inside with the lights on, but now his open-air presence in the darkness couldn't be helped and he felt an insane sense that something stalked through the trees between the walking path and the deep river. He couldn't describe it exactly; it was like knowing a song on the radio but being unable to remember the name until hours later. Perhaps it was just a memory, a key revelation sneaking up in slow and horrific fashion. The tops of the trees rustled in an unfelt wind; their brittle orange-and-brown leaves brushed together in a whispering dirge and then floated to the earth like confetti.

They crossed the bridge out of the woods and into town. Jacob grew tired of walking and Jonathan carried him for a time. More people began to appear. Other parents smiled as they passed, commented on his costume, and, naturally, Jonathan and Mary returned the compliments until, five minutes into the event, Jonathan was already exhausted with small talk. The children, dressed as any number of things both foreign and familiar, looked strange, bumping around on short legs, unsure of their own dimensions. As they reached the center of town Jonathan could see the throngs of people. The weather had been beautiful all year and tonight was no exception. There were easily twice as many people this year as usual, traveling from all over the state. The mass of decorated flesh surged in the night, and the streetlamps seemed like torches in the darkness, flickering between shadows.

The three of them were suddenly absorbed into the mass, and Jonathan felt lost in a strange world, weak and exposed. The people twirled in their costumes, stumbled drunkenly, bumped and jostled, laughed and screeched. It seemed there were more adults dressed in costume than children, bent on some form of mild debauchery, dressed as witches, goblins, ghouls and other creatures born out of myths and ancient tales, their costumes an attempt to expose humanity to the deathly fate that awaits them all. Jonathan saw children dressed as zombies, the desiccated dead risen from the grave, skin sallow or peeling, eyes blackened, bloody and evil, and he couldn't help but wonder what awaited him the following week in Coombs' Gulch. The boy had lain in that sealed case underground for ten years. Jonathan had never seen a corpse that had fully experienced all the ravages of death, except through the special effects of movies, but now it seemed as if all the stages of death crowded on the streets, mingling in a ritualistic gathering of citizenry. From the angelic face of a young child to the bare bones of a skeleton, a pantomime of the life-and-death process paraded down Main Street in the night.

Jonathan's stomach curled: would they open the box? Would they need to? He didn't know. Part of him wanted to treat it like any other piece of luggage to be thrown away, but there was something else burning in his soul, something that said he could never put it to rest until he fully confronted it, gazed into that box and communed with the reality of death.

He felt that somewhere in the crowd, somewhere in this night, the boy was dancing around him, parading and marching, waving and laughing, gray with putrescence, walking on wobbly, dead legs, hand in hand with something much larger and more terrifying in its power.

It stirred both his guilt and wonder. After weeks of researching and his phone call with the Texan, what disturbed Jonathan more were the children dressed as caricatures of familiar things – clowns, farmers, characters from cartoons or movies, and his own little mad scientist. They were real things distorted and accentuated into something *other*. It made him think of those strange images, the children caught on hunting cameras in the middle of the forest in the night, places not meant for people. It occurred to him that the children in those pictures appeared too perfect, like something pulled out of an advertisement, meant to show what children are *supposed* to look like, but rarely do. In that way, they seemed alien and even more frightening than the caricatures of death. Jacob walked beside him, his eyes wide in fright and wonder at the massive, roiling crowd of strange faces. Jonathan felt Jacob's little hand slipping from his own.

After finally reaching Main Street, they shuffled along with the throng of parents and kids. People lined the sidewalks, waving and laughing; cameras flashed, smartphones recorded video. Perhaps when they played the video back later they would see something different, something more powerful hovering in the sky, bearing down on them all. Perhaps they would see what the ancients feared and sacrificed to during these days of descending darkness.

Jonathan heard Mary laugh – a welcome sound – and turned to look. She had her hand on Madison's shoulder. Conner was standing, tall and lithe, beside his wife, and it took Jonathan a moment to recognize him in the strange setting. Conner nodded and they shook hands briefly. Mary was asking why they didn't see more of each other and why they didn't get the kids together more often. Madison nodded her perfect, pretty head in agreement.

Jonathan looked down and saw Conner's children, Brent and Aria. Brent was dressed as a hunter, in camouflage jacket and pants, which were baggy and creased in odd angles on his small body, a bright orange cap that seemed to glow in the darkness, black makeup beneath his eyes and a toy rifle cradled in his arms. His face was smiling, pale, innocent and unbroken, and, for a moment, Jonathan thought that it was all just some tremendous joke, the boy in the woods nothing more than an elaborate prank, his life for the past ten years a reality television farce played out for some cackling audience.

"He saw the old pictures of you guys from your hunting days and wanted to dress up like his daddy and Uncle Mike," Madison said.

Jonathan saw Michael standing a few feet back, looking aloof and lost in the mass of families, his wife, Annie, nowhere to be seen. He came to do his duty in supporting his brother, niece and nephew, but he looked out of place and uncomfortable.

Jonathan looked at Conner. "A hunter, huh?"

Conner put on his proud-dad face. "Yeah, maybe someday."

"Well, I bet you guys are excited to go out together again next week," Madison said, and Mary launched into a speech about how she was always trying to get Jonathan to go out with his friends and do the things that bring him joy – a veiled admission that his life was largely joyless. "You just can't work your whole life," she said.

She didn't realize that for men like them there were no friends, there was no joy.

Jonathan turned back and gazed out at the mass of costumed people streaming around them. The pitch-black sky bore down over the yellowed streetlamps with their dull coronas of electric light. They were halfway up the incline of Main Street, which drove straight toward the steep hill with the cemetery looming over them all. He looked up at the great black hill and wondered at something that escaped his mind. He turned and looked down Main Street, which plunged toward the river and the submerged dam just beyond the street. He heard Madison and Mary talking. He heard the crowds of revelers. There was movement all around, horrific, screeching faces, made up with blood and gore and alien smiles.

Far off, near the river and trees and just at the edge of the light from a streetlamp, a tremendously tall figure stood cloaked in black. Jonathan strained his eyes but could not make out its features, other than it was standing in shadow and its head reached halfway up the lamppost. It did not appear to be part of the celebration, not walking or mingling. Instead, it stood alone in the darkness – a creep, probably, one of those mentally unstable adults who wallow in gothic darkness and get a kick out of trying to convince the world they're psychotic.

But then the figure stepped closer to the lamplight, and suddenly Jonathan could make out its features. The face was a crude mask of wood with poorly carved slits for eyes, mouth and nose and primitive designs of dull color painted on the flat face. Upon its head were the antlers of a tremendous stag, which reached like bony fingers up into the night. Its hands were raised at shoulder level as if offering up a sacrifice – a pagan priest transported from the scene of some ancient rite, his prayers and incantations rending time, existing in both realms simultaneously. A wind moved high in the trees, sweeping down from the great cemetery above, and it carried a deep and haunting dirge. The masked priest called out for them, for blood and sacrifice. He stared out from darkness, and his eyes seemed to shine in the light.

CHAPTER EIGHT

It was just after 3:00 p.m., and the sun shone bright and cold through the office windows on the twentieth floor of the Parson's Insurance building in downtown Hartford, partially blinding Conner Braddick. He had repositioned his desk several times since his promotion, but still, every sunny afternoon, blinding sunlight poured through, reaching every corner of the room. Conner's eyes watered with spiraling sunspots and left him with a mild form of blindness. Twenty more years of this and he would probably lose his vision completely.

Conner pinched the bridge of his nose. A little blindness at this point was fine with him. He couldn't look at his computer screen any longer. The wake-up call he received from his bank this morning was enough to throw him off his work for the day anyway. A month and a half behind on the mortgage; why did they have to buy that house – a house that size – anyway? He couldn't remember at this point. Third child on the way and Madison said they needed a bigger house. Of course. Whatever. That was the way it was supposed to work, right? He had read it in various conservative journals; having children pushed men and women to work harder, to push themselves harder, to get that promotion, put in the extra hours, save and scrape so you move up the middle-class ladder toward…what? He was no longer sure. It was just what people did – what he did. It was like a trap you lured yourself into. No need for bait; delusion and hope would do just fine.

It all went by in a blur, like running as fast as you can until your legs are dead and you're out of breath and there's nothing left and you look around and realize that you're lost and a long, long way from home.

It had all seemed so easy at first, like everything was falling into place. He got that promotion, up here to the twentieth floor, now assistant to the vice president of investments for Parson's. He had worked for that promotion. Not in the usual way one worked for a promotion, but the real way – schmoozing with the managers, long lunches with a lot of backslapping, and junkets to Saratoga Springs and Boston for meetings, which generally consisted of some 'expert' selling his latest theory and everyone sitting around lauding it as the new way forward. For all the media's focus on social progress, insurance was still a good ol' boy club, where promotions were earned through 'lunches' that became late-afternoon booze fests and everyone got sloppy. Those trips to Saratoga and Boston were merely excuses to do what men actually wanted to do: avoid work and get stupid. Everyone sat through eight hours of experts and charts and graphs for the big payoff of an open bar with attractive waitresses. Nothing concrete ever came from those meetings. No plans were ever made. They just stumbled from one place to another in a new city, pretending to know how this business worked, how investments worked, how life in general worked. They had their statistics and algorithms, computer programs that spit out answers, which Conner and his colleagues used to impress everyone with their vast knowledge of *how it actually works*, as if they could simply solve problems with a snap of their fingers. The problem, which had been slowly dawning on Conner, was that all those equations and algorithms, the investment software, the charts and graphs, were merely descriptions. They were like paintings – nice to look at, but changed nothing in reality. They were all, himself included, sitting around looking at and discussing descriptions of how it worked without actually understanding *how it worked*. And because of that, they lacked the ability to change anything. The industry was too big. There were too many people. The entire company and everyone in it were being rolled along by forces bigger than they could imagine and too complex to be understood. Those forces certainly couldn't be changed or influenced as much as the wizards of smart at these meetings thought they could. No. Conner and his colleagues were all just small cogs in a vast machine who thought they were actually running the show. More and more, Conner felt like a fraud. And, he suspected, so did the other corporate executives. That was why these out-of-state trips devolved into such pathetic drunkenness – all these 'powerful' men were sitting in a room, staring at each other and realizing there wasn't shit they could do that would make an ounce of difference in the long run. It was actually scary to witness. He could see it roll over their faces – the sudden realization that you are ineffectual, impotent and small. That the vast machine was terrifyingly large and defied explanation from the likes of you. They realized their own pathetic mortality while staring at pie charts and Venn diagrams.

So, like any competent executives, they pretended to have the answers, pretended these meetings were essential to operations and then drowned their dread in booze. Allusions to plans were discussed, but no one ever wanted to take the reins. In the end, all the money spent on parading everyone out to these meetings resulted in a change of interdepartmental language at best: refer to *this* as *that* and refer to *that* as *this* and somehow profit margins will increase. The structure always remained the same and business remained the same – failing.

Their auto insurance line had been tough lately. They were losing money big-time. The new cars were all now equipped with rear-end cameras, sensors, automatic braking, alert systems. The average car now contained computers more advanced than anything people had in their homes ten years ago. The cost of the cars went up. The cost of insurance claims went up. Now your average fender bender involved replacing a myriad of cameras and sensors, rather than just a piece of plastic. But, of course, no one wanted to pay for it. The insurance industry was plagued by pirates, little companies that operated out of strip-mall offices or – even worse – online, with virtually no overhead. Not like the millions it took to keep this tower running. These pirates offered minimum-cost insurance plans that undercut the bigger companies, deflated the prices, left every customer looking for less. Of course, those pirate companies came with risks, but most people don't factor in the risk of your piddly, little, no-name insurance company not paying out a claim. Most people don't plan for the accidents. They just go about their lives confident that today they will wake up and go through their usual routine unencumbered by the possibility of death and destruction. Until it's too late, and then they're left holding the bag, so to speak.

And now he was holding the bag, too. Conner's income was tied to his performance, which was great in the good times and horrible in the bad. He and Madison planned for the good. Everything in their lives had seemed on the upswing. Now, for the second year in a row, the returns for Parson's were coming in low, and that left him in a bad spot. Conner had managed to squirrel away enough money to make up the difference for a while, but now he was looking down the barrel of a financial gun and the hammer was dropping.

Naturally he kept Madison in the dark. She was from a family of 'means' – as her father would refer to it. Where Conner was from, they were just called 'rich'. She had never wanted for anything, and Conner had to admit, it was part of his attraction to her in the beginning. Seeing her house, the way she lived, the way her parents lived. He hoped that success would rub off on him, that he would be absorbed somehow into a social level where he'd be insulated from situations like this.

Madison had always wanted to be a stay-at-home mother, something that was virtually unheard of these days. But she wanted to emulate her own upbringing for their children. She had gone to college and become a nurse. Her father's world of finance had no appeal for her. Madison didn't want to know where the money came from; she just wanted to live her life as she saw fit. She left the nursing job – an easy $60,000 per year – after Brent was born and stayed home with Conner's awkward and often veiled assurance that everything would be fine. They bought nice cars. They entertained friends and family on holidays. He had to buy a $10,000 lawnmower just to do the yard, which was two acres of beautifully arranged 'butterfly garden' engineered by the previous owners.

Madison was a great mother; he couldn't have asked for anything more. She treated their two children – and the third unborn – as a full-time job with the utmost alarm and seriousness. Every cough or sneeze or symptom other parents would dismiss warranted a trip to the doctor's office. The medical copays grew, and Conner's patience decreased. Now he felt on the precipice of a fall and it was getting hard to breathe. How do you tell the woman you love that the easy ride was over? The dreams of that perfect, upper-middle-class existence might be coming to an end? The penalty payments on the mortgage would continue to rack up. How do you choose between food and housing? The food you need now, and, well, the housing will have to wait. Just keep the lights on, keep telling yourself somehow the rest of it will work out. But in truth, he was trapped by the life he'd built. They all were.

And yet he was struggling, killing himself, to hold on to that trap, to stay alive in it just a little longer. Once, while hunting in his early twenties, Conner happened upon a coyote with its paw caught in a spring trap. The use of spring traps was illegal but the coyotes had been running rampant throughout the area and some people just hated them.

The animal was thin, shaking, its fur falling off in spots from mange, and it raised such a terrible, high-pitched noise in the early-morning darkness that Conner recalled old Irish tales of banshees floating through the trees wailing their death-cries. He saw it there, pulling and pulling against the trap and then, leaning its sharp, thin head down and gnawing at the joint of its trapped paw. It was bloody and worn through and the coyote bit down harder, chewing through the bone. He watched it there for a while, the creature's head pulling back and forth at its own front leg. Conner finally took out his handgun, aimed from a short distance and put a bullet in its head.

Conner thought about that coyote now. Man was an animal, he figured, so that strength to survive coursed through his veins as well.

And now there was the business of Coombs' Gulch. An accident for which there was no insurance, something that couldn't be guarded against with money or an algorithm or a plan. It couldn't have come at a worse time. The final quarter reports would be coming due soon and they were all bad. This trip – trying to keep the lid on something that would ruin him, ruin his family and everything he knew – was smack dab in the middle of his executive downturn. But there was no choice in the matter. History had a way of holding on with long tentacles. Gene's death had garnered him a little sympathy from the bosses and, more importantly, an excuse for them to make their way up into the mountains and finally put an end to this thing hanging over their heads. He was sure of his plan. That lake, deep in the mountains, would keep the secret forever. He knew it would be a tough hike, possibly even dangerous, but it was worth it. He wasn't going to give up. He would push himself beyond his limits to see it through.

The plan, in itself, was an insurance policy, insurance that he would never have to admit to his wife and children and the world what they had done, how he had been so callous and uncaring as to put a dead innocent in the ground and hide the fact. He had long ago worked past the guilt of what happened. The fact that no one ever came forward looking for a lost boy made it easier, made it seem more like a bad dream than anything else, and he pushed it to the back of his subconscious. The others had not been as willing or able to bury it deep enough or rationalize it enough to get on with their lives. Everyone asked why Gene did it. Why he took his own life when he seemed like such a great guy, full of life, and all that other shit people said when mourning a premature death. Conner remembered the night he and Michael sat down with Gene and told him the plan. The look that came over that giant oaf's eyes, as if he were staring into an abyss. Conner should have known right then that Gene wouldn't make it. Two days later came news of his death, but, really, he had died the night he was confronted with returning to Coombs' Gulch. Gene had opted for jumping into that abyss rather than returning to the Gulch.

Conner, Michael and Jonathan understood the necessity of dealing with the issue, of moving the box, of following Conner's insurance plan. Michael was strong. Michael dealt strictly with the problems facing him at the time. A past decision, even a wrong one, was quickly put out of his mind. He was not one to doubt himself or to look much further than the small malfunctioning parts of the vast machine before him. He didn't deal with the guilt and sadness and regret; he dealt with the functionality of it. It was what made him a good engineer.

Jonathan, on the other hand, was a mess. Conner wondered how long it would take before he took Gene's way out. Mary called Madison some nights, crying into the phone, wondering what was wrong with him, why he'd taken to drinking so much and cutting himself off from the rest of the world. Jonathan was down a dark hole. Conner felt bad to an extent, but at some point you have to get a hold of yourself, no use wallowing in the past, particularly wallowing in Coombs' Gulch. There was also the possibility Jonathan would do something stupid and tell someone else what happened. Conner had always worried most about Gene, but as far as he knew, that fat mess had kept a lid on things. Jonathan's downward spiral somehow seemed more pure in its depression and sadness. He had known Jonathan all his life. They all felt what'd happened that night, but it seemed to weigh on Jonathan worst of all.

Walking back into that place would make it real again. Conner had been mentally preparing himself for that, but he was worried about Jonathan losing his mind out there. Conner and Michael were strong, bound by the chain of their brotherhood. He knew Michael better than Michael knew himself. But Jonathan was different. There was always a distance between them, but now it was amplified. Jonathan was burying himself with that boy out there in Coombs' Gulch. He couldn't keep it together and was on the verge of losing his family. The guy just looked pathetic when Conner saw him at the Halloween parade; he looked sick, his skin sallow, eyes dark and sunken into his skull. For all intents and purposes, he looked like one of those former heroin addicts whose bodies never recover, who appear on the verge of death permanently. He wondered if Jonathan could physically survive the trip.

Conner couldn't say he didn't feel the pang of guilt. It was mostly his idea to bury the boy's body. But if they hadn't their lives would have been ruined long ago, never to recover. It was a necessary decision, an executive decision. In this vast machine, he had at least been able to effect some small change that saved their lives. Insurance came with a price, after all. The price was on their souls, but he couldn't risk it becoming more real, affecting things that mattered. A price was paid and another was due. Conner and Michael could handle it. That wasn't theory; that was fact.

Conner was lost in thought, staring at the computer screen in front of him, every stress and concern piling one on top of the other till it seemed a mountain. *Start at the bottom*, he thought, *and work your way up. This trip needs to be done. Get that done, get it out of your life and move on to the next problem.*

There was a knock at the door a fraction of a second before it opened, which meant it was someone higher up the corporate food chain than himself. Underlings always waited for permission; not so with upper management. Tom Doley stood in the doorway, his chinless face like putty pushed into a grin so wide his whole head changed form. But it was a false smile; Conner could see that in his eyes.

"Let's kick off for a while," he said. "Hit the Iron Horse Tavern. This day's over anyway." Tom Doley was one of the cadre of managers who oversaw the investment department. The whole company was layer upon layer of managers, investors, advisors, assistant vice presidents – any sort of title that sounded important was just stacked in and on top of every other title.

"Sure," Conner said. "I was just finishing up." He had been out with Tom before. They would shoot the shit about interdepartmental strife, bitch about how things would be if only their learned wisdom and guidance would be utilized. The usual workplace bullshit every employee, from a store cashier to the CEO of a Fortune 500, engaged in whenever not in earshot of someone who had the ability to fire them. But this seemed different. Despite his entire face being mashed into a smirk, he seemed to be trying too hard, like a grieving family member at a funeral who still has to smile and thank people for coming.

"Meet you there?" Tom said.

Conner didn't even look at him when he said, "Yup." He felt Tom's gaze linger on him a few moments before he shut the door.

Iron Horse Tavern was quiet. A few people sat at its unnecessarily long bar and a couple of senior citizens at the tables. Iron Horse was one of those places that are utterly devoid of character; put some interesting Americana on the walls, slap together a menu and then advertise all these neat local beers on tap so the newly established young generation of beer connoisseurs can pretend their slide into alcoholism is fueled by an intelligent interest in the finer consideration of hops and barley. Generally Conner played right along with that – order some beer that you've never heard of based on the sommelier-type description on the menu. Today he just ordered a Budweiser.

"You drink that shit?" Tom said. He had a double IPA infused with who-the-fuck-knows in a pint glass.

"Sometimes. Roots, you know. My father drank these till the day he died."

Tom nodded, trying to find his opening. Conner could sense it; they weren't here for good times. There was something that needed to be said, but Conner certainly wasn't going to help him get it over with.

"I heard you lost a friend a little while ago," Tom said. "Sorry for your loss."

"Thanks. Old friend. We hadn't been in touch for a while, but we grew up together. Used to do a lot of hunting together. It was one of those things where your buddies all get married and have kids and you don't keep in touch."

"Yeah, I didn't realize you were a hunter."

"Not much anymore. Who has the time, right?"

"I've done that clay pigeon shooting? That was pretty fun."

Conner nodded. "Yeah. A couple times I've done it. It's like golf. They have whole courses set up at some of these clubs."

"You're taking off at the end of the week, right?" Tom said. "I saw that you're going to be out. Where you off to?"

"Upstate New York. Myself, my brother and another friend. Doing one last hunting trip as a send-off for the guy that died – Gene was his name. We thought it would be a good way to remember him."

Tom Doley nodded and looked into his beer, seemingly considering the situation. The whole charade was becoming tedious, so Conner threw him a bone. "Why? Something going on?"

Tom's putty face seemed to scrunch and twist like what he was about to say caused him physical pain. "Well…it's just the timing is really bad. The fourth quarter reports are coming up and…"

"There's always a quarterly report coming up."

"I know, I know. But it's just things in your department aren't looking good this year."

"That's not news. They haven't looked good for three years now. You think I like having to say that? It's fucking killing me."

"Hey. I know it is, brother. I understand. That's why it just seems like now is not a good time to take a little vacation. Some of the managers upstairs are looking to make some cuts. We just can't compete anymore, and without significant investment income we're going to be looking at some hard times to come."

"What are you trying to tell me here?" Conner asked. "Layoffs are coming?"

"That's the word."

"They'd be stupid to lay off anyone in my department. We're the only chance they've got. They want to hire some outside firm? They'll be paying double in fees. You know this. They know this. They're just looking to pin everything on someone or something. Truth is, they have no idea how to get things back on track and they're flailing."

"I hear you, Conner. I hear you. I'm just giving you the heads-up. Now is the time. Now is the time for you to step up and really take control, show them what you're made of. I like you. I think you do a great job. I don't want to see anybody get laid off, but the truth of the matter is we're looking at significant losses this quarter and some heads are going to roll."

"I'm taking off three days, not a month, Tom."

"You're taking three days off during the investors leadership summit in Mamaroneck."

"Jesus Christ. That thing?"

"It's a big deal, Conner. The bosses, they want to see people involved, actively engaged in problem-solving, in mitigating losses, in using the downturn to optimize for leaner and smarter investment management."

"Christ, Tom. I went last year. It's not rocket science; they just make it *sound* like rocket science. Frankly, they make it sound more like a cheap self-help book by a quack psychologist."

"I'm just saying, Conner. You should be there. It would look good for you. It would look good for us."

Conner stared down at his bottle of beer, its red, white and blue label slightly peeling, soft from the condensation on the glass. He pursed his lips in frustration, anger, the fucking idiocy of it all. His life on the line and here he was being upbraided for missing a meeting that amounts to nothing more than a minstrel show for bigwigs trying to hold on to the precipice of imaginary power.

"I can't, Tom. This trip is important for other reasons. I can't make it to the investors workshop. Not this year. I'm sorry."

"I gotcha, Conner," Tom said, holding up his hands as if he meant no offense. Just another slimeball sent on a slimeball's mission, to weasel and cajole. "I'm just trying to look out for you, buddy. That's all. Things are just lean right now and they're going to get leaner."

Tom poured his putty face and fish-eyes into his glass of double IPA scented with shit. Conner pounded the Budweiser and ordered another and another.

Tom Doley left at about 5:00 p.m., his long, lumbering figure making haste out of Iron Horse Tavern while Conner pulled up a stool and sat lonely and angry with his beer – every bartender's worst nightmare. The pretty girl behind the counter avoided conversation, standing near the service bar; she chatted with waitresses and a guy from the kitchen before enough people showed up that they had to get back to work. In a way, Conner envied them. Sure, there wasn't much money in it, but at least at the end of the night you left it all here; it didn't follow you home, sleep with you in bed and wake you up at four in the morning just to remind you that you are owned. A job like this, he thought, one that was vastly simpler, meant for the young or those without the stress of mortgages and growing families, implied a simpler life, one not connected to status, cocktail parties, pointless meetings in faraway places and the idea that you must succeed or die trying. It was something he missed. He had worked jobs like this as a teenager and through parts of college. Still the best times of his life. And merely saying that to himself made him feel old and bitter, as if he were already on the downward slope of life.

The tavern finally became too crowded for him and his thoughts, so he paid the bill – on a credit card, no less – and left. The drive home was nerve-racking. The traffic was always bad this time of day, plus he had to contend with the hazy onset of inebriation blooming in his brain. All he would need was an accident, his fault or not, and one of the last supports of his life would be kicked out from under him. One of the guys in Sales – Peter Selchick – got pinched for a DUI last year after a 'lunch' with a number of other salesmen turned into a shit show with five bottles of wine and tequila shots. He got canned after a departmental review. Hell, one of the guys on the review board had been in the bar with him that very day. But what can you do? Blood in the water and everybody wants a bite. Something like an arrest just brings the feeders. Conner wondered if this little trip and missing the Mamaroneck meeting was a spot of blood finding its way to the upper echelons of Parson's. This little talk with Tom Doley made him wonder, left him feeling vulnerable.

Coombs' Gulch had to be put to rest. He'd spent enough of his life bleeding internally from that goddamned night. First there was the fear – the weeks and months after that night spent in suspended animation, waiting for the guillotine to slam down on his neck. Panic. Wondering when he would see that first story of a little boy missing in Upstate New York, see the picture and recognize the face, the outline of his head, wondering when he would stare at a picture of a boy with two living eyes, rather than one dead eye and a bloody hole. That time never came, and as Conner's panic began to subside after six months or so, the guilt set in. Of course he felt terrible. Only a sociopath wouldn't. What they had done, covering up their crime, was the same thing anyone would have done. Sure, people like to pretend they're honest and caring, believe they would fess up right away to such an incident, but when they actually see their entire future about to be ripped away, self-preservation kicks in. Conner told himself it was only natural what they'd done. Simple numbers: ruin four lives at the behest of one death? No. It didn't add up.

But still there was something missing in that equation. It was a child. It wasn't a natural death. What the fuck was that kid doing up there, in the middle of nowhere in the middle of the night? Where were his parents? Why was no one looking for him? Dear God, the boy wasn't even dressed for the cold, probably would have died of exposure if he hadn't caught a bullet.

And what about that bullet? Conner hadn't fired the shot. That was all on Gene, who had now given up all his responsibility by putting a bullet through his own head. Same rifle no less. Now Conner, Michael and Jonathan were left holding the bag if that box was ever found – and it would be, if this new development went through. Conner had seen the plans. He had pored over them during late nights, staying after 5:00 p.m. at the office just to root through the proposals without anyone noticing or asking questions. Some guys wondered why he took such an interest in their latest underwriting project, but he just brushed them off. The box had to be moved. The boy had to be buried someplace where no one could find him. Conner hatched the plan himself and it was a good plan. He suddenly felt a surge of optimism, as if he were about to turn his life around. Peaks and valleys, mountains and gulches. Life is going up toward one or down toward another. This would put it forever behind them, clear the way for him to get his life back, unencumbered by the sins of the past. He would have to skip these stupid meetings for the sake of a long-dead boy and thereby continue working his way up the ladder of success. He would continue making enough payments on the mortgage to keep the foreclosure dogs at bay. *He could do this.* One step at a time, as the drunks say. One step at a time up that hill, up that mountain, with a dead body in tow, toward a lake in the mountains where it could all be put to rest.

Conner took the exit, leaving the tumult of the highway and driving onto the dark and winding back roads toward his little enclave in the hills. He stopped for gas and a coffee, hoping the caffeine would help right his brain and cover up the beer smell on his breath. He crossed into his hometown at seven. Clouds moved overhead and it was officially night. He had never left his hometown and he wondered why. Was that pathetic? He wasn't sure. It just was and at this point there was no getting out of it.

His neighborhood was set high on a large hill, and his SUV burned gas plowing up the steep incline. During the day there were great views, but at night it was just rolling blackness occasionally dotted with headlights from Route 4 below. But as he approached Ridgeline Drive he saw different kinds of lights. Red-and-blue strobes bounced off the trees and mailboxes of his road. He turned the SUV and suddenly his mind went into overdrive. Two state police vehicles parked outside his house. He gunned the big engine and raced the few hundred yards to his driveway, jumped out of the car and ran to the front door. Terrifying images ran through his mind of what lay on the other side. Why would the police be here? What had happened? Were Madison and the children okay? Down the road he could see neighbors standing at the edge of their driveways, trying to catch a glimpse.

Conner opened the door and saw Madison standing in the tiled foyer with two hulking troopers. Her eyes lit on him for a moment and then turned back to the officers. He knew this look. She was all business right now. She was concerned and in charge and leveling expectations on those gathered around her. He could already see the deference in the faces of the officers.

Conner was practically breathless and trying to control himself, keeping the smell of alcohol at bay and praying the coffee had done enough to keep the booze off his breath, praying his hazy brain wouldn't betray him right now.

"What the hell's going on?"

The officers looked at him with that professional air of bored authority he despised so much, like he was a bug to be quashed, but for their mercy.

"I was trying to reach you," Madison said. "You weren't answering your phone."

Conner was suddenly confused. He hadn't heard his phone, hadn't felt any vibrations. He instinctively searched the pockets of his jacket and pants. The phone wasn't there. The last he had seen it was – *shit* – sitting on the bar at the tavern. He had been so lost in his thoughts he'd walked out without it, and now, suddenly, it was like a vital lifeline was missing.

"Your daughter was approached by a man when she was playing in the woods out back," one of the officers said.

"What do you mean 'approached by a man'?"

Madison, now brimming with anger, said, "He said he knew you. That he was a friend of yours and offered to take her away. Take her on a trip."

"What?"

Madison continued. "Aria was playing out back in the woods behind the swings. And she says that a scary man came walking through the woods and talked to her and told her he was a friend of yours and could take her on a trip far away from here."

"Jesus," Conner said. His stomach was suddenly brimming with acid, his arms and legs hollow with the thoughts of what he could have lost.

"Your daughter is fine, Mr. Braddick," the other officer said. "She's just a little shook up. She was able to give a description, and we've got other officers driving through the area right now, checking with neighbors and seeing if we can find anyone that fits the description. If he was on foot, then he's probably still in the area. We're also checking any unknown vehicles in the area that might have been parked along the roads."

Conner looked past Madison to the living room. He spotted his son and daughter watching them. Aria's big brown eyes shone wet and strange, watching the drama unfold of which she understood little to nothing. Standing there in that room, his four-year-old daughter watched the ring of adults who, in hushed tones, discussed the events of the day under the gruesome shadow of what could have been – kidnapping, molestation, rape, death, dismemberment – all the evils and horrors that befall children who wander through this world as if lost on a highway at night.

"You don't happen to know anyone that might try something like this, do you?" the officer asked.

"No. Of course not." Conner brushed past the officer and Madison, picked up Aria and held her close to him, gripping her tight.

"She's fine," Madison said. "She was just scared."

"It's a typical line men use when they try to lure a child away from home," the other trooper said.

"What was scary about the man, honey?" Conner asked her. He

wanted to know what he looked like, this man who'd said he knew him, the man who'd said he would take Conner's little girl someplace far away.

"His face looked broken," she said.

"Broken?"

One of the officers chimed in. "We think maybe scarring. Or perhaps he was just beat up and ugly."

"Like a doll that's been smashed," Aria said. "I don't want to go away, Daddy."

"No, honey," Conner said. "You're not going anywhere."

"He said he was your friend."

"No, honey. He's not my friend. That would never happen."

"I ran away and told Mommy."

"That's good, honey. You did the right thing. You did great." For the first time in a long time his emotions welled up enough to bring him to the point of tears. The thought of losing her overwhelmed him, pushed everything else to the back of his mind. Everything except that boy in the box in Coombs' Gulch. That boy's face was broken, too. That boy was gone from someone, gone far away. Just like his little girl was almost gone from him.

"Everything will be fine, Mr. Braddick," the officer said. "Like I said, we're combing the area. We take these things very seriously, and we're going to put out a warning to everyone in town, using the description your little girl gave us. We'll figure this out, but in the meantime please let us know if you see anything suspicious or if Aria remembers any more details, anything at all."

Conner nodded, and Madison began with the thank-yous and assurances she would be vigilant in alerting the neighbors and keeping watch, something of which Conner had no doubt. The officers left, their presence of authority suddenly gone, leaving the uncomfortable feeling of having just brushed shoulders with the law. Even when it's on your side, the law leaves one feeling helpless and victimized. Madison shut and locked the door behind them.

Conner still held Aria, slightly bouncing and rocking her in his arms.

"Where were you?" Madison asked.

"Why was Aria in the woods alone?" Conner said and immediately regretted it. Madison stared at him with cold, brown eyes for a moment, internally considering this last comment, and then silently walked past him. Once a woman had children, he thought, you become second rate, just a piece of shit dragged along to help the mother rear them. His voice had no consequence here. His purpose in this family was to provide financial security; her purpose was much more important, and he'd just criticized her – a small uprising against the queen, all the more damaging because it affirmed his place in the family hierarchy.

"We shouldn't argue," he said. "I'm sorry. I didn't mean that."

"They're allowed to play outside, Conner," she said. "I can't watch them every second of the day. It was just behind the swing set. I could see her through the window. I have things to do around here to keep this house functioning, you know."

"I know," he said. "I'm sorry. I'm just shook up, is all."

"And where the hell were you? Why weren't you answering your phone?"

Now he would get to look like a real shit head. An actual family emergency, and where was he? Downing beers and forgetting his phone at a time when he was actually needed.

"And now you're going to be gone for five days," Madison said. "Great. Really great. Run off with your buddies to God knows where." She lowered her voice to a whisper. "Fucking enjoy it."

That night Aria woke screaming in her room and Conner and Madison stumbled through the darkness, switching on lights, and found the girl sitting upright in her bed, sheets and blankets twisted like snakes around her. Her eyes were open, but she could not see them, even when they sat beside her on the bed and held her tight.

Conner kept saying Aria's name, trying to catch her eyes with his, but she kept staring at the window facing the trees in the backyard.

"It's a night terror," Madison said. "You can't wake her up."

Aria kept screaming, "The broken man," as if her mouth were detached from her brain.

Conner held her tight.

"Maybe I should call a therapist in the morning," Madison said.

CHAPTER NINE

The morning Conner and Michael picked Jonathan up for the trip, the air itself seemed suffused with a shade of blue. Jonathan woke early, unable to sleep. The sun had not yet fully risen, but the air glowed as if through a colored lens. He kissed Mary goodbye, and she gave a half-hearted smile, while busying herself with coffee. Jacob wandered down the stairs as Jonathan gathered his rifle case and pack. Always a bit groggy in the morning, the boy was rubbing his eyes. "Are you leaving?" he asked.

"Yeah, buddy, but I'll be back in a couple days."

"Are you going to shoot something?"

"I don't know, buddy. Maybe." Jonathan faked a smile, trying to let the boy know everything was okay. He pulled his son close and hugged him, the boy's head just above his waist. Jacob let himself be hugged but was too tired and unaware to fully reciprocate. It was okay, Jonathan thought. *This is all for you anyhow.*

Conner's SUV pulled up the driveway. Mary stopped him as he was walking out the door. "You forgot this," she said and lifted his rucksack with all his hunting supplies, minus the rifle. Jonathan was lost for a moment and then took the rucksack from her hand, his charade momentarily interrupted like an actor forgetting his line for a split second. Mary looked at him, suspicious, knowing something was off. "What kind of hunter would you be without this?"

"Not much of one, I suppose."

"I found it still locked away downstairs. You didn't even bring it up. Were you not planning on taking it at all? No bullets, no knife, anything? You're not even taking your tree stand."

"Don't use stands up there. We'll be on foot." He stared into her eyes and she stared back through his soul. He had no more lies left to give. The truth was too close, it was burning through his skin.

After a moment of looking into him, she said tenderly, "I hope you find peace out there."

And because he could not lie anymore, he only said, "Me too." He kissed her for what felt like the last time of their marriage and then walked out the door to the waiting Suburban. Maybe he was confronting it, but then maybe he was burying it deeper. He was confused. He no longer knew if what they were doing was right. He had lost sight of what was right long ago. He only knew what was wrong, particularly what was most wrong for himself and his family. Nothing in any of this was right, but the boy being found by the authorities would be the most wrong thing that could happen to him. Nobility and morality had been buried ten years ago; only half-truths and survival remained.

He loaded his rifle and gear into the back of Conner's SUV. It was packed mostly with camping gear and the small inflatable raft – a tightly wrapped piece of canvas and rubber that could be hauled on a backpack – they would use to bring the coffin to the center of the lake before sinking it to the bottom. His stomach dropped as he shut the door and Conner started the engine. There was no turning back; they had stepped off the cliff and were being pulled by gravity toward their final destination.

The three were silent in the morning hours, contemplating their ugly purpose, feigning tiredness as an excuse not to speak. Conner's SUV was new, a big Chevy Suburban outfitted nicely with leather and all the accoutrements of modern life, a testament to his success in the insurance industry. Money to spare and show. Jonathan knew he was the third wheel in this equation. Even in silence the unspoken, psychic connection between the Braddick brothers filled the space between them. Jonathan attempted small talk, trying to rekindle the friendly, jovial banter they'd enjoyed as children and young men, and Conner did his best to accommodate, while Michael stayed largely silent. Jonathan finally turned and watched the passing landscape, wondering what else lay beyond their grasp of reality. Michael turned on the radio and scanned through static to the self-assured voices and music that had been popular when they were kids.

"Sometimes I wonder if we're just stuck in a time loop," Michael finally said. "Same damn music has been playing for twenty years. It never disappears, just keeps playing on some other channel."

He finally shut it off.

They stopped for coffee before getting on the Mass Pike. They drove west into New York and then shot straight as a bullet up I-80. It was the longest part of the trip, an easy five hours even with the sparse traffic. Albany was the last glimmer of civilization before the southern half of the state locked its doors and the land began to heave – first hills, then mountains where double-hitched tractor-trailers struggled up inclines and barreled down long, winding passages, nearly out of control. The hills just north of Albany were still colorful, filled with the red, orange and shades of brown that paint autumn. Farther north, along Lake George, the leaves fell away. The bare trees reached bone-gray branches into the sky, coating the mountains in a deadly dull pallor. In the old days, it would have been a thing of beauty to the three of them, the leafless trees making it easier to spot a deer. Now it just added to their desperation.

On a long, straight stretch of highway, as the engine climbed a lumbering incline, Conner told Michael to reach in the glove box. Michael pulled out some maps. He looked at them briefly and then unfolded one like a small accordion. Jonathan could see from the back seat hundreds of lightly colored lines lying on top of each other at varying degrees of separation, revealing the topography of the mountainous region around Pasternak. The map was marked with a line running west from a region of depressed elevation to a splotch of blue buried between two steep peaks.

"That's the route we're going to take, as best as I can figure it," Conner said. "I used satellite images to find the location – our starting point. At least I think it is. Hard to tell, but I'm pretty sure I remembered it right."

Jonathan sat up in his seat, poking his head between the two front seats so he could see over Michael's broad shoulder. The route was traced with blue marker. The cabin was marked north of Pasternak at the edge of the negative depression of the Gulch. Not far from the cabin was an X – the body. From there the blue line followed the lowest country available to the lake. Even on the map it looked long.

"The cell service is shit up there," Conner said. "So I thought we should all have identical maps in case we get separated for any reason."

"Separated?" Jonathan asked.

"You never know," Conner said. Jonathan couldn't imagine these two brothers, who had been each other's best friend since the day

Conner was born, ever being separated. Even after the incident, as they all drifted away from each other to erase the past – as Jonathan slipped into loneliness and Gene tried to drown his memories – Conner and Michael never separated. It wasn't in their nature; they worked in tandem.

"This looks rough. A long haul," Michael said. "You remember what that country was like. Dragging that case with us, getting through that thick ground cover. It isn't going to be easy."

"It's seven miles," Conner said. "Even if we're only doing forty-minute miles, we can make it in a day. I kept our path in the lowest elevation possible so we're not climbing those mountains. If you look, there's a corridor between two of the peaks on the western ridge. There's a field there, just tall grass, as best I can tell. We can make good time there." Michael traced the route with his finger until he found the flattened section of meadow before a slower, more casual descent toward the lake.

"If we start in the morning, we can make it to the lake by nightfall. Camp there, head back and then get the hell out of town."

"I don't know," Michael said. "It's going to be tough, slow-going. Might actually be a day and a half's hike with everything in tow. Tents, guns, food, the box." Michael took out his phone and pulled up satellite images of Coombs' Gulch. He focused in on the passage between the peaks. "It's thick brush. It won't be easy no matter what."

"Let's not make this longer than we have to," Jonathan said. "Early up, get it done. Don't stop moving till it's over."

"It's the best route," Conner said. "The only way there is between those two peaks, unless you feel like climbing a mountain – which I don't. It's kind of the long way around, but any other route would be too dangerous, too difficult."

Michael was still on his phone. "There's going to be bad weather moving in by day three," he said. "Should be all right till then, but that gives us three days before the temperature really drops, and it's either rain or snow, depending." Michael dropped the phone and then stared at the topographic map with its hypnotic lines and swirls that masked the true nature of the place. "I don't like it," Michael said. "Can't say why."

"Nobody likes any of this, Mike," Conner said, and for the first time Jonathan felt a tension between them that seemed almost murderous in its betrayal. He remembered how fast tempers can flare between brothers who have everything to lose between them. "The plan will work. The route will work. I've been planning this out for months. We just need to man up and get through it. I never said it would be easy, but it has to be done."

Conner's SUV ate gas fast enough to warrant two stops, the first just past Albany as civilization began to stretch thin. They pulled off at a quiet Shell station overlooking the highway as double-rigged tractor-trailers passed below, burning diesel and rattling jake brakes in their descent. The few cars on the highway echoed in the cold, sharp air. The sun was bright but without warmth, and there were few shadows. Jonathan crawled from the back and stretched his legs. It was a lonely place. The sound of the highway died in the trees and every second seemed like the last.

Michael and Jonathan walked inside the small store while Conner gassed up the Suburban. Jonathan retrieved a soda and pawed at some bagged snacks but didn't have much of an appetite. He looked at the newspaper headlines, national and local, but at this point nothing could occupy space in his head.

Michael came around the corner of the aisle. He carried a case of canned beer and was loading up on chips and pretzels. "It's gonna be a long trip. Probably another couple hours and then another hour or so to get Bill and get to the cabin. Might as well be stocked up." Michael had an edge to him, as if the small rift between him and his brother ran deeper than Jonathan realized, or at least shook Michael enough to put him in a foul mood.

"Really?" Jonathan whispered. "I don't think…"

"Do you really want to be dead sober this whole time? You of all people? Do you really want to remember all this?" Jonathan felt that old dread wriggling at the back of his mind, an excitement that welled up within him at the thought of drowning out reality, even if only for a short time. He took a ten-dollar bill from his wallet and gave it to Michael. Conner saw them walking from the store with the beer and seemed annoyed he would be chauffeuring them through the mountains like he had ten years ago.

Jonathan stayed stretched out in the back seat, drinking the beer, letting his brain go numb and thoughts cloud over as they continued past Lake George. His mind softened and returned to dark ideas. Jonathan hadn't told the brothers anything about his most recent online searches, about his insane suspicions, a line of thought he toyed with for no other reason than a lack of options. He had searched for so long, through so many missing person reports, that he'd finally veered off the well-worn path of rationality and spun a fact-based fiction. He had a creative mind; he knew he was subject to an imagination easily dismissed by someone with the opposite tendency like Michael, for whom the simplest explanation would always suffice. Jonathan could picture Michael's response already and couldn't blame him. Michael had been known to become visibly angry when confronted with irrationality – emotions and stupidity set him off like gasoline to fire. Conner would probably dismiss any explanation out of his need to just be done with it and get back to his life. But Jonathan needed some kind of reason, some rationale as to who the boy was or what he was doing out there on his own. It was like following a pathway as far as it would go, only to find that it led to the edge of an abyss. Was it Nietzsche who said something about the abyss staring back?

So Jonathan decided to stare into the abyss some more. While Michael rifled beers in the front, Jonathan began searching through children who went missing further in the past than any of them had bothered looking. He found websites that preserved old missing files from decades before the internet and transferred them into searchable data. He pushed further and further into the past – news articles, bulletins, photographs of 'missing' posters, grainy, pixilated photos on the back of milk cartons. His eyes sagged from the beer and the early morning. The images blurred. He kept scrolling and scrolling; the pictures flashed by like television commercials.

And then, like a dream, the moment came to him – the moment that had eluded him for so long. A flash of recognition, a clenching in his gut before his mind could even register the tiny image on the screen. *His face.* Young and flesh-colored and whole. Jonathan saw him smiling with small white teeth, boyish hands soft and curled in his lap of corduroy pants. His plaid shirt in muted, earthy colors, born out of the Seventies when every color seemed a shade of yellow and brown. It was a school photo of Thomas Terrywile, and it was attached to a newspaper article from the *Desmond Dispatch* out of Pennsylvania, dated 1985. The headline read, 'Local Boy Missing, Police Find Signs of Cult Activity'.

Thomas disappeared after school on April 28 over thirty years ago. He was last seen walking home from school, setting out across the football field behind the Edward McNally Middle School in Desmond, PA. His home was a short quarter-mile walk on a path through a small, crooked finger of trees connected to an expansive forest to the north. He took the path to and from school every day, not uncommon at the time. Several other schoolchildren took the same path, all hailing from the same small neighborhood, but this day he was walking alone. Some kids noticed him leaving but paid little attention, a small figure disappearing down the path, nothing out of the ordinary. But by eight o'clock that night, his mother, Candace Terrywile, called the school, friends, neighbors and finally the police.

A search party with flashlights turned up nothing that night. The next morning came the dogs that followed his scent from the school, along the path through the woods and then somehow lost the trail. The search expanded into a massive town-wide undertaking by the third day. Helicopters brought in by the Pennsylvania State Police hovered low over the forest, and police were taking tips from anybody and everybody who could offer some kind of information.

Rumors and whispers started trickling into the police and washed like a flood across the town – people in the forest at night, the sound of chanting carried on the wind, strange glowing lights that emanated out from the trees, strange individuals clad all in black with wide eyes and ugly skin seen roaming through parking lots at the edge of the trees. It was a dark time during the history of the nation. The papers and television were rife with claims of killer cults, Satanists who would kidnap children and sacrifice them in occult rituals. The rumors and stories reached the blood-sucking media, and soon national news helicopters joined the Pennsylvania police search and ran over miles of forested land that stretched out beyond the town. Headlines splashed fantastic rumors and speculation; special detectives were called in from other counties.

The hysteria of Thomas Terrywile's disappearance finally culminated in some grainy photos of a clearing in those woods. The supposed site of some kind of cult ritual. The leaves were clearly raked out of a circular area. Rocks, partially set in the ground, were arranged in a circle surrounding a rather elaborate geometric design, and then formed a series of crisscrossing lines – some of which extended beyond the edge of the circle, with a final, rectangular space in the center. The detectives were at a loss to explain the design. It was not the typical pentagram found on heavy-metal album covers and spray-painted on abandoned bridges. An altar was set to the side, built with stones placed one atop another and stained with a dark brown substance. Supposedly occult symbols were carved in the trees, small animal bones were piled together to form particular, peculiar designs, and there was evidence of a fire. The police found a small, ramshackle cabin beyond the clearing. Syringes on the ground, more strange symbols spray-painted on the plywood walls, candles dripping dark wax. There was children's clothing on the floor of the cabin, but none of it matched up to Thomas Terrywile. Fingernails had carved deep gouges in the wood walls. The police did the usual for the time – rousted some of the local teenagers and weirdos with long hair and black T-shirts and questioned them, revealing sordid tales of marijuana use and rebellion against the moral majority. But there was no sign of Thomas Terrywile anywhere. No one the cops questioned could explain the symbols in the woods. None of them had any connection together, despite a desperate search for a larger conspiracy. In the end, there was nothing. Thomas Terrywile was gone without a trace.

And then, like a shooting star, the story disappeared. The media moved on to the next big headline, satisfied with an answer that was not an answer at all. Jonathan found a final article about Thomas Terrywile – not so much about him but about his mother, left afraid and alone. It was one of those 'still looking after five long years' stories, and pictured in that newspaper was Thomas's mother. She was only thirty-seven years old but looked fifty, lips caving into her dry and withering mouth, her big, Eighties-style perm translucent in an obvious and sad attempt to cover up her hair loss. Even in the photograph, Jonathan could see her scalp. A dress from the dollar-store rack hung from her shoulders. She looked like a ghost, and her words, though printed, were the words of the dead and defeated. Reporters asked her if she was still looking. "I'll never stop looking," she told them. "I still get people calling me every year saying they saw him. In a crowd in the city. In a park all alone feeding some ducks. Walking through a campground in Nebraska. He's out there somewhere, I can feel it. It's like he's there and gone at the same time; it just depends on when you look. I just feel like the whole world blinked and he was gone. But maybe if we all blink again, he'll be there."

Jonathan forced Conner to pull to the side of the road. He fell out of the back seat onto the cold asphalt and the sparse, dying grass that smelled of rubber and oil, and vomited up whatever was left in his stomach. He wished he could purge more just then – organs, blood, memories.

Michael was still drinking a beer in the passenger seat, and Conner was mumbling something to himself, his normally cool facade giving way to a brooding anger and frustration. The brothers looked down at him in a mixture of annoyance and disgust. It was an impossibility; Jonathan knew they would never believe him. He didn't believe it himself, but he knew it was the same boy – something primeval in his mind screamed in recognition. His hands dug at the pebbles on the side of the road; his mouth sucked in cold air tinged with bile. The wind shook the trees.

Jonathan turned and looked back at them in horror.

CHAPTER TEN

They arrived in Pasternak a little after 5:00 p.m. with the sun inching below the western mountains and the town preternaturally dark. It was a place that seemed to grow up out of nothing, like a patch of moss on a giant rock. It was a dying place, not long for this world. Pasternak was forever losing – people, business, life. It seemed to shrink in the cold shadow of the mountains but somehow remained populated with stragglers who found ways to get by with virtually no major industry in the area. The town was originally settled in 1850 as an iron mining and timber town, but social and governmental changes ended it before it could ever really begin. The Adirondack logging industry was pursued by the government, while large and brutal corporations sought to capitalize on veins of iron that coursed through the mountains and played havoc with explorers' compasses. The iron industry, however, never truly materialized. Only five years into opening operations and building over one hundred factory houses in Pasternak, the Witherbee-Sherman Mining Company closed up the mines and shuttered its blast furnaces. The deposits around Pasternak were too deep, the iron veins too thin to follow to their source. A small collapse, which claimed the lives of five men, finally ended operations, and Witherbee-Sherman decided to focus on their other factory towns like Mineville and Moriah. The logging industry held on for two decades before famed topographical engineer and environmental activist Verplanck Colvin issued his poetic and apocalyptic report to the state legislature, saying the Adirondack wilderness warranted preservation. The state reacted quickly and decisively, creating a state forest preserve that exists to this day. Pasternak was ruined virtually overnight, and the townspeople burnt an effigy of Colvin during a disturbing night of unrest. Old-timers, steeped in the history of the town, still sneer at the mention of his name, and the collective loathing ran as deep as the iron deposits beneath coniferous mountains, which remain untouched.

Few new houses had been built since the 1800s, and the 'town' consisted of Main Street and two bisecting roads that created a small square of commerce. The 'commerce' consisted of one gas station (there was a second by the freeway), a diner, a bar, VFW, a small supply store, and some specialty shops that sold guns and ammo, bait and tackle, musical instruments and home decor. The white steeple of a one-room church was the highest point, reaching just above the trees at the western end. The small, brick elementary school was around the corner. There were two more blocks of houses in either direction, but there wasn't much keeping Pasternak running besides spite and a continual need to hang on to the last remnants of a forgotten life. At least an hour's drive from any populated area that could actually give someone a career, it seemed to exist outside time and culture, a place that would probably never die but was never truly alive to begin with. If anything supplied Pasternak with lifeblood it was, in one way or the other, the wilderness itself. A river crisscrossed with small bridges ran alongside the town square. The water was low from lack of rain, shallow swirls of darkness around gray-white stones. The trees crept in from every direction. One could turn a corner and find themselves face-to-face with a vast wilderness, constantly lurking at the threshold.

Conner pulled into the parking lot of a small Piggly Wiggly, which did its best to supply everything the townspeople might need before they had to get on the highway and drive several miles south to an actual store. Pickup trucks lined the sidewalks. There were a few small cars in a Cumberland Farms parking lot. Michael was slightly drunk, Conner's eyes bloodshot from driving, Jonathan's face drained, withered and white. He felt like he was seeing the world – the real world – for the first time, shocked into existence by the ghost of Thomas Terrywile.

In that way he resembled the residents of Pasternak – at least the few who were wandering the aisles of the small grocery. Obviously single, unshaved older men limped slowly with handheld baskets; abandoned women leaned heavily on wire shopping carts with chattering wheels to support their aged bulk. They all seemed in a similar state of shock, as if the bottom had dropped out from beneath them and they were lost in a new weightless, worthless world. The only sign of life was the girl working the checkout register, waiting for a customer, her thumb swiping at a smartphone.

Jonathan and the brothers bought food they could carry – jerky, candy bars, trail mix – and then food for the cabin – eggs, bacon, bread, peanut butter. Conner planned on a massive breakfast before setting out in the morning. The girl at the register was probably sixteen, blond hair in a ponytail and disinterested eyes. She could have been found anywhere in America, but she was here and resented that most of all.

Michael stopped briefly at the neighboring liquor store and bought three bottles of whiskey, mumbling, "We'll need these." Stress fractures were beginning to show on his stony face. Conner remained business as usual, keeping up his slick demeanor, but Jonathan suspected that by the end they all would be revealed, stripped of their phony facades, like a gutted deer, opened to show its inner workings to the world.

Bill Flood's apartment was just above the Olde American Diner on the corner of Main and Black Bridge Road, which crossed the cold and frothy Wilbur Creek. Darkness came early as the sun dropped below the mountains, and light from the diner showed a few couples seated in Fifties-style booths and men in trucker caps drinking coffee. A hastily constructed wooden staircase climbed the side of the diner to a small landing outside Bill's apartment. Conner knocked while Jonathan and Michael waited a couple of steps below. They waited and knocked again and waited.

"Are you fucking kidding me?" Conner said.

"He knew we were coming?" Jonathan asked.

"I talked to him last week," Conner said. He took out his phone and called. They could hear the phone ringing just beyond the door. He then tried Bill's cell phone, but it went straight to voicemail.

"Goddammit," Conner said. "I just want to be there already."

"Does anyone remember how to get to the cabin? Maybe we could go out there without him," Jonathan said.

"Hell if I remember. The road isn't even on the map, and even if we found it, what are we going to do, break in?" Conner said.

They stood for a moment longer, looking around the dark, lonely town accented with streetlights. It was cold, approaching freezing. Trucks and cars rolled down Main Street; figures with thick jackets and jeans trundled along the sidewalk in and out of the glow of shop windows and the Olde American Diner. From only the second floor, they could see over the tops of the century-old buildings to the surrounding mountains.

"We're going to be out there with all that," Jonathan said.

"With all what?"

He nodded toward the heavy darkness. The brothers looked and understood, on some level. At least at home there was the knowledge that civilization was right around the corner, but here there was no such refuge. In the mountains, night was still as ancient as when man first sparked fire and prayed to strange gods. And now they were here, dressed as hunters like Conner's young son at the Halloween parade, pretending they could go out and live that dark life, complete their sacrifice. New fools in an old world, staring into the immense black of a moonless night.

There was no sign of Bill in the diner, and the waitress said she hadn't seen him all day, but that he was a regular in the mornings. She suggested trying a tavern just down the street where he was known to frequent. Conner kept shaking his head and cursing Bill beneath his breath.

Jonathan called Mary to check in and tell her they had arrived safely but were still waiting on the cabin owner. He talked with Jacob and told his only son that he missed him. It was true; he missed them both terribly, the purpose of the trip adding to his burden, his fear of losing the only good things in his life if the plan went awry. Already the signs were not good. They were all tense. Everything needed to function perfectly in order for them to complete their task and return home before the weather set in. Jonathan told Mary cell coverage was limited at the cabin, so this was probably the last he'd speak to her or Jacob for three days. He told her he loved her and then told himself it was all for her and Jacob. It was both the truth and a lie.

Finally, Michael said, "Fuck it, let's get some food and beers. Maybe we can find that old bastard at that bar." Conner drove the SUV across the small town and parked outside The Forge, a tavern with small windows shining Pabst and Budweiser neon into the night. The Forge was a small place. It looked ramshackle even in a place as poor as Pasternak, the kind of place that probably spurred numerous public safety complaints but would never be touched because all the men drank there.

The inside was all dim light and smoke, New York's anti-smoking laws ignored in this quiet cave. There were several tables in the front, and the bar ran the length of a narrow, wood-paneled interior. Men wrapped in shade and flannel, with thick hands and forearms, sat in booths and on barstools. The bartender was bone thin, scraggly hair dripping down his skull; he wore only jeans and an undershirt. The air inside was hot and stale and smelled of old grease and beer. A group of five men were talking at the corner of the bar, laughing loudly, beers in hand, looking up occasionally at a television running football highlights. They went silent when Conner, Michael and Jonathan walked through the door. It was right out of an old Western. Some things never change; in a neighborhood bar, when strangers walk in they get looked up and down. Ten or twelve years earlier it would have been the three of them back at home standing in the corner of the East Side Tavern, swilling cheap beer and staring down the newcomer. Yet this seemed different. The place literally went silent, and it wasn't until after they sat down at a table that the talking began again, this time in slow and low murmurs.

"You sure you want to eat here?" Conner asked, but Michael was already thumbing through a plastic menu on the table. Conner gave up and looked at Jonathan. "You want to go get some beers?" Jonathan nodded and they walked to the bar. The bartender took his time coming down. He looked worse up close, lips cracked, the skin of his arms marked with puncture wounds.

"Kitchen open?" Conner asked.

"Sure thing, you just let me know what you want." They ordered two pitchers of beer and paid cash. Conner left a good tip, which seemed to soften the bartender up a bit.

"You boys just get in from out of town?" he said.

Conner settled into his social easiness, like water around any obstruction. "Yeah, we were supposed to meet up with Bill Flood, but we can't find him anywhere."

"Bill Flood? What do you want with that old bastard?" The bartender was practically laughing.

"We rented his cabin up in Coombs' Gulch. He was supposed to take us out there tonight to open it up, but he isn't home and isn't answering the phone."

"You guys ain't trying to hunt up there, are you?"

"Why?"

"Place is dead as a grave. I don't think anybody's shot anything up there in a decade. Bill done took you for a ride if you're paying good money to go hunt the Gulch."

"Really?" Conner said. "We did pretty good last time we were here."

"When was that?"

"'Bout ten years ago."

"Well, things have changed up there," he said. "Listen, friend. Don't give Bill Flood your money. I got a couple buddies here that will take you out to some real hunting spots, show you around a bit. They're kinda like guides." He gestured down to the end of the bar. Four thick-faced men with small shiny eyes raised their beer glasses to them, and Conner nodded back. One had a big, red beard, hands thick as a bear's paws and sweat pouring down the sides of his head. He smiled and stared at them. Jonathan felt a deep discomfort in his stomach. The bartender gestured over his shoulder. "Larry here knows these woods better than anybody. Takes folks out hunting all the time."

"I appreciate the offer," Conner said. "But I think we'll take our chances as it is. Have you seen Bill at all?"

The bartender suddenly cooled, seemingly offended at the rejection of his offer. "Nah, I ain't seen him since last night when he was tying one on. He's probably up at that cabin right now, drunk out of his mind." The bartender leaned over the bar, in close, and Jonathan could suddenly smell him, flesh and sweat. "Listen, you guys don't want to go up there. Last group that went up there, they lost a couple guys. Got all turned around; two of them died of exposure, stuck outside all night. You boys don't want to go there, 'specially if you don't know what you're doing. They're gonna pave over that whole section of forest next year. In my opinion, it can't come soon enough."

Michael came to the bar and interrupted the awkward moment, changing the subject to food. They ordered burgers and wings, loading up for the night, and then took their seats, pouring out draught beer into pint glasses.

"So that was interesting," Conner said.

"What happened?" Michael said.

"They pretty much warned us off of Coombs' Gulch."

"Fuck them," Michael said.

"It doesn't matter," Jonathan said. "We just need to get this done. We need to find Bill."

"There must be somebody who knows where he is."

"Like the guy said, he's probably at the cabin right now, drunk off his ass." The bartender talked with the good ol' boys down at the end of the bar, occasionally glancing at their table, probably trying to figure out how they could make some money off of the newcomers aside from their failed 'hunting guide' offer.

They ate simple food, nothing the kitchen could screw up too badly. Conner kept trying to call Bill Flood.

Michael went up to use the bathroom at the shadowed end of the bar, and Jonathan sat dazed, staring into his beer. Conner was sending Bill an email telling him they were looking for him. Then there was a commotion, activity that bled into Jonathan's vision from the corner of his eye. Michael, one arm extended, shoved a big, red-bearded lurcher back into his barstool. It seemed to happen in a separate moment in time, the rest of the world waiting to catch up. Then everything went fast and loud. The others pushed Michael back against the wall, and someone reached over and grabbed him by the shirt collar. A quick punch was thrown. Beer glasses spilled and broke. Michael threw a fist over someone's shoulder, breaking a nose. Jonathan and Conner were up, pushing chairs out of their way, rushing toward the melee at the end of the bar. The bartender got out a piece of pipe. Everything was hazy and smoky and blurred. They rushed into a mess of arms and shoulders that felt like rock, pushing them off Michael. A fist the size of a ham caught Jonathan above the eye. He swung out with a left, and then a battery of hands and arms flew at him; he ducked his head from the barrage. An arm wrapped around his neck from behind and squeezed, and Jonathan suddenly couldn't inhale. He panicked, trying to pull the thick arm away from his neck. Jonathan pushed the big man back against the bar and rammed his lower back into the wood, punched him in the groin and nearly tore his own ear off pulling out of the chokehold. Jonathan stared the man in the eye for a moment – black, glossy marbles, dimmed with alcohol, a black-and-white goatee that reached his Adam's apple, a look of violent intensity in his face – and then punched him square in the mouth. His fist scraped against whiskers and ripped across teeth, and the sheer violence of it suddenly made Jonathan want to quit and just take the beating. Conner and Michael struggled against Larry and two bigger, meaner-looking men, and then Jonathan saw the bartender, with his piece of pipe, wrap one of them around the throat and pull them off Michael. He grabbed them by their collars and pulled them away as if it were an old game he was accustomed to playing, like a woman with a lot of dogs who occasionally has to keep them from killing each other. His voice rang across the bar, and suddenly it all seemed to stop. Jonathan was tossed to the ground and landed hard on the old wood floor. He could see legs and jeans and boots and heard the bartender telling them to get the fuck out. "I've had enough of this shit every night, Larry! Get your shit and get out. Got enough trouble here!"

"Fuck yourself, Andy. You're no fucking good anyway." Larry was practically lunging at the bartender, who held up his pipe, ready to strike.

It was quiet, but there was electricity in the air; they were all panting, eyes bugging out of their heads, hearts pounding, blood pulsing, pulling at their clothes to put them back in their proper place, waiting for the next move. Jonathan stood up so he was ready, and the three of them stood facing the five locals with a pipe-wielding bartender holding the tentative peace.

Finally, Larry looked away from Michael and back to the bartender. Larry was bleeding from the nose, his red mustache and beard looked wet and tinged with darkness. "Fine, Andy. We'll leave. But I didn't lay a finger on that fucker. He hit first. You saw that."

"You know what you said, Larry. I can't be having this shit on a nightly basis with you."

Larry pointed a finger at Michael. "This shit ain't over. You fellas better watch your back."

"The fuck is that supposed to mean?" Michael said.

"You all are strangers here. Don't forget that shit. Enjoy Coombs', you peckerwood pussies."

Larry and his friends shouldered through and went out the rickety door into the night. Jonathan finally let down his guard and breathed and started taking account of any damage. He'd been hit a few times; he just wasn't sure how bad yet. He rubbed a hand across the side of his face. His knuckles were bleeding where they'd cut across teeth. Blood leaked from the corner of his mouth, and his left ear felt like the skin had rubbed off. A knot formed on his forehead above his right eye. Michael and Conner were in similar shape. No missing teeth, no apparent broken bones, everyone tuned up and coming down and restless. Michael fumed.

Conner thanked the bartender, but he only stared, pipe in hand. "You don't get too welcomed up here by getting into a fight with those boys. Some of them are all right. Some of them ain't. Just sayin'. You boys best be finding Bill Flood and get the hell out of town."

Defeat began to set in, and they sat back down at the table, still wanting to be anywhere but here.

"What the fuck happened?" Conner asked.

"He said something," Michael said. "He was saying... I don't know. Strange things. He threatened us."

"So what?" Conner said. "It's not worth pissing off guys like that up here."

Jonathan could now see that Michael was drunker than he let on. He'd always had the ability to hide it well, his glazed-over eyes the only telltale sign.

"We'll be lucky if we go up there and they don't kill us in our sleep."

"We have guns," Michael said.

"They probably got a thousand guns!" Conner said. Then he lowered his voice to a whisper. "We can't afford to be making mistakes. We can't afford to be remembered. We can't afford to have the police talking to us. Don't lose focus on why we're here. It's certainly not to fuck around with the local wildlife."

Jonathan watched the bartender for a time. They had pretty much chased out all his business for the night. He stood up and went to the bar to pay the tab. The bartender looked him up and down and seemed repulsed.

Jonathan paid the tab and tipped him a twenty. "Sorry about all that," he said. "But thank you for not letting us get killed."

The bartender's eyes burned bright and huge beneath his long hair, as if he were riding some insane beast that only he could see. "I can't stop you from getting killed, friend. I can only stop you from getting killed in here."

Jonathan nodded. "Do you know how to get to Bill Flood's cabin? It's just we have nowhere to stay tonight and if someone could show us how to get there..."

"Never been there myself. Never had reason to. Place isn't any good these days anyway. But there might be someone I can call. Bill's good friends with this guy Daryl Teague. I know he knows how to get out there."

Jonathan tipped him another ten. "It would be a big help," he said. "It would get us out of here anyway."

He took the ten and said, "Probably for the best then," and walked to the phone.

Conner groaned the second they walked outside to wait for Daryl Teague. All four tires of his Suburban were slashed, and the SUV sat on its rims like a beached whale. The night grew longer and longer. In ancient times it would all have been a warning of disaster, the various problems, big and small. The rhythm of the trip was all wrong. The ancients would have turned back by now, knowing that the time for this undertaking was not right with the gods, but then, they had no other time, no other way.

"What the hell do we do now?" Michael said.

"We have to keep going," Conner said. "There's no choice."

CHAPTER ELEVEN

Daryl Teague was abnormally huge. He arrived in a Ford F-150 about the same time the wrecker showed up from Cerutti's Tire and Auto shop, and the truck righted itself when he stepped out of the driver's seat and onto the pavement. The bartender didn't offer to call the police and Conner didn't ask him to. Conner was deeply angry. He folded his arms behind his head like a runner at the end of a marathon and sighed.

Daryl Teague had the air of a man who did not give a shit about anything and was too big for anyone to make him. Daryl's pinky and ring finger were missing from his left hand – something they saw immediately as he brought a cigarette repeatedly to his mouth. He noticed their eyes watching his hand and held up his three-fingers and wiggled them, smiling, seemingly proud. He said he lost them from frostbite – the result of driving during the winter with the window down while holding a cigarette. "My fingers went numb and I didn't even realize it," he said. "It gets real cold up here." That was his story, but they all knew it was untrue. How could someone not realize his fingers were being frozen black? It was impossible. Conner and Jonathan just smiled and nodded, anyway.

"Why didn't you just roll up your window?" Michael asked.

Daryl Teague smiled. "Don't want the truck to smell like smoke." For a man that size, everything could be a joke. He barely took a breath without cigarette smoke. Daryl raised his three remaining fingers to his lips and removed the second cigarette he had finished since arriving at The Forge. They could smell the inside of the truck from ten feet away, ash and wet dirt.

Mario from Cerutti's Tire and Auto gave the SUV a look over and was then on the phone with his brother at the shop. A tall, bent man with a permanent Italian five-o'clock shadow, he finally walked over to the group. "I don't have this size tire in stock right now. It'll take me twenty-four hours to get them up here. Gotta ship them in. That's as quick as it can be done. Everything's closed now anyway, so I can't order them till the morning. I'll tow it tonight, put them on as soon as they get in."

It was nearly eight o'clock at night now. They needed to be hiking through Coombs' Gulch by six in the morning to keep pace with Conner's plan.

Jonathan and the brothers turned to a small huddle. "I don't see how this is going to work," Jonathan said. "This just isn't happening."

"We need to stick to the plan. Everything can be fixed, paid for. It's just a bump in the road."

"It's a bit more than a bump. I got a bad feeling about all this."

"Did you ever have a good feeling about this? Don't get superstitious."

Daryl approached like the shadow of a mountain in the night, and they all turned and looked up at him. "Listen, I know you guys had a deal with Bill. He told me about it a few days ago. If you all want, I can drive you out there so you can get started on your trip." He inhaled deeply on another cigarette. "Tell you what. Leave the keys with me. When the truck is fixed, me and my buddy will drive it out to the cabin and drop it off for ya; how's that sound?"

Conner was still rolling his eyes in anger.

"Yeah. Yeah, that'll work," Michael said. "We'll pay you for your trouble."

Daryl smiled. "Damn right. I'm sure Bill is still out there right now, anyway. It's been a while since anybody rented the place, so he was going up to give it a once-over. Can't say I'm surprised he forgot to come back. Load your gear in the back." He looked at the three of them and nodded at Michael. "You, big fella, you grab the front seat, and you two smaller guys can squeeze in the back."

Mario was waiting on a final decision, saying he had another call. Daryl seemed to consider the three outsiders for a moment. "Don't worry yourselves about the car; I ain't going nowhere with it. You pay, you'll get it delivered. Hundred bucks will do it."

They all ponied up and paid him, then moved their stuff out of the Suburban and into the bed of Daryl's truck. Mario hooked up the winch and pulled the SUV up onto the wrecker.

Conner and Jonathan had to bend their legs and practically lie against each other to fit into the back of Daryl Teague's Ford. Daryl drove with the window down, his three-fingered left hand hanging out the side of the truck, a tiny cigarette clutched between them. They all shivered in the cold. The cigarette glowed in the night air.

"You boys look a little banged up. Rough night?"

"Long day," Michael said. "Couple assholes."

"Huh. Larry can be that way sometimes. Him and his group, that's their way. People up here get territorial, is all. Especially now with the new highway system coming through. Gonna be lots of development in the coming years. Lot of people were pissed at Bill for agreeing to sell his land. He was standing between the town and the whole project. They weren't going to be able to build without his thousand acres in Coombs' Gulch. They offered him enough money that he's gonna move outta Pasternak and probably buy a mansion somewhere down south."

"Good for him," Conner said, returning to his friendly, winning self. "We figured we'd get one last trip in while it was still here."

"You know there hasn't been much wildlife out there for a while, right?"

"It's more for posterity's sake," Conner said. "Old times we had there."

Daryl nodded and grunted. "I couldn't help but notice you fellas had tents and hiking gear in there. Just a friendly warning, you gotta be real careful up in Coombs' Gulch when you're hiking. Bill usually tells people not to wander too far from the cabin. People get turned around up there, suddenly don't know where they are, and next thing you know we're calling out search and rescue to find some weekend warriors lost in the woods."

"The bartender said a couple guys got lost up there a few years back?"

"Yup. That's the case. Two of them died of exposure. They was here later in the season than you guys. Snow was tough that year and they were stuck in it. Still, it was a rough scene when they were finally found."

"How so?"

"Whelp. There was four of them at first. Hunters, like yourselves, but they kept pushing farther out because they weren't finding any deer. So they pushed farther and got turned around. You know the general layout of the Gulch, right?" Daryl said, and they all grunted in approval. "Looks simple enough, right? North to south, ridged with mountains to the east and west. Seems like it should be easy to navigate, right? Well, one thing the rescuers found when they were out looking for those boys is because of the way the two mountain ridges look from the valley; they're practically mirror images of each other. Makes east look like west, north like south. People get all turned around and that's what happened to those guys."

"Jesus," Jonathan said beneath his breath.

"Nah, he ain't out there," Daryl said with a smile, "at least not for these guys." But Jonathan was more concerned about their trip sending them into uncharted territory.

"Anyway," Daryl continued, "when they found those guys, the ones who were alive were damn near starved to death and frozen. The other two had nothing to worry about anymore. But the two fellas that were alive – ain't never seen nothing like it. They were barely able to speak, just kept mumbling about the mountains. We traced their tracks through the snow back to the other two. They were stone cold dead, sitting upright. The look on their faces – I tell you something – looked like they died of fright. Mouths wide open, eyes wide open, blue with frost. That was the last time anybody went wandering around Coombs' Gulch. When the state and those developers came in looking to buy it up, Bill saw the opportunity, milked them for as much as he could. That's Bill for ya, though. Never met a deal he couldn't milk for something better."

They listened to Daryl Teague drone on and on. He wasn't the strong, silent type. The black trees blurred as they traveled; Conner and Jonathan bounced in the back seat over the potholes with spine-jarring shocks as they turned onto the dirt road toward the cabin.

"You guys know the history of Coombs' Gulch, right? How it got its name?"

"Christ, there's more?" Conner said. "Don't tell me you're going to spin some Indian legend?"

Daryl eyed Conner and smiled from the corner of his mouth. "Nah. No Indian legends up here. They avoided the place except for wars between tribes. Nah. The Gulch got its name from Charles Coombs III – a very peculiar fella."

A soft glow appeared out of the trees ahead. The outdoor lights of the cabin cast an electric glow in the darkness, the trees like ghosts, the ground beneath bare and lifeless dirt. The inside of the cabin was lit as well, the windows like yellow eyes. Parked in front of the cabin was an old rusting pickup.

"See? What did I tell ya? Bill's up here. He's just a forgetful old drunk, is all. Probably mixed everything up and thought you were coming out tomorrow."

"I thought Bill had a memory like a steel trap," Michael said.

Daryl glanced over at Michael. "Eh, some memories chew their legs off to get out of that trap."

Jonathan didn't care, though; he was just happy to finally be at the cabin, to unload their gear, bed down for the night and get this journey over with. Already, he dreaded the long battle ahead. The hike would be difficult enough, but having to dig up that box and haul it the miles and miles over wilderness terrain was something he felt physically unprepared for. He was tired, but he feared going to sleep because he knew in the morning they would have to begin.

Daryl banged on the door to the cabin with his massive fist, yelling for Bill to wake up. "He's got a spare key hidden around here," Daryl said, and he walked around the side of the cabin. In the darkness, they could hear the drone of the gas generator in the shed behind the house – the same shed where they'd hung their deer ten years ago and stripped them of skin, the same shed where they retrieved the pickaxe and shovels to bury the boy in that box. The faint cracking of the generator was better than the pure silence and darkness that awaited.

Then Daryl was standing in the open doorway of the cabin, having entered from the back door. "Don't know where he is. Don't see him anywhere in here." He took a flashlight and said he was going to look for Bill.

Jonathan didn't much care, none of them did, and they began to haul their gear inside. Michael stacked some of the boxes and grocery bags on the kitchen table. Jonathan fell down into the old couch, relieved after a full day of sitting in the car and then experiencing the incident in town. Conner was opening a beer, clearly trying to kill the stress.

Then Daryl was once again standing in front of them in the yellow light of the cabin, taking up the whole room with his presence. But somehow, in that moment, he seemed diminished, as if he were fading or shrinking.

"Bill's out back," he said quietly. "He's dead. Stone dead."

Bill Flood – seventy-two years old – sat upright on a simple wood bench beside the stone-circled firepit, shrouded in darkness behind the cabin, staring out into the deep expanse of Coombs' Gulch. At first, from behind the bouncing circles of light from the flashlights, he looked like any old man sitting on a bench – someone you might see in a park on a lonely, overcast day, throwing breadcrumbs to ducks in a pond, shoulders stooped, silver hair combed back and kept trim with regular visits to the barbershop, which were usually unnecessary but offered an excuse to converse with others. The firepit was filled with leaves and refuse that spilled over the rock perimeter. Bill sat there, his back to the cabin – to them – and, despite Daryl's insistence the man was dead, Jonathan still held the expectation that Bill would turn around and look at them with foggy eyes and croak some distant, hollow words from a constricted throat.

They circled the firepit to see his face, but he did not move. He sat still as a statue, frozen in time and somehow balanced on the bench, his frosted-over eyes staring out at dark mountains. They all stood in a semicircle around him, running the flashlight beams over his body, looking for any sign of what had happened and seeing nothing obvious. Their breath formed clouds in the cold night. A chill passed through Jonathan like a frozen spike touching the base of his spine. He followed Bill's dead gaze and turned to look out into the forest of the night, and there, in the darkness, he saw it.

The world twisted and fractured and opened up like a doorway through time and space. He saw trees reaching through; he saw figures, impossibly tall, cloaked in stars, like an elaborately designed fabric. And in the twisting darkness, he saw the face of Thomas Terrywile appear, formed out of the trees and mountains, pieced together like a child's puzzle. His eyes were large as the moon, his mouth grinning with a thousand teeth. An image of death veiled with the skin of an innocent boy.

CHAPTER TWELVE

Charles Coombs III claimed the Gulch in 1824 as the Dutch were moving into the northern New York region with mining and timber operations. Coombs was a third-generation heir to a British textile manufacturing empire, but he eschewed his father's and grandfather's business to create a great new society, a society of communal living that would allow him to be at one with nature. In effect, he rebelled against his father and family, seeking a new life overseas with a vast amount of wealth at his disposal. He traveled to America, where he became enraptured with the transcendentalist movement, with its focus on the natural world and the perfection of humanity through communing with nature. The presence of and access to Native American tribes and belief systems drove him upstate as he sought out the Iroquois, north of Lake Champlain. He stopped for a period of time in Albany, where he purchased a hotel and created the Society of the New Dawn, drawing a few members at first and then progressively growing as Coombs made trips back and forth into the wilderness, seeking native wisdom and returning with stories, prophesies, and insights he shared with his followers. Although the Society was largely an intellectual endeavor at first, as it grew it began to change. Historians of the United States' transcendental movement noted that much of Coombs' teachings did not appear to mirror anything he could have gained from the Iroquois, who, at the time, were consolidating their people – decimated by war and infection brought by European settlers – and looking to abandon New York for the West.

In fact, no one is really sure who Charles Coombs was talking to during his trips into the wilderness. There is brief mention in a fur trader's journal of an Englishman making numerous attempts to speak with Iroquois leaders and being turned away. At that point, the Native American tribes had grown tired of dealing with European settlers and deeply distrusted them for obvious reasons. Still, Coombs would be gone for months at a time and return to Albany dirty, haggard, half starved and seemingly delirious. But he also came with visions and philosophies, preaching against the rise of industrialism, capitalism and greed. His Society of the New Dawn began to take on religious connotations. He led members in prayerlike rituals that began to grow loud and ferocious, leading to complaints from surrounding city dwellers. Like other groups that sprouted during that time, Coombs and his followers began moving toward a completely open society, one in which families were communal arrangements, marriage was abolished and child-rearing was shared. But his utopian ideals were anchored by something darker. He talked of gods in the wilderness, beings that moved through the trees and haunted the mountains. Supernatural forces that could touch humanity, move the world with an unseen hand. Very few people recorded his teachings; what remains is a compendium of loosely linked, circular ramblings with no apparent underlying mythology. He tried to talk about time but made little sense. He talked about gods, but they were all foreign to any formal religions. The largely Christian population in Albany became concerned.

Following an incident in which Coombs was accused of 'crimes against morality', he and his followers were forced to leave Albany or face possible arrest. Coombs took his group, now numbering nearly one hundred and twenty, and fled for the Adirondack Mountains, a place where he said they could commune with the true gods of nature and life. The choice to relocate to the harsh and uncharted Adirondacks was also strange. The native tribes avoided the mountains except for the purposes of war. The harsh terrain made farming difficult and the winters brutal. The Society of the New Dawn traveled as far as they could by train and then wagon and then finally by foot until Coombs finally found the Gulch – a seemingly self-contained area of woodland with a brook flowing through the middle – and declared that this was where they would settle and create their new society.

They lasted only two years. Fur traders at the time – and families seeking out loved ones who had absconded with the Society – described a few ramshackle cabins that would likely not hold up for the winter, a meager attempt at a farm, and strange nightly rituals that involved worshippers gathering to form geometric shapes and chanting in low, deep tones in an effort to 'commune with the Great Spirit'. Visitors who witnessed the events usually left the commune shaken and disturbed, refusing to return to the area. "What they summoned, I could not begin to say," wrote Daniel Jansen, a fur trader and woodsman. "Only that it was an abomination to the one true God. Following their ritual, they engaged in unspeakable carnal acts as if possessed by spirits. The whole land is haunted with witches and demons they have called forth. It is not safe. Coombs' Gulch should be avoided."

Indeed, it was not safe, as members of the Society of the New Dawn began to die off quickly during the harsh winter. Accidents plagued the community as high-minded intellectual elites attempted to tame the wilderness with few survival skills. Hunger ravaged their ranks. Those who attempted to leave that first winter became lost in the mountains and died quickly of exposure during an unusually bad winter. Suicide became rampant as some, delirious with their beliefs, tried to become one with Coombs' gods.

But it was over the course of the second year that the children began disappearing into the woods. Infants, toddlers and adolescents began, one by one, to be unaccounted for, seemingly vanished, sometimes in broad daylight, sometimes during the night. Their frenzied parents and community leaders searched the Gulch endlessly and found nothing. Their rituals grew more fevered – violent, at times – as worshippers tried to appease the spirits to bring back their children. Visions of strange worlds and horrific beings became commonplace. The death toll rose.

Following the second year in the Gulch, all communication with the outside world ceased. A Dutch timber company working its way north eventually found the cabins but no signs of life, except for a few journals and remnants of a community. Among the journals was Coombs' own diary. After reading the last entry, the timber company turned away and left to find other areas. "*We see them in the night,*" the diary read. "*The dead come forth, the children play. Time is nothing to it. Mankind merely a toy. It takes many forms, but none more terrifying than our own…. It was all a great mistake.*"

"Jesus, fuck," Jonathan said. "We can't do this anymore. This is dumb. We should just leave and risk it."

"Fuck that," Michael said.

"This place is bad. This is all bad. It's like luck or a curse or whatever, but it follows you, and it's damn sure following us!"

"Shut the fuck up; that doesn't even make sense."

The three of them were inside the cabin now, sitting at the table in the small kitchen. Daryl Teague had gone to fetch the police. Now their names would be recorded in some kind of official report, a record of their trip to Coombs' Gulch a matter of legal proceedings.

"I saw something out there. I know this sounds crazy, but I saw—"

"You saw nothing. This is just an exercise in stress and you're cracking."

"Listen. I'm not cracking. I'm not losing it. I'm telling you that we've already had enough problems. This is not going the way it should be. There's some kind of curse following us. Call it whatever you will."

"There you go. I'll call it crazy, thank you."

"Let's not go off the deep end," Conner finally said.

Jonathan's mind was fracturing and spinning like a child's kaleidoscope. He tried to tell them about Thomas Terrywile, about how other missing children suddenly appeared on hunting cameras in the lost reaches of the world where only avid hunters would venture; the blued image of that little girl, dressed like it was 1972, kicking up her leg in a joyous leap; the Texan whom he spoke with on the phone, who had no reason to lie and little desire for attention. He told them, but it just came out as gibberish, and he couldn't blame them for not believing – who would?

What he had seen outside, in the forest and mountains, was like looking into a shattered mirror, the world in a thousand different angles and pieces, and yet, somehow, it provided a truer glimpse into reality – the true world. But it wasn't just the shattered mirror – something that could be perceived as a twist of fate or a spate of bad luck – it was the fact that behind it all he saw a malevolent force, a face dressed like little Thomas Terrywile. It was a pantomime, an exaggerated Halloween costume, a mask worn by something awful to mock them. The eyes were black holes, the teeth like a shark's mouth implanted into a boy's face. It was grotesque, an abomination of what is and what should have been.

"It's getting late. Too late. Maybe you should get some sleep," Conner said.

Jonathan tried to right himself, to get his mind back, but it felt as though his sanity were spiraling down a drain.

"We need you right. We need your head right," Conner said.

"You sure your head is right with all this?" Jonathan said. "I don't think *right* has anything to do with any of this."

Jonathan stood up and brushed soot and ash from his clothes. They said he had stumbled backward, tripped over the rocks lining the firepit and fell. They said he was screaming, but he didn't recall any sound or any voice, just that vortex of darkness taking in the trees and the mountains and the face grinning ear to ear.

Bill sat beside the firepit, staring into the Gulch. They hadn't moved the body and could barely make out his form or the pastel colors of his plaid shirt in the light from the cabin. But it was impossible not to notice him sitting there. Somehow, he was constantly in sight, whether from the corner of your eye or in the background, just over someone's shoulder. No matter which way you turned, where you looked, there was dead, dumb Bill sitting on a bench outside in the cold. Daryl Teague had left in his pickup truck, surprisingly distraught for a man who looked more animal than human. There was no cell phone signal to call the police; none of them knew how to get the radio to connect with any receiver beside the one at Bill's apartment, so Daryl drove off into the night and they were left babysitting a dead man.

Jonathan grabbed a bottle of whiskey from the grocery bag and took a long drink. He slammed the bottle on the table. "Fine. I'm better now. I'll shut up. You don't want to listen to it, that's fine."

Michael was shaking his head, on the verge of belting him.

"Do you remember what it felt like that night?"

"Shut up. We all remember things differently. It is what it is, and there's no use remembering it now."

"Do you remember the night? Do you remember what it's like out *there* at night? We're going to be out there – far out there – with no way to get back here."

"It's just the woods," Michael said.

"It's not just the woods. It's heavier. It's like being at the bottom of the ocean."

"This is bullshit."

"There are things that live there, too," Jonathan said.

"And that's how you explain the boy out there?" Michael was yelling now. "What did we do, fish him up from the bottom of the ocean?"

"Maybe it wasn't the bottom," Jonathan said. "Maybe it was just somewhere else. Or maybe it was both. It doesn't have to make sense to us."

"Well, thank God because you're not making sense to me."

"Think about it," Jonathan said. "What is your best explanation for what he was doing out here in the middle of the night? What is your explanation for why no one ever looked for him? If he went missing in 1985, no one would be—"

"Do you have the picture? Do you have the article so we can read it?" Michael asked. Michael stood up, looming over Jonathan now, hand reaching out, asking for Jonathan's phone. "Can we see all this research you've done?"

"There's no service here."

"Brilliant."

"Doesn't answer my questions."

"It's fucking simple – he was a lost kid with shitty parents who didn't care, that's it!"

Somehow that seemed infinitely worse, and suddenly, after Michael said it, the whole cabin grew as silent and lifeless as the body of its former owner. They stood face-to-face with each other in a moment of truth they couldn't comprehend, split between two horrifying possibilities.

The cabin lights began to dim, and they could hear the generator again, sputtering, running low on gas.

"I'll go take care of it," Michael said and walked outside to the shed.

"He'll cool down," Conner said. "You know how he is."

Conner sat down beside Jonathan, took the whiskey bottle, unscrewed the cap and took a long pull.

"I hear what you're saying," Conner said. "I've had similar thoughts. Wondered whether there might be something else going on. It always sounds insane. It has crossed my mind, but there's another way of looking at all this."

"And?"

"I know that we all grew apart after your wedding."

"It wasn't the wedding."

"It wasn't. But I'm sorry that happened. It was just difficult."

"I know. I was there."

"I wish we had been there more for Gene."

"So do I."

"This incident, this accident, could devastate everyone around us, people we love," Conner said. "It would ruin Gene's memory, send us to jail, destroy our reputations. You know all this. It's not worth it. As much as I feel terrible about this – and I do – it's a matter of simple calculation. What's done is done, and no amount of regret, guilt, punishment or embarrassment to our families is going to change that, so we might as well spare them from going through hell." Conner took a breath from his speech and seemed to collect his thoughts. His eyes changed, no longer the salesman, no longer playing for the crowd, no longer closing a deal. He looked at Jonathan the way he had when they were young.

"It's our job to go through hell so they don't have to. That's what all this is," Conner said. "Why would it ever be easy? Why would hell make sense? We were damned before the bullet left Gene's rifle."

Jonathan took the bottle of whiskey back and tilted it back. He looked at Conner, sitting across from him at the table, Bill's body floating in the heavy darkness in the background.

"That's the only honest thing I've heard you say in the last ten years," Jonathan said.

Michael came back inside and sat down, and they passed the bottle back and forth until the ambulance arrived to cart Bill's body away.

CHAPTER THIRTEEN

Dawn, deep and cold. Even in the cabin Jonathan felt the chill. Through the windows he could see the land touched with frost. The air grew light, but the forest of Coombs' Gulch remained in shadow. He was sore and hurt from last night. A bruise darkened the side of his face. His skin sore from being pummeled in the bar fight. They scrambled a dozen eggs and fried a pound of bacon. The greasy smoke swirled in the morning light. Conner and Michael laid out the gear on the table. Michael would carry the three-man tent. They each carried a sleeping bag. Jonathan would shoulder the inflatable raft, which would carry the boy's makeshift coffin to the middle of the lake. Each of them took a hunting knife and rifle; the topographic map of Coombs' Gulch; flashlights, trail mix, jerky and sandwiches stuffed in Ziploc bags; canteens filled with water; lighters and lighter fluid. They dressed in layers beneath their camouflaged coveralls. They would sweat during the day and freeze at night.

The police and paramedics had long since left. They already suspected Bill died of a heart attack. Daryl told the police that Conner had rented the cabin and clearly couldn't get their deposit back now, and besides, they had no transportation yet. The police agreed Jonathan and the Braddick brothers could remain at the cabin for now, happy to leave and be done with it. Daryl left saying he would deliver Conner's Suburban in two days. By that time they hoped to be able to pack their things and leave forever.

They dressed in their gloves and hats, and donned their backpacks. All told, they probably carried an extra eighty pounds in gear and clothing. They felt bad already.

Conner opened the rear door of the cabin, and they walked out into a pale light and biting cold. Coombs' Gulch fell away before them, a vast and dark expanse of black spruce trees born out of acidic soil. The twin ridges of mountain peaks glinted in the sun, catching the first direct rays. Jonathan stood for a moment looking out at the Gulch and felt his fear and history wash away: none of it mattered now. There was only the long walk ahead; there was only the job to be done. Conner was right. This was their hell to walk through. It was mountains and dirt and trees. The weight of the gear sagged his shoulders. He hefted up the rifle and pack, pulled them tight against his body.

The sun was not yet over the eastern ridge. They took shovels and a pickaxe from Bill's shed. They would dig the site, leave the tools, and retrieve them upon their return. The three of them walked to the edge of the woods where the tree line stood sentry before the Gulch. It was a solid wall of thin, dark conifers pointing to the sky like fingers from the earth. Half of them appeared dead. Spikes of broken limbs jutted from their trunks, flat and sharp. It wasn't until the very highest reaches that the black spruce would suddenly sprout living branches and dark needles, which sagged like cloaks draped over old women. Dead pine needles covered the ground that was riddled with exposed roots and fallen limbs; blankets of moss covered wet rocks. The trees formed layer after layer upon each other until it resembled a three-dimensional picture on a sheet of paper; there was no depth, merely the illusion of it, a false world.

"I don't remember it being this thick," Michael said.

"No wonder everyone says it's gone dry up here. It's absolute shit."

"Wasn't there a trail before?"

"I can't see anything."

They walked the edge of the forest until they reached the corner of the cabin grounds, just past the supply barn and the firepit where Bill's body had sat upright staring into the trees, and then paced back again. The forest had retaken everything, covered every previous step and trail, twisted and rearranged the landscape like a puzzle put together all wrong.

A slight entrance into the trees appeared to open to them, and they could see fifty feet into the dark woods. They plunged inside like returning to the womb. The sun glimpsed over the mountains and was then hidden from them.

The gear slowed them. Dead branches pulled at their packs, trashy shrubs grasped at their coverall sleeves. They maneuvered the long, wooden handles of the shovels and pickaxe between the trees and branches. The barrel of Jonathan's rifle caught on brush. The ground was still soft and damp, not yet frozen for the winter. The pine needles made their footsteps nearly silent. The only sounds were their breath and the morning breeze through the Druid-cloaked canopy.

"You hear that?" Michael said.

"I don't hear anything."

"Exactly. Nothing." There were no birds. It was silent as a grave, and they were the only living creatures walking among the tombstones.

Jonathan followed behind Conner and Michael. He couldn't say if they were heading in the right direction. They had not traveled very far into the darkness that night ten years ago, just to a hillock overlooking the creek bed. But they had been drunk, intoxicated with bravado, trying to face childhood fears of the forest at night, and they pushed out – boys dressed as men. It had never been a serious attempt at hunting. Looking back, he wondered if they had ever taken anything truly seriously. But that night, beneath the booze, they had been afraid – afraid of what, Jonathan couldn't be sure. Perhaps it was the sense of dread that lingers in the back of everyone's mind, the thing that drives men and women to engage in all sorts of activities meant to stave off death or, at the very least, distract them from the coming silence. Everyone rages against it in some way, trying to keep it suppressed so it doesn't explode. It drives them like an engine. He thought of joggers bouncing up and down the side of his neighborhood road at all hours of morning and night, mere inches from the certain death of passing cars; he thought of writers, composing books so their thoughts and words will somehow live on after they die; of industrious men and women who build companies to outlast their tiny lives; of politicians who craft pointless laws so they can look into the abyss and tell themselves they accomplished something – anything – to make the world and humanity a little better. They all lie to themselves.

And Jonathan thought of himself and Conner, Michael and Gene. What did they do? They confronted death by bringing it to other living creatures, plunging those lives into the abyss and taking their skin and crowns.

Jonathan wanted to leave something behind, something good. He wanted to recover what was lost when they stared into the awful reality of life, a reality in which a random bullet strikes a random child and the world fractures into a million tiny reflections of what could have been.

How far had they truly wandered that night? His memory was flashes of a remembered nightmare. It was only a fiction at this point.

The only truth was a boy buried in a box somewhere in Coombs' Gulch.

"I don't remember it being this far," Michael said. "And I had gone back for the shovels. It wasn't this far; there's no way."

"It's kind of sloping that way, toward the east," Conner said. "Everything's grown over. We had a trail that night."

Jonathan offered no opinion. They had been hiking for an hour at this point, and he was already growing tired from the overburdened backpack. The brothers' history of being strangely good at nearly everything they tried seemed to mean little in finding their way through the Gulch.

Conner took out his map. "There's no way we were this far north. The stream is closer than this. We head due east and we'll pick it up."

They walked into the sun as it blared between the peaks of the eastern ridge. The light shone down in rare patches. The sky was a deep, cold blue. The temperature climbed from its nighttime low of twenty. The ground was still soft.

The land sloped imperceptibly toward the lowest point of the Gulch. The forest appeared to open up briefly, the trees spaced apart and the shrubs became larger, taking in sunlight. They passed through dying wild grass; the sun warmed their faces. Suddenly Jonathan felt so far from home and lonely. He thought of Mary and Jacob and was scared. He checked his cell phone, but there was no signal, no way to reach them.

The three of them were silent and Jonathan realized he missed the Braddick brothers and Gene, as well. They had grown up on the same block together during a time when mothers weren't terrified to let their children disappear for a whole day. A neighborhood riddled with small, ramshackle ranch houses that appeared out of the heavy forested greenery at odd intervals. It was a community pieced together over a century and kept cheap, meant to house tradesmen. Their friendship seemed inevitable, four kids roughly the same age living on the same block. They pressured their tired fathers with calloused hands into buying Daisy BB rifles and ducked into the woods that bordered the neighborhood and descended toward swamplands that puddled in the depressions between rolling New England hills. It smelled of muck and rot. Reeds and willows grew fast and far and crowded the ground. They shot at birds, occasionally knocking a small swallow out of a tree or annoying the crows. A tinge of boyhood guilt came with their first kill – a small chickadee that fell dead to the ground. They poked and prodded it with sticks before finally trudging home and lying awake in their beds, thinking suddenly on life and death with a nausea in their stomachs. On summer evenings they gathered at a cul-de-sac of their neighborhood that was devoid of houses and near an old gravel pit. Surrounded by high trees, they tried shooting the bats as they flapped across darkening skies. It was an impossible task; the bats sensed the BBs coming and in their blindness avoided death.

Michael and Conner were the first to take up hunting. Their uncle took them on a trip for pheasant. They were fifteen and sixteen at the time and returned with two fat, brown birds to eat that night. The uncle took them again and again – for deer, turkey, anything that walked or crawled across the face of the earth that was legal to shoot. The uncle had no children and a lot of money, and he wanted to pass on his love of hunting to his nephews.

Even when they left for college and Gene stayed in town, they returned during weekends and holiday breaks, woke early in the morning, shivering in the cold, and ventured into the old and well-worn hunting grounds together.

It all seemed so far away Jonathan could barely recall it, but he felt he was still that boy, young and afraid. He feared then the life he had now – one of separation and solitude, distance from the camaraderie of youth. He worked at a desk and grew fat and soft. Years slipped by without a true word spoken, with nothing shared. All that existed was work and schedules and a family that he felt incapable of supporting. At some point there had been a trade, one made without his knowledge that left him trapped, painted into a corner by expectations and desperation. Like a creature whose base instinct lures it into a cage baited with food, their lives would have progressed quietly and quickly into adulthood – but for the boy buried in the woods.

His childhood fears had been replaced with something different, and now he fought *for* the trap; he struggled into the woods to keep the only life he knew. It was all he had, and for that reason he loved it. It was a strange dichotomy, which tore at him.

Michael and Conner were ahead in the distance now, dressed in their camouflaged hunting gear. He strained to see them. The black, gray and white of their jumpsuits blended with the trees. They seemed to melt into the forest, revealed only by their motion. They slipped in and out of their surroundings like ghosts.

He heard the fast-moving water of the brook that bifurcated the Gulch up ahead. The sun reached down through a break in the trees and touched them all. The brothers stopped and turned to stare at him.

CHAPTER FOURTEEN

The brook waters ran cold from the northernmost edge of Coombs' Gulch through the center of the valley, growing in size and force as it flowed south into Pasternak. It was the same flow of water they had seen twisting around the dead town, the same snakelike stream beside which they had buried the boy with the star-shaped hole for an eye.

They had traveled too far north and backtracked along the brook where the dense undergrowth gave way to grassy tuffets and the rocky riverbed. The trees retreated far back in this section of the stream, leaving a long, low flatland of scrub brush and tall grasses turned gold in their autumn dying. The lowland area stretched a quarter mile before disappearing into the spruce forest again. It was quiet and brown and seemingly untouched by life in the bright sun. It was a place where the wildlife would gather to drink from the stream and nip at the fruit-bearing shrubs. It was here Jonathan had bagged his first buck of their trip ten years ago. The brook seemed to talk. It drowned out their silence.

They followed the stream now, unsure of their location, unsure of where they had been that night they buried the boy. They wandered, frustrated, feeling lost, their packs heavy, shovels and pickaxe awkward, their energy draining before they even began the most arduous part of the journey.

Toward the southern edge of the lowlands, turning a bend in the stream, they saw a small rise at the edge of the trees – the hillock from which they saw those yellow eyes glowing bright and alien in the darkness at the very edge of the spotlight's range. They all remembered the giant northern raisin bush where they found the boy and buried his body. Michael eyed the hillock and traced an imaginary trajectory with his finger to a dense patch of shrubs. They saw it there – the raisin bush, grown large as an explosion, heavy with leaves, the ground before it overgrown with grass and weeds. They walked to it and stood momentarily in silence before putting their gear to the side. Michael took the pickaxe, swung it high over his head and buried the blade into the rocky soil. A wild scream went up from somewhere in the distance, high-pitched and awful, like a woman dying. It seemed neither animal nor human.

They stopped and waited. Sweat brushed their brows.

"Fisher-cat?" Conner said. "Didn't sound right. Too long and drawn out."

"Vixens," Michael said. "Bobcats. They make that kind of sound."

Jonathan raised his Remington to his shoulder and sighted in the edge of the trees one hundred yards away with his scope. He ran it along the tree line. The forest was dark with shade. A slight breeze came from the north.

"It sounded far away," Conner said.

Jonathan watched for a time, letting his breath out slowly, finger resting on the trigger guard. He glassed the lowlands to the north of them. The scream went up again, the unworldly sound an animal can make in the throes of death or sex. He lowered the rifle to take in the whole area.

"Anything?"

Jonathan shook his head.

"With the damn echo of this place, it could be a mile off or right next to us," Conner said.

"We wouldn't see it anyway," Jonathan said.

"Fire a shot. Scare it off," Michael said. "Last thing we need is some big cat following us."

Jonathan hadn't fired a shot in ten years. He pointed the barrel in the air, turned his head down and to the side and squeezed the heavy trigger until a blast roared over the valley and the gun bucked in his hand. They waited a moment while the high-pitched ringing in their ears died down and the echo rolled off the mirror image mountains to the east and west.

Jonathan brought the scope to his eye once again and scanned the limits of the lowland grasses. The reeds shifted in the morning breeze; amber waves of grain ran through his mind. He saw nothing, but he felt something, a presence in the lonely solitude of that place.

"Anything?" Michael said.

He shook his head silently. Michael raised the pickaxe and plunged it again into the dirt.

They dug three feet down until Jonathan's spade finally struck the makeshift coffin, and he leaned down to brush away the earth. The black, heavy-duty plastic case suddenly revealed itself, and he recoiled, his heart racing, the guilt and terror overwhelming. He stepped back, away from the dig and into the surrounding brush. He wanted to melt back into the forest. Conner and Michael dug around the edges until they could find the handles to grasp it and pull it up from the ground and into the light.

The case was two feet by five and two feet deep, made of military-grade high-impact polymer – the very kind of equipment on which survivalists, hunters and those who venerate high-impact military gear would drop a small fortune. Conner purchased it as a much younger man, free from family and mortgage, and when too much testosterone pumped through his veins. Everything he owned for his hunting adventures had to be the best – military grade. It was airtight, waterproof, designed for long-term outdoor conditions and overseas transport, and able to withstand being dropped out of a plane. Nothing – air nor moisture – went in or out when it was completely sealed.

It looked no different from when they buried it ten years ago other than being coated in a layer of dirt. It sat on the ground before them, and for all its tactical grooves and ridges it sat absurdly plain and simple. For a moment they collectively marveled how a plastic box – dumb and meaningless – could cost so much, could hold so much. Like the rifle slung from Jonathan's shoulder, its reality was so small compared to its consequences. They stood in a semicircle around the case, staring at it. It looked as if it could do no harm to anyone, and yet the bullet that split Thomas Terrywile's skull and left a star-shaped crater in his eye weighed mere ounces. That fact rang true between them; their situation – the sum of its parts – was not determined by the present, but by the past. The bullet only mattered when it was fired; its size and shape and corporeal reality were meaningless compared to the history left in its wake.

"We should open it," Michael said. "What if this is all for nothing?"

Somehow, staring at the case on the dirt and grass, the point of their task no longer seemed worth it. Jonathan thought briefly of

Schrodinger's cat and wondered if the box was never opened, the boy would be alive somewhere.

"Nothing?" Conner said. "How's twenty years in prison sound? Does that seem like nothing to you?"

"Things are meant to come apart," Michael said. "That's the way things are – everything breaks; it's just reality."

"Only if we let them break," Conner said. "Since when do you talk like this?"

Conner was angry now. He sighed and put his arms over his head. "This isn't difficult. It's a seven-mile hike. Anyone can do this. It doesn't matter what happened in the past. It only matters what will happen in the future if we don't. They're going to run a road and buildings right through this place, and they're going to find this if we don't move it now."

"It's the same either way," Jonathan said.

"Fuck you both," Conner said. "I'm not losing everything over a hike through the woods, and neither are you. This is just insurance. I do this every day. This is worth it! There are few things that translate to even money, and this? This is better than even money! We come out on top with this! Be logical!"

Conner reached down and seized a handle. He lifted the side of the case off the ground, and they all heard the contents slosh toward the lower end. Conner dropped it and stepped away with a look of revulsion on his face.

He stood silent for a moment. "I didn't think it would weigh so much," he said in a quiet voice.

"No air in or out," Michael said. "It isn't just bones in there."

Jonathan had researched what happens to a body left in a sealed container. The bacteria feast on flesh and organs, releasing various gases into the small amount of air in the case, and leaving a sludge of putrescence. The gases, the chemicals, the living tissue – everything that had formed Thomas Terrywile's body – existed simultaneously in three different states of matter. Jonathan tested the weight – easily eighty pounds. The ghost of Thomas Terrywile was heavy.

It was nearing 10:00 a.m.; the sun was over the mountains, glaring down on Coombs' Gulch, the air warmer, but still they shivered as sweat dampened their skin. Jonathan looked to the northwest, trying to place the corridor between the peaks that led to the mountain lake, but he could not see beyond the pines. On its face, the scene was postcard beautiful, but he felt something working on them, the same way it had worked on Thomas Terrywile and turned his body into sludge.

Conner stood with his hands on his hips, breathing hard and sweating now in the cold air. His sharp jawline was accented by a close-cut beard, and his lithe frame nearly bent in worry and fear, his brown eyes looking desperate, rimmed with tears.

"If you guys won't do this with me, I'll just do it myself. I swear to God."

He looked back and forth between Michael and Jonathan, eyes reaching across the divide of the case containing a dead boy's body.

"I don't care if it takes me three days to drag this damned thing to that lake; I'm going to do it. With or without you guys."

"I didn't say that," Michael said. His words came out low and mumbled together, as if his jaw were clenched shut. Michael would never let Conner go off without his help. The fact that Conner doubted his brother's commitment was a source of pain.

"I didn't say that, either," Jonathan said, but he lied. He wanted to leave this place, leave it all behind.

But he couldn't leave them behind. Not yet. As much as they may have separated in the past ten years, as much as they had become strangers, he could not let them go into this alone. They were bound together in this – they were as close to brothers as he would ever know.

"I'm in," he said. "All the way. It's just... I wanted to be sure."

"We are sure," Conner said. "We didn't imagine this shit. We need to be on the same page here." Conner was practically begging. "We need to follow the plan and just do it, no questions asked."

Jonathan reached down and grabbed the side handle of the case and looked at Michael, who walked over and took the other side. "Due north, right?" Jonathan asked.

Conner was holding back and couldn't form the words. He just nodded.

Michael and Jonathan lifted, and together they followed the stream north and plunged back into the black spruce forests of Coombs' Gulch.

CHAPTER FIFTEEN

It was more difficult than they imagined. Their shoulders burned with the strain. The case was heavy. It knocked into their knees as they hobbled through the underbrush. The sludge inside would shift and move in slow waves as they rocked back and forth. Although it was only eighty pounds between two men, the constant weight pulling down, the need to shift it up and over shrub brush and rock outcroppings and desiccated branches that could impale a body, turned eighty pounds into a hundred, then two hundred, growing heavier the longer they traveled. They worked in half-hour, three-man rotations, switching sides to give each shoulder a break, keeping one man free with the rifle. They kept pace and time through the rotation, and it quickly became the only time in the world worth measuring – a clock kept by pain and weariness.

The terrain changed. At first they followed the creek, keeping to the soft ground before it gave way to the rocky creek bed. The long grasses disappeared and were replaced with the dark expanse of the coniferous forest, with visible root systems spread like spider veins, popping from the soil to trip them, before plunging back below the surface. Dying ferns, shrunken and brown, carpeted the forest floor. Were it spring or summer, those ferns would form an impenetrable green blanket over the whole area; now their boots crushed them to dust underfoot. Massive boulders from the last ice age appeared like gray ghosts, sheer rock faces wet with lichen or moss, dotted with small, thin, impossible trees whose roots wrapped like hands over the stone and sprouted at strange angles toward patches of sunlight.

The case knocked into the side of Jonathan's knee, which was already raw and bruised. They had hiked for three full rotations, and the constant jostle and bump of the case against his knees, the heavy tugs on his shoulders when Michael or Conner walked out of pace with his own gait, had grown to a point of eruption. They continued to follow the creek, stepping down occasionally into the rocky creek bed to navigate around underbrush. The slippery rocks twisted their ankles, caused them to stumble and splash into small pools of cold water.

The strain of the journey pushed Jonathan to his limit. Branches swiped at his face, thorn patches gripped and tore at his sleeves, and all the time there was the shifting slosh of the boy in the box. His breath was heavy and hard. Sweat soaked into his hat until he finally removed it, and then his head froze in the air. The soles of his boots bent and slipped. The case pulled again at his shoulder and rammed into the side of his knee. He felt a murderous rage and then marveled how easily the desire to kill fell upon him, how such a minor thing could drive a man insane like the slow drip of water torture.

They dragged that thing over rock, water and earth for three hours, passing in and out of darkness and light.

They were already carrying at least eighty pounds of camping gear on their backs and now the case with the full weight of the boy's body inside. This was US Marine Corps stuff – not for a few guys who rode desks for a living. In the months leading up to the trip, Jonathan had thought little of the physical strain of the hike, but now it seemed impossible. When it was his turn to be free of the box and walk in the rear, he felt a small modicum of relief – just enough to renew his spirit and body for another rotation.

The creek became thinner – the water slowed to a trickle between rocks. It twisted snakelike through the trees, took long, undulating curves and then returned to them. They followed it for hours. Conner kept watch on the mountain peaks above, waiting for the point when they would stop and turn west to climb the mountain and reach the pass. It would be a harder leg of the journey, but at least it would be progress. He felt like he could gather more energy if they could just move in a new direction. But even a renewed energy would not be good enough. There was a growing knowledge between them; their pace was too slow.

"How far have we come?" Jonathan asked.

"About three miles," Conner said. "We're almost there."

"I don't know if we're going to make it," Michael said. "Not today anyway."

Conner sighed long and heavy again.

"Three more hours of this shit and I'll be near dead," Michael added. He breathed heavy; sweat and steam poured from his head.

"I know," Conner said. "Just a little farther. We need to get to the passage. At least that. If we need to we can camp there for the night. The rest is downhill toward the lake."

"Weather is coming," Jonathan said.

"It's at least another day out. We'll be okay."

Michael was calculating their chances of making the journey in his head. Jonathan could tell; his blank eyes were lost, his mind running logistics. Michael knew the actual chances of making the journey free from injury or death, the chances of not getting lost or getting caught in the coming snowstorm – diminishing numbers.

They switched for another rotation. The case rocked against the side of Jonathan's knee again. They kept hauling through the woods. Everything seemed so far away now. They were beyond the point of no return.

Conner stopped them. "Here. That's far enough north." He was looking at his map and then trying to see through the canopy of spruce trees to the mountains. "Let's stop for a bit," he said. "Eat, take a break." He checked his watch – nearly 2:00 p.m. It would be dark by 5:30. "Just a few minutes. It's not far to the pass but it's uphill. We have to at least get there by dark."

Jonathan and Michael unceremoniously dropped the case and collapsed. They all scrambled away from it to find a place to sit – a rock or fallen tree. Conner began to hike up a ledge to get a better look at the ridge of mountains to be sure they were in the right spot. Jonathan dropped his backpack and felt the soaked back of his shirt lift from his skin, sending shivers down his spine. He took two sandwiches from his backpack and ate quickly.

Michael stumbled off into the underbrush, and Jonathan was left alone in Coombs' Gulch. He sat back on a fallen pine tree till his face caught a sliver of light in the shadow. He put his head back and stared into a patch of sky. The trees seemed like dark gray lines, the blue of the sky so deep it seemed to give way to space, stars. His mind flowed upward, away from the earth. In his exhaustion, all was stripped away.

Then a voice called to him, at first from a distance, and then closer.

Michael's voice telling him to come down to where he was, closer to the mild trickle of the stream.

"Down here!"

Jonathan sat up. Conner came bounding down from the rock ledge. Jonathan saw him and paused, blinking his eyes, trying to come back to reality.

"Down here," the voice came again.

They followed the sound of Michael's voice toward the stream with their rifles. They pushed aside saplings and dense, sharp underbrush.

Michael stood in the center of a large clearing completely devoid of plant life, brushed clean of any fallen leaves or pine needles. The forest seemed to stop dead at its borders; the trees and bushes surrounding it formed the barrier of a perfect ring that reached into the sky. Even the tops of the trees refused to extend into the range of its circumference. Conner and Jonathan approached the center. The air felt thin, as if a portal in the atmosphere formed a single, strange vacuum. Michael stood in the center of an elaborate design formed by rocks embedded in the ground. Jonathan recognized it, a circle of white stones the size of footballs, with parallel lines of rocks running through the middle, crisscrossing in geometric design, an empty space in the center. Michael stood near the center, staring down at the remnants of a fire – ash, soot and blackened pieces of burnt wood. At the far northern end of the clearing was a rock face and, below it, three large, flat stones arranged to form a flat, table-like surface. Above the stone table was written 'TIME IS A VEIL TO THE SHATTERED WORLD' in a faded white paint, scrawled with a childlike hand, as if the author had just learned to form letters.

Jonathan's stomach twisted. Like a ghost from the attic of his subconscious, the grainy black-and-white photo from the newspaper article detailing Thomas Terrywile's disappearance sent panic coursing through his body. It had been difficult to make out the images in that old report, but the basics were there – a clearing in the woods, a stone altar, symbols that hinted at occult practices.

"What the hell is this?" Michael said. He appeared dumbfounded by it, as if he'd just opened a door and found himself at the edge of a cliff, staring into the drop. "This can't be possible." But it was the fact anyone would believe in something enough to make a ramshackle altar in the woods that truly baffled him.

"This far out here?" Conner said. "This can't be right. Who would go this far?"

"*We've* gone this far," Jonathan said.

Michael was turning himself in circles now as if he was searching for something.

"Who would travel this far out here to do this?" Conner said.

"It could be old."

Jonathan thought of that night ten years ago, thought of the box of remains sitting just a few yards away. "Maybe that's what he was doing up here," he said. "We thought there was no way in hell anyone would be this far out in mountains at that time of night. Maybe there were people up here. Maybe this is what they were doing."

"That still doesn't make any sense," Conner said.

"These kinds of things never make any sense."

"They said it to me," Michael said. "They said it. I didn't know what they were talking about."

Conner crossed into the body of the star and took Michael by the arm. "Hey! Hey! Get it together. What are you talking about?"

"In the bar," Michael said. "Those guys. They said it to me."

"You said they were saying weird things," Jonathan said.

"They told me to stay out of the Gulch. They told me something about this place. I don't know; I can't remember exactly. It all sounded fucking crazy. I thought they were drunk or high or something. Then he said, 'Your face looks familiar, boy. I's seen you before. It'll be your bodies they're hauling out of there next.' That's when I shoved him."

Your face looks familiar, boy.

It rang like a deep and terrible bell in Jonathan's mind. So much familiarity, repetition, motions repeated over years and years, the reappearance of lost children.

"It makes no sense," Conner said.

"It doesn't have to make sense to us," Jonathan said. "If they were out here that night, if they saw us, if this is where they come."

"You're just telling us this now?" Conner said. "Fuck this redneck bullshit. There's no trails leading here. There's nothing out here!"

"Except for this," Jonathan said. "They know we're out here. They could be following us."

"We would have noticed."

"Why? Because we're such expert woodsmen? These guys live up here."

Michael stepped through the circle and wandered, dazed, to the stone altar set at the base of the rock face. The stones were stained with a rusty brown color. "What does this look like to you?" he said. The stains were thick and circular, with lines that flowed down and over the sides of the flattened stones. "I can tell you what I think it looks like."

Everything seemed still in that moment. Jonathan looked to the ground where the white stones lay in their terrifying design. He saw something he mistook for rocks but was actually a twelve-inch section of deer spine, the vertebrae still linked together, picked clean and bleached white from the sun. He bent down and nudged it slightly.

"This is...I don't know what this is."

"It's nothing, is what it is," Conner said. "It's a bunch of hicks goofing around in the woods, pretending they're Satanists or pagans or whatever you call the people that do this shit. We need to keep moving. We'll keep a close eye out behind us for any signs someone is trailing us. It's doubtful, but we need to get moving."

They each turned in their respective spaces, took a last look around and then pushed through the underbrush toward their gear and the heavy, black coffin.

CHAPTER SIXTEEN

The earth sloped gently at first and then grew steeper. The pitch changed their trek from a slow walk to an uphill battle. Like infants, they crawled on hands and knees up the incline, dragging the box behind them, grasping saplings for purchase to pull themselves higher, boots slipping in the blanket of dead leaves covering the ground. They were too tired to keep their heads upward to look up the mountain, so sheer rock ledges appeared as if out of nowhere, suddenly stopping them in their tracks and forcing them to either backtrack and circle the ledge or attempt to scale it with their gear and the box.

Conner climbed to the top of a rock face and lowered a rope. Michael and Jonathan tied the case by using the handles, and Conner pulled it up while they watched below, fearful it would break loose or burst open and rain down its contents. They circled around the small cliff and met him at the top. The brief repose left them colder now; the sweat soaked into their underclothes chilled them to the bone, sapped their energy. Their legs burned. The rocks were slick with wet moss, their feet slipped, and they went on all fours again like animals. Conner sat on the ground beside the coffin, waiting for them, panting heavy. They could make out the stream below through breaks in the trees. They rotated carriers again and moved up toward the pass. The black spruce trees were slowly replaced by yellow birch, hardwoods, which had shed their leaves during autumn. Their bony fingers reached into the sky and swayed slightly in an unfelt breeze. Bursts of dead honeysuckle and crawling tendrils of witch hobble tripped them. The sun moved closer to the horizon and shone in their faces. Blind, they stumbled up the mountain, backs bent, heads down, the case just a few inches from the ground. Their stops became more frequent. Each rotation was like a runner's last burst of energy at the end of a marathon. The mountain grew rockier, the pitch increased, and they strained under the heft of the thing, which felt like hundreds of pounds now and forced them to stop every few minutes. Fallen limbs rolled underfoot and caused them to stumble. The air was tinged with decay, the faint smell of fire somewhere in the distance. Time raced and stood still.

"We have to make the field," Conner said. The sun cut through the trees, stabbed at their eyes. They couldn't see anything ahead. There was no hope of making the lake by nightfall. "At least there we'll be in the open."

With every step, they traveled farther from that place, that place of belief and ritual, where the hands of man tried to convey some kind of meaning.

They stopped for a moment. Jonathan turned around to look back. The land fell away in a long, downward slope. Shadows reached out from behind the trees. The air around them seemed a dull blue, suffused with remnants of daylight sliding into dusk. The depths of the Gulch were already deep with shadow.

"What do you think it all meant down there?" Jonathan asked.

"Nothing. It meant nothing," Michael said, but then he was quiet.

"We still have time," Conner said.

The trees thinned out ahead. The pitch was steep but there was less underbrush. Through shards of light the forest opened, and long brown grasses swayed in the evening breeze from off the mountains. The closer they came to the meadow that crested the mountain pass, the stronger the wind became, and now the trees chattered and moved like deadened wind chimes. Their branches knocked together, hollow and flat. The trees seemed to speak.

"*Time is a veil to the shattered world*," Jonathan said.

"It's metaphysical bullshit," Michael said. "Something someone read in a book."

"Why would they write it in a place like that?"

"How should I know? Time is just a measurement," he said.

"A veil?"

"It's what we see, but not what's really there," Michael said.

"So what is really there?"

"Nothing. God, if you want. Something eternal. Whatever you imagine, I suppose."

"This is pointless."

"Something that's eternal would see everything, all of time, at once.

Everything from the big bang to however things end up would all exist simultaneously," Michael said. "Time wouldn't make any difference. The sun going down –" he gestured to the sky "– day, night, years, millennia, none of it would make a difference. It would all just happen at the same moment."

"Maybe that's what it's about."

"Stop."

"The shattered world?"

"Who knows? It has no application. It's meaningless."

"Like firing a shot in the middle of the night?"

"Shut up with that."

"We never actually talked about what happened."

"There's nothing to talk about. It is what it is."

"Didn't look like they were hoping to find God down there."

"I'd say not."

Jonathan waited a moment, thought about that night, his memory of it. Things got murky. None of them could understand or agree on what happened, how a boy was wandering the woods at that time of night. Did that make it fact or fiction? Jonathan stood and lifted a side of the case to feel its weight again. The contents moved.

"I can see the field up ahead," Conner said. "We can make it to the top."

In the short time they sat on the forest floor, it had grown darker.

"The opening is up ahead. One last push. Tomorrow will be easier."

The sun had passed below the horizon of the mountains, and the field seemed to glow. Just a bit farther and they could rest for the night, put it down for a time and then put it down forever into the lake. Jonathan wanted it over now. The trek purged him. He was too tired for guilt, fear and remorse. It poured out of him like sweat.

The forest was dark and cold. Somewhere below them, a tree bent and snapped, breaking slow at first and then falling fast to the forest floor, dry wood exploding and crashing against other trees. The sound died in the valley.

They stood now. Conner and Jonathan let go of the case and took up their rifles. Michael had his eye to the scope. He stood at the edge of a rocky outcropping that jutted outward from the mountain like a stone face. They listened, but there was only the sound of the tree branches touching in the evening breeze. The dense forest of the Gulch lay before them like a pit.

"I can't see anything through all this shit," Michael said. He watched deep and hard, looking for breaks, looking for the things that could fall apart so he could sweep it away. Dead silence again. Nothing to see but the gray bark of countless trees melded together.

"Bear?" Conner said. "What else would take down a tree like that? Can't be a person."

"I don't see anything. Maybe a deadfall."

"Fire a shot," Jonathan said. "If it is a bear, maybe it'll turn tail and run."

"No," Michael said. "Let's wait, let's move, let's get in the clear. I don't want a warning shot; I want a kill shot."

"Stay back," Conner said. "Keep an eye while we get out and then follow."

Michael kept his eye to the scope, the barrel of his Remington tracing slow arcs across the dead expanse of Coombs' Gulch below. "Go," he said.

Conner and Jonathan shouldered their rifles, took up the box and began to move quickly up the hill, leaving Michael behind to stand watch. Jonathan could nearly count the yards till they reached the field. The birch trees thinned into small saplings. The last remnants of the forest grabbed their clothes, scratched their faces. Jonathan and Conner pounded up the slope another thirty yards into the full blaze of the sun. The dry air smelled of dying grass and released the damp cold from their lungs. The massive, open land rolled like ocean waves toward the crest of the hill.

They reached the top and stopped, dropped the case, fell to their knees in the last light of evening. Their lungs screamed, hearts raced. From here they could see down into the Gulch to the east, and to the west they could see glints of sunlight dancing across the surface of the lake. Mountain peaks rose high above them to either side.

Below, in the darkness, Michael followed. His back was turned to them, and he scanned the tree line with his rifle.

Finally, he lowered the gun, turned and began to jog slowly up the hill through the field.

Behind him the forest twisted and turned in the dusk. From his knees, Jonathan raised his rifle, put his eye to the scope and looked just over Michael's shoulder. Something moved in the darkness of the tree line.

Another strange scream went up from the valley, and they turned to look all around them, to the sky and field and trees, as if it originated from the air itself. It sounded so human, and yet, in its pain, it took on an animal ferocity.

The forest behind Michael gave way to something he could not see – it shifted in the shade and underbrush.

The scope lifted from his eye as Conner tipped the barrel of Jonathan's rifle skyward.

"What are you aiming at?"

"Nothing," he said. "No shot. Just making sure."

CHAPTER SEVENTEEN

Michael stood on the crest of the field in the last light of dusk, patient, immobile as a statue, the binoculars at his eyes.

"There's something there," he said. "I see something in the trees, but I don't know what it is. Doesn't want to show itself."

"How can you tell?" Jonathan asked.

"Just can. It's like it's there and then it's not."

The case with the boy's body sat atop the rolling brown meadow. Their gear sat in the tall grass where they had dropped it. They breathed heavy for a long time and waited until they'd mustered enough strength to set the tent. The grass was above their knees and moved with a dry, grating rustle.

"Fire a shot. If it's an animal, it will either run or be dead," Conner said.

"And if it's human, we'll be dragging two bodies off this goddamned mountain," Jonathan said.

"I want to draw it out," Michael said.

"What animal behaves like this?" Conner said.

"Bear would be my guess," Michael said. "Seems different, though. Hard to tell if there's anything really there or I'm just imagining it."

"I thought everyone said this place is dead. No deer, no bears, no nothing," Jonathan said.

"No forest is ever dead," Michael said. "Not completely. There's always something."

The meadow seemed huge and lonely in the dying light, as if nothing in the world were so large, and the three of them small and without consequence. The tree line appeared miles off across the rolling pasture; the withering stalks shimmered in the evening breeze. Far below, Coombs' Gulch changed color. The dull gray of the leafless birch trees darkened. The temperature dropped, and they could see their breath and shivered in the gathering cold – sweat-soaked, wet to the bone.

Across the Gulch the moon seemed to appear in the sky like a specter slowly rising from the grave, full and huge, hanging just over the eastern peaks. It cast a ghastly glow over the field, leaving the tree line a black barrier to the unknown.

"Why does it change size like that?" Jonathan said. "The moon. Sometimes it seems so huge and other times small and far away."

Michael still watched the trees. "It's an illusion," he said. "The moon looks bigger near the horizon. No one is really sure why. It's a trick of the light."

"A million miles away and it looks right on top of us."

"Later it will look no bigger than a dime."

"Can't trust your own eyes, I guess," Jonathan said.

Jonathan took his cell phone from his jacket and turned it on. He waited a moment, and then it buzzed and chimed with messages.

"You have service?" Conner said.

"Some."

A message from Mary asking that he call home as soon as he received it. A photograph of the front door of his house – a heavy oak door stained dark, but through the middle of it were five claw marks, deep and broad, as if a human hand had somehow torn into it. He looked closer at the image and saw small drops of blood; whatever it was, it had clawed itself bloody.

He called and the phone broke between static and her faded voice. He heard Mary's gentle, calm voice for a moment, and then she was gone; he wished he was with her now, wished he was with his son and that they were all home and all of this was over or had never been.

He turned atop the high meadow in the Adirondacks and said her name again and again into the phone until her voice came back to him.

"You're breaking up," she said.

"I can hear you now. Is everything okay?"

"Everything is fine. Something was at the door last night. I called the animal control people. They think it was a bear."

"Bears have four claws," Jonathan said.

"What? I can't hear you."

"Never mind. Did they find anything?"

"No. You know how these things go."

"Is Jacob all right?"

"Jacob is doing just fine."

"Be careful. Don't let him outside alone."

"I won't. He'll be fine. He's in school all day tomorrow anyway."

"I forgot tomorrow was Friday," he said.

"Are you okay out there? Are you guys having a good time?"

"We're fine, just out of range most of the time."

"Will you be okay when you come home?"

He didn't answer. Instead he looked out at the trees and watched them move gently, imperceptibly.

"I want to tell you something, but I don't want to ruin your trip," she said, and Jonathan closed his eyes, worried that she would tell him she had filed for divorce.

"Tell me anyway," he said. "I don't think anything could ruin this trip."

"It's going well then?"

"Perfect. What do you need to tell me?"

"Something strange happened here in town. Someone dug up Gene's body. It's gone. The whole town is in an uproar about it."

"Dug it up?"

"It's in all the papers and the local television news," she said. "His poor mother."

Jonathan looked at the two brothers, checking their own phones, trying to call their wives.

"I have to go," he said. "I want you to keep an eye on Jacob."

"Of course. It's all gruesome."

"Is he okay?"

"He's fine. The usual night terrors, though. He slept in bed last night with me. It was the only way I could get him to calm down."

That somehow made him feel better.

"I love you," he said into the phone.

"I know," she said, and then her voice was gone and he was alone again with the brothers on the top of a lonely field in the freezing night. He looked at the phone in his hand, angry and afraid. The brothers wandered aimlessly and stiff-legged in the field, their phones to their ears, trying to find the sound of their wives' voices, talking in low, conciliatory tones.

The cold evening wind seemed to carry the darkness down to them.

They tamped down the long grass and rolled out the tent. Michael took a large flashlight from his pack, nearly bright enough to light a sports field, and sat waiting in the darkness, flashing it out to the tree line, scanning the field. They watched the long, dry grass bend and roll and rustle in the light, their shadows like a thousand worlds hidden behind each stalk. His breath billowed out in the cold air. The moon was far away now, a distant pinprick of light.

It was below freezing and they shivered and shook. The grime of the day froze to their bodies.

"We can't build a fire," Conner said. "The whole field would catch."

"Should we leave someone to stand guard?" Jonathan said.

"And see what?" Conner said. "Even if there's something out there, we won't be able to see it in time. Whoever is standing guard would just be bait. Better if we're all inside. Whatever it is would have to come through the tent first."

They took their rifles with them into the three-man tent and crowded in close in their sleeping bags, each of their bodies pushed up against the other's.

Jonathan's body was tired, already asleep, but his eyes kept moving, seeing, as if in a dream. He thought of his son and the boy's nightmares – when he would scream while staring at the world, at his parents who were trying to comfort him. The tall grass brushed against the canvas of the tent and seemed to whisper to him. Jonathan stripped down to his sweatpants and sweatshirt, previously soaked with sweat, now just cold and stiff. He lay in his sleeping bag, Michael's bulk pressed against his back. The darkness inside the tent was deeper than it was outside. Jonathan's rifle, cold and hard, lay beside him. He folded his arm beneath his head and closed his eyes and listened to the sound of their breathing.

He thought of Gene's grave. He wondered if the stone was overturned. He wondered at the piles of dirt that would have been removed to dig down to the casket. He wondered at the willpower of such an act, what drove such depravity. He remembered the night when the boy was killed. Michael and Conner had left to bring the airtight case, and he was alone with Gene, standing guard over the body. Gene was shaking, racked with panic and guilt, tears pouring down his chubby face. "I never wanted this," he said, voice trembling, staring out into the dark trees. "I never wanted any of this. It's not right. None of it is right. Something is wrong. It's all wrong."

Gene's words stayed with Jonathan through the years. He thought about them and wondered, years on, what exactly Gene was saying that night, what he was talking about. Was it just the boy? Just the shot he fired? Or was it something more, something bigger?

Jonathan woke in the deepest part of the night. His eyes could not see, but he felt the damp cold of the tent canvas reaching through his skin, and he could hear Michael's harsh whisper in his ear – "Stay quiet." He realized the brothers were awake; he could feel them sitting upright in the tent, tense, breathing quickly, staring at the zippered entrance.

There was a sound outside like a great rushing wind, swirling around the tent as if they were caught in a tornado. The canvas wall bulged inward, then shuddered and rippled. Outside, the rush continued, and he could feel vibrations in the ground beneath him and remembered the night in Coombs' Gulch when it had seemed every animal suddenly came awake and stampeded through the darkness. Suddenly it seemed like time was repeating itself over and over – a different situation, but the same nonetheless. It all kept coming back. Michael slowly chambered a round in his rifle. The tumult swirled outside. The tent shook.

Then Jonathan felt hands – small, but immensely powerful and cold. He turned his head toward the tent wall beside him, which glowed in the moonlight. Two palms and ten small fingers pressed through the canvas harder and harder, reaching inward for him. Beneath the sound of the swirling force that rushed through the grass, a whisper came, slight and high-pitched, childish and achingly familiar – "Daddy."

Conner and Michael tried to stop him as he rushed for the opening of the tent. They pleaded in desperate whispers, but Jonathan felt something deep in his core pulling him outside, something he could not deny, something that did not know fear or trepidation. It moved inside him, twisted like a worm impaled on a hook. They pulled at his arms, but he thrashed against them.

Jonathan fell out into the darkness, onto his hands and knees, the long grass brushing against his face, slowing his movements like water, and he screamed Jacob's name into the night like an insane man might cry out at a hallucination.

But all was silent and still. There was no wind. There was no noise or stampede of animals. He was alone in the night, only his own frenzied breath falling into the air. He scrambled to his feet and ran around the tent, searching and screaming, but there was nothing. The distant moon cast a ghostly pallor. The field seemed to stretch on forever. The grass shone and sparkled with frost in the pale light. Jonathan's voice died in the distance.

Then Michael and Conner were outside with their rifles raised. Jonathan stopped, like a man suddenly waking from a dream, returning to the mundane world. They waited in silence, breath exhaled in clouds of mist, cold overtaking their bodies.

"What the hell happened?" Conner said.

"It was him," Jonathan said. He struggled for breath. "It was Jacob; I heard him. He was here. He spoke to me."

Far off in the field was a deep, throaty chuff and heavy footsteps through the grass. Michael raised the flashlight, but it did not reach far enough into the night. They listened as it moved east, back toward the Gulch, slouching at a slow, heavy pace down the slope of the meadow. A vixen scream went up from deep within the valley and reverberated in the air. It sounded more human than animal now. Jonathan felt cold hands close around his heart. There was no air. He could not catch his breath.

"I don't know what that is," Michael said.

He took the flashlight and searched the field around the tent for tracks, but the sea of grass was undisturbed; it swayed lightly in the cold breeze, whispering, as it had for a thousand years.

"We didn't just dream that, did we?" Conner said.

"I can't tell anymore," Michael said.

Somewhere in the depths of the Gulch, the high-pitched scream rose again, shocking and anguished, full of fear and longing.

CHAPTER EIGHTEEN

The man from the woods was outside the window again last night. Jacob had watched him walking stiff-legged along the edge of their backyard in the darkness, stopping and staring at the window where Jacob sat on his bed and watched. Then he would turn and continue his strange walk and disappear back into the darkness, just like the past few nights. Jacob was never able to truly see his face. Somehow it looked familiar, and Jacob combed through his memory of adults – neighbors, friends of Mommy's and Daddy's, parents of other kids at school, teachers – but he couldn't find that face anywhere. It looked different, almost broken, like when he had knocked over a ceramic stein on the bookshelf and he and his mother tried to piece it back together with glue before Daddy returned home and became angry.

Maybe it was some kind of monster. Normally he would be scared, but monsters didn't walk like people. Monsters were large, fanged, multi-legged things that stalked in the darkness, in closets and under beds. This was just a man – one he thought he recognized – walking along the woods.

When he first began to see the man several days ago, he told his mother. "Did you have another bad dream, honey?" she said and kneeled down so that she was eye level with him.

Jacob was told he had bad dreams at night, but he couldn't remember them. He would just suddenly wake, sometimes in another room, usually with his mother and father standing over him with tired eyes, looking worried or possibly annoyed. Sometimes, he would wake to his father yelling at him, telling him to snap out of it, but Jacob wasn't sure what he was supposed to snap out of. It was like being transported by magic to another room in the middle of the night. His face would be wet with tears, his body would be shaking, and he would be terrified, but he didn't know why. He couldn't remember anything after lying down in his bed and falling asleep. But then he would be awake, and all the night was disturbed and it was his fault. His body and his brain were doing things he couldn't control and didn't remember. But he knew they were scary things. He woke with the terror inside him. He woke knowing something had happened; he just didn't know what. He supposed if you couldn't remember them, then maybe it didn't matter.

"No. I don't think it was a dream. I don't usually remember scary dreams."

"Some you remember and some you don't." She looked tired, and Jacob wondered about those nights when he woke in fright and saw his parents standing over him. She looked tired but also sad, and sometimes he would catch her just staring out the window into the trees for long periods of time – the same trees the strange man disappeared into each night. He wondered what she was thinking. He wondered if maybe she had seen the man, too. Or maybe she knew him and that was why he seemed familiar.

"I'll keep an eye out for anything, okay?" she said. "But if you see him again, you come and tell me and show me, okay? It might just be one of the neighbors."

The police had been here yesterday because some animal put scratches in the door. The police were big, strong in their stiff uniforms, and Jacob, like most boys, focused almost exclusively on their guns, the shape of them in those holsters, wanting to one day be able to proudly walk around with that kind of power at his fingertips. He didn't know why; he just did. Daddy had guns, but they were locked up in the basement and he hardly ever took them out, except for this week when he went on a trip.

Jacob had watched his father clean those guns one time. He took them out of the safe and methodically, silently went over them bit by bit, taking them apart and wiping the metal with a rag and spraying its precise parts with a can of special oil that gave off a smell and left Jacob with a headache. He wanted to hold them, to feel the metal and pretend to shoot bad guys.

"Some other time," Daddy said. "When you're older." Jacob wondered if that would ever happen. Daddy would always say 'later' when Jacob wanted to do something with him, and later never seemed to come. His father would just sit on the couch, drinking from one of his 'Daddy drinks' until after Jacob went to bed. It was like lying, but not quite. That was the strange thing about his father – he always seemed to be lying, to be hiding something. It was nothing that Jacob could actually point to and say 'liar' but just a feeling that there was some great big secret and everyone knew it but him.

But his father was gone now on his hunting trip, and for some reason Jacob felt a sense of relief, as if he could breathe easier without this large, lumbering man who seemed to be angry all the time, stalking around inside the house. At least the man from the woods was outside, beyond locked doors and windows.

It was Friday morning, and Jacob ate a bowl of cereal grown soggy with milk. His mother was drinking coffee and tapping on her phone with her thumb. It was almost seven thirty in the morning, and she finally told him to get ready for school. Jacob tried in vain every morning to pretend school wasn't coming, but his mother always remembered, always told him it was time to get ready and go, and then he would wander out into the cold, walk to the corner with the stop sign and wait with the other kids for the big, yellow bus. His mother would watch him some mornings from the driveway. Other mornings when it was too cold, she would sit with him in the car at the corner. Jacob didn't like school. It was a lot of sitting, being forced to do work, being made to pay attention to things that didn't interest him. He liked his imagination. He liked to spend all day in his room, imagining adventures, playing with Legos, creating worlds in which he was a powerful hero bent on overcoming an enemy and saving the day.

School was strange. The teachers, the other kids, all seemed to be in on some big secret, too. They all seemed to know so much more than him, even the kids in his same grade. They gathered in circles and talked and laughed, and Jacob generally had no idea what they were talking about and why it was funny. He tried to laugh along, to pretend that he was part of it, that he knew about a particular television show or video game, but he didn't, and it usually showed fairly quickly; the other kids would look at him as if he were an alien and move on. He was invariably left out. Jacob asked his parents for a phone like his mother and father had, but they refused. He asked for a video game system, but they said they didn't have the money. He asked to watch particular movies, but was only shown movies for little kids. He was left out of the *know*; everyone else had a head start and Jacob couldn't catch up.

The teachers were nice enough, but they insisted he do work and learn things that all seemed foreign. Perhaps he was an alien, accidentally left here for some reason, or transported from some other time and place, the same way he would close his eyes and wake in fright in some other part of the house.

Jacob wasn't sure where he was from, what he was doing in this world. He didn't feel a part of it. He didn't really feel a part of his family. His father seemed angry about something, his mother tired and sad and he, above all else, felt alone with the feeling that something wasn't right.

Jacob dropped his shoulders, cleared his bowl and spoon, and shuffled off to his room to put on the clothes his mother had laid out for him the night before. His room was bright with sunlight now. He looked through the windows to the trees beyond the small space of yard in the back. The leaves were all different colors, and every day there were less of them and he could see deeper and deeper into the woods. In the spring and summer, he played out there. There were large rocks to climb, bushy enclaves he used as forts in his imaginary games and battles, but he hadn't been out there much since it turned colder. After the police came, his mother told him he couldn't play outside alone anymore. There was some animal or something out there – perhaps a hungry bear. There were lots of bears out there, supposedly, but he had yet to see one.

He was more concerned about the man who came from the woods at night and walked along the perimeter of the yard in that strange way, like one of those puppets held up by strings; the parts move and you have to pretend it's alive. He had seen a puppet show like that at school once. There was a tiny stage and curtain in the front of the classroom and this weird, funny, fat man was there making the puppets dance and move on stage. Jacob watched the puppets but he also watched the man whose face hovered just over the curtains as he told a story and the puppets acted it out. The man smiled in a strange way and the puppets moved by his unseen hands. Maybe that was who was outside the window at night, Jacob thought. Maybe it was the puppet man.

His mother kissed him goodbye and watched him from the driveway as he stood with three other children at the stop sign, waiting for his bus. Jacob said hello to them but didn't speak much after that. He kept his hands busy by adjusting his backpack. It was cold out today. Not cold enough to see his breath, but cold enough to make the wait seem eternal. The bus could be heard across the whole neighborhood. The rolling hills and trees didn't block its big diesel engine and squealing brakes. When it pulled up he was the last to climb the steps into that big tube on wheels that smelled like vinyl and rubber. His mother stood at the top of the driveway, arms crossed to keep her hands warm, and watched him as he passed by encased in glass and steel.

Jacob had yet to fully understand the large building that was the Region 12 Consolidated Elementary School. Their town was small and shared the school with neighboring Burlington. It was his first year at this place, which still seemed huge and strange despite his having come here nearly every day for the past two and a half months. The first few days left him in tears, trying to find his way to his classroom, trying to understand the rules, trying to decipher the orders from his teacher and the directions his classmates constantly spilled out at him as if they had been attending classes for years. Now, at least, he knew the routine. But still, the school branched off into long, dark hallways, doors appeared out of nowhere, and in the bathrooms older kids would mingle and laugh and stare as he stood before the urinal. When he had to pee, he waited until the midpoint of class so that he could be relatively sure he'd be alone. Without the throngs of other kids stumbling through the hallways, bumping, talking over one another, pushing him this way and that with their over-large bodies, the cheaply tiled hallways seemed to yawn like the open mouth of a cave, hiding doors to other worlds. His first week at this school, Jacob accidentally went to the wrong class and sat down at a desk. He still couldn't understand why they had to go to different classrooms to learn different things; why didn't the teachers just walk to the classroom he was in so he didn't have to navigate the maze of doors and classroom numbers? But he sat down with a sick, uncomfortable feeling in his stomach. Somehow, he already knew he was in the wrong place. Things just didn't look right. The kids looked slightly bigger than him, slightly more knowledgeable. They looked at him and then seemed to purposely ignore his presence, but he was lost at this point and didn't know what else to do, so he waited.

As soon as the teacher began her lesson, he knew he was in the wrong place. But now, with an entire classroom of older boys and girls, all with two eyes with which to stare at him, he kept his silence. Finally, the teacher's eyes found him sitting in the second-to-last row.

"I don't recognize you," she said. Her hair was so blonde it was practically white and there were lines in her face that deepened when she spoke to him. "What's your name?"

"Jacob Hollis."

"Are you sure you're in the right class, Jacob?"

"Umm…"

"How old are you?" Now he was being grilled, and he felt his stomach tightening.

"Seven…"

"No. You're in the wrong class. What class are you supposed to be in?"

Jacob didn't know.

"Well, march down to the main office and talk to them. They'll get you to the right place." Her voice was harsh, and she watched as Jacob stood from the desk that wasn't his own and walked back out the door. The other kids laughed quietly as he left. No one held his hand; no one told him where to go or what to do. It was just him, alone, in this monstrosity of a place.

That feeling had not yet left him and he wondered if it ever would. He wondered what this place was supposed to do for him, why there was so much emphasis on coming here, enduring here. In this place, surrounded by other kids, he felt alone.

There was something different about today, though. Although he was never happy or comfortable here, he had begun to grow accustomed to it. It had at least become a familiar, unwanted feeling, but today he felt something else, something more twisted and frightening than the usual alienation and confusion he normally felt. Maybe it was his dad being gone – the way he had packed up his things, his instruments for killing animals, and left early for some faraway place. Maybe it was the memory of the man from the woods still stalking through his mind. With his father gone, that lumbering figure in the darkness suddenly seemed more frightening. Even though Jacob always sensed something wrong about his dad, he at least knew that his father loved him and would protect him, protect the house. He was big. He was strong. He could do that. Now, with his father gone someplace far away, Jacob had an unsettled feeling that everything was wide open, like the door to the house was open and anyone could just walk inside. Perhaps it was the look on his mother's face as the bus pulled away on the street. It was like a photograph in his mind; one thing about looking at pictures is that you look at them to remember people you haven't seen in a long time. He missed her suddenly, overwhelmingly, and wanted to be in her arms, to have her hold him in his house where he could feel safe.

Or maybe it was something else. Perhaps, those dreams he couldn't remember were slowly sneaking their way into his thoughts. He knew he would wake screaming; what did he see? Did he even want to know?

Jacob watched two boys giggling over a phone in a corner of the hallway, and their faces seemed suddenly sharp and devilish, their smiles too wide, their cheekbones like blades trying to cut through their skin. They looked at him for a moment like they could kill him. He looked away. No. There was something wrong today. He felt it, and he wanted more than anything to be home. It made him feel sick to his stomach.

In Ms. Cracco's class, they learned about telling time on a clock, the small arm and long arm moving slowly across the numbers on a circle. They made their own clocks out of construction paper, wrote in the numbers with marker, cut out hour and minute hands and fastened them to the paper clock. They moved the arms into the correct position to match times Ms. Cracco announced to the class. Next it was on to shapes – squares, rectangles, stars and circles. Again, more cutting with scissors and arranging the shapes into neat patterns. Jacob enjoyed that lesson. He laid out different shapes over each other, their edges and angles intersecting, forming things that resembled objects in real life. A triangle and a rectangle to form a house; a circle with a square below it resembled a hot-air balloon. He even used the shapes to form people – a circle for the head, a triangle or rectangle for the body, two smaller rectangles for the legs – like the 'boys' and 'girls' signs in the hallway beside the bathrooms.

He placed the star inside the circle and sat staring at it for a while. It reminded him of something he couldn't quite remember but somehow seemed important. He took the clock he'd made and then laid the star over it. He traced the lines of the star to the different numbers the five points touched.

"What are you doing, Jacob?" Ms. Cracco hovered over him suddenly, stern and foreboding.

"Nothing," Jacob said. "I just thought it looked cool." It wasn't necessarily that it looked cool, but it looked like something.

The teacher kneeled down next to his desk. "You see how all the points intersect? And those points go to the numbers on the clock? What do you think about that?"

"You can go from one time to another," he said, "and skip over the other times."

"Maybe one day we can," Ms. Cracco said. "You're a smart boy. Maybe you'll figure it out."

Jacob looked at her. She seemed older than her face would suggest, and he thought he saw disappointment in her gray eyes. Was it with him? But she had just said he was smart, so it couldn't be disappointment with him.

She stood silently and continued walking down the row of desks, overseeing the projects of her students. Jacob wondered what it took to be a teacher. He suddenly wondered about her life. It was a momentary flash of empathy. Wondering if Ms. Cracco was married, if she had children of her own, if she really wanted to be a teacher. Like most adults, she seemed to be hiding something. There was a lie somewhere. Maybe she was sad like his mother or disappointed in something else. The world of adults was strange. They always had information, knowledge, which they held back. When they looked at him, it always seemed like they were looking at someone to pity. It made him feel like a burden, that perhaps their lives would be easier if he didn't grow up in their presence. The way his mother hugged him, clinging to him like he could be lost at any second, made him wonder what was out there, what waited for him in this strange world.

It was a day like any other. But it was Friday, and Jacob was glad that he wouldn't have to come back tomorrow or the next day. He could stay home, play in his room with his toys and use his imagination to construct other worlds where there were no secrets because he had them all. They were boy's games made of Legos and action figures, spaceships, trucks and cars, imagined heroic personalities and villains bent on world domination. In those worlds he had control over the action figures, what they did, what they thought, who they battled and why. He could reach into those imaginary worlds, pull characters out and put them back in, shift time and location and even planets. His was the hand that moved them into situations and either let them live and conquer or suffer under an unseen enemy. That was how he spent his time on those long days of solitude. When he would go outside, he went to the woods where he explored the rocks and trees, imagined monsters waiting in the shadows, and acted out scenes of bravery and control he wished he possessed in real life.

His father would sometimes say he should be out playing with the other boys on the block, but he never saw them. It was as if they were all locked up in their separate houses. Besides, since he was only seven years old, his mother wouldn't allow him to just wander up the street, looking for other kids to play with. Most of them were older, anyway. Their eyes were focused on phones and screens, which did fascinate him when he had the opportunity to see them, but because he had never played with them, he was instantly lost, outside the circle of understanding, unable to be engrossed in them like other kids.

At the end of the day he was hungry and tired and wanted to be home again. The bus bounced on the old back roads of his neighborhood, a place where nearly every house was partially hidden. Jacob was momentarily lifted off the seat, bounced, and settled back into the vinyl. He could feel the cold coming off the window, touching his forehead. There were very few children on the bus, and, with each stop, there were fewer; the brakes squealed, and their little bodies with big backpacks jumped off the bus stairs and walked quickly and confidently in the direction of their homes.

Jacob's mother sometimes waited at the top of the driveway for him to arrive, but other times she merely watched him from the windows. He liked those times. Walking from the bus stop to his house on his own made him feel more grown up. He also liked the brief moment of solitude. It was cold and bright out today. The sky was a deep blue, and the leaves were dry and brittle, falling from the trees in a dancing rain of brown and yellow. His stop was next, and he could see the intersection ahead. Jacob pulled his backpack up on his shoulder and readied himself to stand up and exit as quickly as possible. The other kids were already standing in the aisle, holding on to the back of the seats, waiting for the full stop and the doors to fold open. Jacob looked through the windows. His mother wasn't on the driveway today.

After he got off the bus, it pulled away down the road, and Jacob watched as the two other kids walked away from him in the opposite direction. Normally there were three other children who got off at this stop, but Dori wasn't here today, so there was only Logan and Bella walking down the street with their backpacks high on their shoulders. The road sloped gently downward toward their houses, and the two other children disappeared out of view. He could hear them talking to each other. They had said nothing at all to him, though he wished they would. He wished that maybe one day he could walk with them and they could talk like friends.

Jacob waited for a moment and watched the bus disappear around another corner. He looked to his house but couldn't see his mother at the window. The wind pushed cold air across his face and with it a strange, pungent smell – something thick and raw.

There was a small copse of trees separating Jacob's house from the neighboring one, which was occupied by an old woman who needed a tank to breathe. Jacob began to walk toward his home, but, in that copse of trees, he saw something. Buried in the dry fallen leaves was something bulky, with light brown fur that moved slightly in the light breeze. He stopped and stared at it for a moment and then slowly stepped off the road and walked a few feet into the brush. Overhead, the trees moved slightly with small, twisting sounds of wood. The sky was deep blue above their long, thin branches, and, even in the daylight, the moon was visible but almost see-through, like a cold, distant ghost.

Jacob saw the fur ruffle again in the leaves. He walked to it and looked down and then cautiously moved the leaves aside.

It was a rabbit, but it no longer looked like a rabbit. The insides had been torn out, and the blood and gore had crusted on the ground and stuck to the dead leaves like glue. Its head was attached by only sinews. Its doll eyes had glazed over with a bluish-white tinge.

He rolled the rabbit over completely with the toe of his shoe. The inside was hollow and black. Strands of muscle and gut were hardened and crusted and old. Jacob stared at it for a while longer, the body splayed open, the life rotted away, and wondered at it. He wondered if that was how it looked when you died. If there was really nothing left but this empty shell, crusted to the ground, hanging with partial bits of what was once stomach, lungs and heart.

Poor rabbit, he thought. Then the same thick and raw smell wafted over him again. There was a shadow on the leaves. A shadow big enough to engulf both him and the rabbit as one. He turned around to look, and the afternoon sun shone bright in his eyes.

CHAPTER NINETEEN

The high mountain lake shone through the leafless trees in the light of the cold, early dawn. Jonathan, Michael and Conner stood at the crest of the meadow and saw the water sparkling, and, for a moment, everything seemed beautiful and good. They turned to look at the black case sitting in the long grass, tinged with frost, and the air seemed to grow dark around them. They pulled out the tent stakes, folded the rods and rolled the tent back up, but they couldn't get it right. They tried again until Conner finally stuffed it into its carrying case. Jonathan rolled his sleeping bag. It was sloppy. He let it be and strapped it to his backpack. He was too tired to care. Michael stared with his cold eyes at the lake.

"What do you say? About a mile?" Michael said.

"Mile and a half," Conner said.

"We should have been walking back by now," Jonathan said.

Michael looked at the sky. "Snow is coming."

They searched again for animal tracks around the tent and near the coffin, but there was nothing. Jonathan tried for a cell phone signal, but it was gone.

"We should just bury it here," he said.

"With what? We left the shovels back in the Gulch," Conner said.

"Fine. Then just leave it and go," Jonathan said.

"Just out in the open? No. We finish this. Stick to the plan."

"Are we even going to talk about what happened last night?"

"I don't know what happened last night. I don't know what that noise was. But what I remember most is you acting insane."

"I heard something."

"We all heard something. An animal, the wind, doesn't matter." Conner picked up one side of the case. "Let's get on with it. Mile and a half and we're done. We can be back by nightfall."

Jonathan looked back over the meadow to the Gulch and shook his head. It was cold, even through his coveralls. Beyond the mountains to the west the sky seemed to be building toward something; there was a gray haze where the deep blue disappeared into a fog. He walked to the other side of the box. His legs were sore and he walked slow and stiff. He picked up the side and tried to walk and then put it down to catch his breath. "It's heavy as hell."

"We're just tired, is all," Conner said.

Jonathan waited a moment and then picked it up again, and, together with the weight of his pack, clothes and rifle, tried to start walking with Conner. Their steps were awkward. The case bumped into the side of his knee, the same raw and bruised spot as the day before, and he became angry again. They walked down the slope toward the lake. Gravity pulled them through their steps. They walked together like a broken animal, stumbling, hobbling down the hill. The long grass scraped against the underside of the case and moved around them, and it sounded like a crowd of people speaking in hushed tones.

He tried to hear it. He tried to make words out of the long, rustling grass the way one might try to discern conversation in a crowded room. The sound seemed to come from everywhere, carried down from the mountains on the cold, open breeze. He stared at the tree line; long, broken fingers, a maze of pale trunks and branches, reached up to claw at the distant sun. He heard the whisper of the grass against the plastic case again. It sounded like the voice of a child, and he listened harder.

He looked at Michael, but Michael was staring into the trees. He looked at Conner beside him, but his head was turned, looking into the distance. There were no faces, and he suddenly felt as if he were alone with this burden. Jonathan turned to look everywhere, to the whole expanse of field and mountains, but he saw nothing. The world seemed like a picture or a painting. It looked so unreal that, for a moment, he wondered if it was all an elaborate hoax, a maze for lab rats. The wind moved the trees and the tall grass. He reached out his hand to try to touch it, but there was only air and distance. The boy in the box shifted, sloshed to the other side, and the weight of it pulled him sideways.

The lake disappeared behind the tree line and Jonathan sweated in the cold sun. The dark trees rose up before them. They stopped at the edge of the field and waited, breathing heavily. The woods seemed to slide up to meet them, and they peered inside. The ground was rocky and covered with leaves and devoid of underbrush, which had choked and died long ago. The tree trunks were thicker and spread apart. Lichen grew patchworks on the bark. It smelled wet. The tall branches were thick and darkened the ground, and roots rolled above and beneath the surface, like thick snakes.

They weren't walking now, but the whispering grew louder. It sounded familiar. They tried to look past the trees – another mile to the lake, but they waited, catching their breath before taking the final plunge. Jonathan thought of Thomas Terrywile in the box; the thought of dropping it into that lake forever suddenly terrified him more than being caught, than living with it.

The end somehow seemed worse. He wondered if there was an end.

Jonathan turned away from the trees and looked up toward the top of the field, to the ridge of the meadow, the sky pouring across the horizon, and saw a humanlike figure standing dark against the sky, staring down at them. From this distance it was a small, erect shadow, but he could see it. He could feel its eyes. He heard the whisper through the meadow, through the trees and through the box by his side. Something spread across its unseen face.

Jonathan tapped Michael and Conner and nodded up the slope. "About five hundred yards off." They turned and looked. The wind pushed against them. Michael raised the rifle and looked through his scope. The figure at the top of the meadow did not move. Michael stared through the scope for a long time but kept his finger on the hilt.

"What is it?" Conner asked. Michael was silent. His face paled; the skin around his eyes softened as he opened his left eye and slowly lifted his head from the scope.

"Too far of a shot," he said, but his voice was dead.

"But what is it?" Conner asked again.

"We should go."

"Just take the shot anyway, goddammit." Conner took the rifle from Michael's hand. Michael didn't resist. His limp body let the sling slide off his shoulder. He stumbled and swayed slightly in the wind. Conner raised the rifle toward the shadow atop the meadow, but it was gone, and there was nothing but the rounded horizon.

"I don't see it," Conner said. He slowly scanned the cold field for any sign of movement, life, but there was nothing. "What did you see? A person? A bear?"

Michael stared off into the trees, as if seeing something in the air, in the spaces between. "I don't know what it was. It was too far off."

"Bullshit," Conner said.

"We should go now," Michael said.

Conner looked at Jonathan and then back to his brother. "Let's just get this done," he said and lifted the side of the box. Jonathan took up the other side. Michael stumbled into the forest. They lost sight of the lake when they dropped below the tree line. It wasn't far off.

They moved quicker. They ignored the pain in their legs and shoulders. The new forest opened up and swallowed them, and they were lost in a limbo of thick trees. They kept a quick pace. There was no undergrowth to slow them down. The downward slope carried them, but it seemed endless, and they could not see more than fifty yards in any direction. Time and space seemed to stand still. Jonathan thought they passed the same rock outcropping several times. Nothing changed; the forest scrolled past them like a broken film. The deep blue morning sky faded, and the sun was now hidden behind a desert expanse of low gray clouds. The colder air came quick and sharp. Sweat seeped out from beneath Jonathan's wool cap and froze to his cheek.

"We won't beat the snow," Michael said.

"We will," Conner said.

The cold air brought a heavier wind. The tops of the trees danced and swayed, knocked against each other. The sound came from above them and in every direction and echoed hollow, cold and dead. Michael and Conner carried the case now. Jonathan kept the rifle ready. Behind the clatter of the tree branches was the sound of heavy footfalls. Jonathan motioned for them to stop. He turned and watched the trees behind them and was lost in the cascading maze. He felt something but saw nothing. He looked through the scope, but it made him more blind, limiting his vision and perspective. There were only hints of movement, something sliding behind the wall of forest, nothing more than a fleeting shadow from the corner of his eye or the sound of a tree limb snapping or a branch breaking free of its moorings. He let the brothers move ahead and waited for what followed; he waited for what had uttered those words to him the night before and what stood at the crest of the meadow staring down at them.

He wished for other times and places, for other lives where that night ten years ago had not happened, where the bullet was five inches to the right and missed the boy completely. Everything inescapable hinged on precise moments, tiny factors that change the world. He watched and waited and felt something beyond the trees calling to him.

He whispered something to the trees.

He heard Michael and Conner calling for him in the distance. He turned with his rifle and began moving quickly down the mountain toward their voices, which seemed far away, lost in the wilderness. He rounded a tree and saw them, rifles raised, sighting the barrels directly at him. He stopped dead and thought they would fire. The two brothers could keep a secret for eternity, no matter what haunted their lives. Their faces were stone cold, expressionless. Jonathan raised his hands gently, and they lowered their guns.

"Yell out when you're coming," Conner said.

"We're here," Michael said.

The trees thinned out, the ground turned to wet stone and frozen mud, the smell of condensation and dead fish. Jonathan stared down at the box with the dead boy inside. A mirage of dark and haunting water called to them from between the trees; the surface of the cold lake wavered and rippled and gave way to its depths.

CHAPTER TWENTY

A narrow and rocky shoreline traced north and south from where they stood, bending in and out of sight and then jutting far out into a peninsula before disappearing. It was a thin line of dark gray before the water, which ran black beneath the gathering clouds. They placed the box at the water's edge and sat down to collect their breath. The damp rocks penetrated through their coveralls, touched their skin, but they sat anyway. Jonathan filled his canteen with water from the lake and drank. The water was cold, near freezing. The daylight temperature was below thirty now, and already he was shivering after hauling the coffin down the slope. They stared out at the lake, and it seemed suspended in air, as if a dark, flat cloud hovered in the mountains. The peaks on the other side rose to the sky. All was silent. The water rippled slightly in a breeze.

"It goes down at least a hundred feet from here," Conner said. "It feeds the river that runs down through Pasternak. It isn't going anywhere."

The lake seemed prehistoric, outside of time and beyond the reach of civilization.

"It will stay secret here," Conner said, but neither Jonathan nor Michael replied. Jonathan was hungry, drained from the past two days. He looked in his pack. There were only two sandwiches left, and he ate them both, shivering in the wet air. He could smell the approaching snow.

Michael and Conner ate. Conner looked at the sky and said, "We need to get this over with." He unstrapped the portable raft from his pack and spread the flat, thick rubber over the round, wet river rocks. He took out a battery-operated air pump, and the small machine roared to life with the sound of a large vacuum cleaner. The rubber began to move the way a carcass left long in the sun will start to undulate slowly with life eating away at the insides. The raft slowly took form as Conner filled it with as much air as possible. It became a large, dark gray oval and seemed to hover in the air just above the rocky shore. "It will hold up to three hundred pounds," Conner said.

They turned and looked at the box sitting crooked and uneven on the rocks.

Conner nodded toward it. "We're gonna have to open it up, weigh it down with some stones and then cut some holes in the sides so it sinks."

"Who's rowing out there?" Jonathan said.

"I am," Conner said.

"You sure it will hold?"

"I've fished in it before. Had Brent out in it with me. I might get a little wet, but I'll be okay."

Michael looked to the sky. "Let's hurry," he said. Jonathan kept feeling the insides of the box moving back and forth like swamp mud as they had carried the case across the mountain, the way one's body remembers the rocking of the ocean after a day on a boat. They all stood over it in a triangle with the makeshift coffin for Thomas Terrywile in the center like an all-seeing eye. The metal fasteners were covered in dirt and rust from a decade in the ground. The wind whispered through trees. Jonathan looked up into the forest but saw nothing. Everything had grown dark with cloud cover. He looked back down at the coffin.

"I want to see," Michael said. They turned and looked at him, but he was focused on the box. He bent down and tried the first fastener, but it did not give. He took out a hunting knife and wedged the tip between the handle and the case itself and tried to wrench the metal latch upward – at first gently and then with a growing anger – until it squeaked and groaned as he unfastened the latch and lowered the metal hoop that held the lid to the body. He moved to the second latch and used his knife again and then moved on to the side latches. They all came unwillingly. Finally, the case sat unlocked, seemingly relieved of a massive tension.

Jonathan looked to the sky but couldn't see the sun. His watch said 10:32 a.m.

Michael reached into the pocket of his coveralls and took out a camouflaged hunting mask that covered his whole head, mouth and nose. Michael and Conner buried their faces in their collars. They watched as Michael kneeled at the box and lifted the lid.

A great rush of gasses poured out of the case and rose into the air, dirty green and speckled with swirling particles like black stars. A wretched, humanlike scream rose up from the mountains, carried over the lake and echoed, so it seemed as if the whole earth were screaming in a terrified rage. The smell overtook them, sunk like liquid through the fabric of their coveralls, into their nostrils and down their throats. Jonathan gagged. His stomach tightened with nausea. He backed away for a moment, choking, hacking, and then, when his body stopped convulsing, he waited a moment and walked forward. He looked into the blackness of the coffin – the black sludge of what had once been a boy. It was so dark that no light escaped, and in it, *he could truly see.*

Jonathan felt his body drift upward, as if in a dream. He saw the three of them lying on the rocks, faces upward, pale and cold, the open box in the center, its contents still and dark. He felt himself rising away from his body, prone on the riverbed, like the stories told by men and women who have died, only to be brought back to life. He was drawn into the trees. The world twisted and turned like mirrors in a carnival funhouse. He was pulled by a great force through the forest they had just traveled – up the slope, across the meadow and plunged back into Coombs' Gulch. He stood in the center of that strange, occult design, the white stone lines intersecting before him and firing out to the edge of the circle. He looked up at the perfect ring of sky. The clouds were stripped away as if erased by an unseen hand; the sun disappeared, and there was only the blackness of Thomas Terrywile's melted body.

A face took shape in the darkness, merging together like spots of color behind tightly closed eyes. It gazed down on him, and its strange mouth spread wide as a severed throat. It shifted and changed and swirled. Now it was his own face staring at him from the darkness of the spaces in between, but it was distorted and strange, like a rubber mask slipping down from the skull of a child.

Jonathan suddenly found himself back in Collinsville at the Halloween parade. He stood alone among a thousand children, and they all wore a Jonathan mask, and they squirmed about his legs, pushing and shoving through, writhing like maggots, slippery and wet and covered in some kind of decaying slime. They were packed so tight against him he couldn't lift his legs to move. He looked out over the whole town. The land itself seemed to move with those children, like so many ants bearing his face – skittering, running, moving together. Then they began to fall apart; a limb would drop, a leg collapse, the skin of a tiny hand slide off the bone to the ground – a thousand little lepers all falling to pieces. They did not make a sound; they did not take off their masks.

And as they fell apart and dropped to the ground, he saw one child still standing at the top of the hill beneath the cemetery. His little hand reached to the top of his head, and he pulled the rubber mask away. It was Jacob, and he was falling apart, melting away. The mask dropped to the ground along with his small, delicate hand. Jonathan screamed and tried to get to him, but there were too many bodies, too many little arms and legs and heads, and he could not force his way through the mass grave of faceless children. And then the demon-god rose out of the muck and mire, its expressionless, wooden mask staring down at him, seemingly held aloft by puppet strings from the dark storm clouds that rolled overhead.

Then he was gone from that place, and now he saw only a single dull light bulb illuminating a smoky stage. Mary was there in the circle of light. She started to move, to dance, undulating and gyrating like a cheap stripper. She removed her clothes. Her shirt fell to the ground, then her bra. He could see her breasts – sagged from childbirth, nipples rigid and calloused from breastfeeding, her stomach still fleshy and loose, but lovely all the same. Her underwear dropped to the stage, and she swayed and danced in all her human imperfection. Amid the sexual farce, she dug her fingernails into the skin of her forearm and pulled. Her skin peeled back and tore loose with a soft, rubbery snapping sound. Blood poured out, and she quietly and calmly dropped the strip of skin to the floor. Jonathan cried out like a drunken barker from the audience, but she kept stripping away her skin, slow and bloody, like the dance she performed beneath the dull spotlight, until her body was stripped bare, down to muscle and tendons. In the dim light he could see her face wet with tears, but she did not make a sound; she did not utter a word. She stood before him, open to the world.

Then he was back in Coombs' Gulch. Michael and Conner were spread out in pieces across the spiked branches of the black spruce trees. They were alive and in agony, and he heard their cries and saw their anguished faces distort with pleas for an end, but no end came for them. They moved their heads and somehow moved their feet, even though their lower limbs were spread ten feet away on another tree. All the feeling was there, all the pain, every inch of their bodies ran with it like blood. A cold wind swept through, and the trees swayed back and forth and pulled their desiccated bodies in different directions. They screamed, but the sound was lost in the woods. He reached out to pull their bodies down, but he could not reach them.

Then Jonathan felt himself fall into nothingness, the silence deep and thick. He felt his eardrums would explode from the silence. He heard his breathing; he heard his heart beat, the rhythm louder and louder till it was all he could hear. Then he detected something else, another sound behind the beat of his heart – something deeper down within, so deep it seemed a million miles away.

Screaming. Fatal, terrified screaming.

He understood it then. Hell is not a place. It distorts all time and space and dimension. Hell is within – deep down, filled with the agonized screams of everyone we love.

Jonathan stood again in the center of the occult design in Coombs' Gulch. All was silent and dark and cold but for the white stones, which glowed like lights on an airport runway. He could feel a terrible presence with him, and he turned to look. He saw the outline of a distorted and massive figure standing at the edge of the circle. Its wooden mask glowed in the moonlight, its arms and legs vaguely human, but with rootlike tendrils crawling up and over and changing the demon-god's form.

It spoke with a deep, garbled and croaking attempt at human language.

Do you see?

Jonathan was silent – dead with fear, shaking and alone.

This time, its voice boomed over the mountains and rose up from the earth.

Do you see!

"I see!" Jonathan screamed out, but then the figure was gone and there was no one there to hear him.

Suddenly, he was in the light of day again. A sunlit afternoon in a quiet hamlet of forest at the edge of a school sports field. The day was warm but promised a cool night, the air sweet with moisture and decay. The sky was a deep, autumn blue. And Jonathan was there. He felt the light on his skin; he breathed the air and smelled the turning leaves and the grass giving up its life. He was walking, but not of his own volition. He was trapped behind a pair of eyes, an observer. He walked through a cheap football field toward the trees, which stretched along the field and then up a hill, spreading like a blanket over the land. He wore jeans and an old shirt. He carried a backpack, and his sneakers were old, a design from decades ago. His hands were small and light, unblemished by years. His hair was thick and shaggy, full of life. He found a path into the trees and started down into a patch of forest. The trees had not yet given up their leaves, and the short stretch of forest was darker and cooler. He could see the houses of a neighborhood up ahead, with the sound of cars rolling over pavement, and his eyes were set on that place. He moved with a lighthearted happiness.

On the ground near the edge of the path was a small clump of fur in the leaves. He stopped and wandered closer. He picked up a stick to poke the furry thing gently, to make it move, but it did not move. He pushed harder with the stick until it finally flopped over and showed its exposed and hollowed insides, crawling with maggots and other infestations. He dropped the stick and jumped back in disgust. A smell rose up and overtook him. Then a shadow fell over him and a heavy, dirt-laden hand gripped his shoulder. He turned slowly and looked up. A bearded man in a dark hood with wild, shining eyes stared down at him. The man leaned down close, near to him, and whispered, "Do you see?" and his face seemed to move and swell and deflate, as if those same infestations were moving beneath his skin. Two other hooded figures appeared behind him, as if materialized out of the trees.

Jonathan tried to scream, but that heavy hand, ripe with dirt and oil, clamped down over his mouth. The figures picked him up and carried him through the trees. He fought and struggled and cried, but the grip was so strong – the arms a vise over his small body – it was useless. They seemed to fly through the trees. They traveled far, far into the woods, and he struggled until shock finally set in and his body went limp. His eyes were open, but he could not move. The procession went on endlessly into the night. Darkness swelled up from behind the trees.

They took him to a place, a clearing where everything was silent and still, and white rocks gleamed in the moonlight in a circle with lines tracing through, which formed an empty square in the center. They set him down in the center. He stood with the man behind him, each of his powerful hands clamped on Jonathan's shoulders. The three figures began to chant in words he did not understand, their dark hoods over their heads, their faces writhing and crawling.

The rocks glowed in the night. The chanting filled the cold air until it was all he could hear.

And then there was a new presence in the circle with him, massive and stinking with death. He felt it, heard its strange breath. The man released his grip on Jonathan's small shoulders, and two long arms with clawed hands reached around and embraced his tiny body.

Then he was gone – gone from this world, gone from time and space. The sharpened tips of its claws danced over his body, and he seemed to melt, spreading out into those interstitial spaces. It was all like a never-ending dream, or perhaps a nightmare, in which he was everywhere and nowhere at once.

He faded in and out of reality, in and out of places and times, materializing in strange forests and disappearing again. He would see people – campers, hunters, hikers at various times – dressed in clothes he did not recognize. He could see them, but he was far from them. He would scream out and cry for help, and they would turn to look but never see.

Other times he came to in a forest at night, and he would wander, trying to find his way home, lost and terrified. But the woods were not his own, the places cold and endless. He wandered through these forests in the night, and it would walk behind him like some strange guardian making sure he did not run off. He could feel the branches and leaves; he could touch the cold ground and breathe the scented air. He could see the animals that stared at him and then bounded off in fright. His clothes were not enough to keep him warm, and he trembled and cried and shivered in the darkness.

Then he would disappear again, melt into time and space, and his small body was racked with pain; there was nothing but frozen, empty space. His eyes could see, but there was nothing – absolutely nothing – to be seen. He couldn't tell if those blank spaces lasted seconds or millennia. The incomprehensible pain overwhelmed all time and thought. It was as if his bones were trying to escape his flesh. He cried for his mother during those times, but there was no answer, only more cold and pain and timelessness.

He wandered along a brook in the night, with the presence following his steps as if marching a slave. It was freezing. He shivered and walked to stay warm, but all he truly wanted was to lie down somewhere and die so the endless torture would end. He wandered near a giant bush, and suddenly, in the darkness, he saw a bright light. It was like looking down a long and dark tunnel. The light turned toward him, blinding white, and he turned away for a moment. The creature behind him croaked in a deep and unknown language. There was a flash of fire in the distance, and something struck the back of his head. Then, suddenly, he felt release and freedom, freedom from pain and bondage and suffering.

For a moment – an immeasurable increment of time before he was finally released – he heard the sound of men's voices whooping and cheering in the night.

CHAPTER TWENTY-ONE

Jonathan woke with relief and terror, shivering and cold like poor Thomas Terrywile on that night. His back was wet with lake water from the small pools nestled between rocks on the shore. The water soaked through his jacket. Small, light snowflakes fell from an expanse of gray clouds, which rolled like ocean waves overhead. He woke with a gasp, terrified that he was still alive, like being born again, from one hell into another. Now he was among the living, though unsure what that meant. Here in the cold, he could feel the gravity of the world again and realized now the trap laid for them – the trap they had built themselves, stick by stick with guilt and fear throughout their lives. They had imprisoned themselves for the hunter.

Jonathan had never even put up a fight.

It was not a cage. Rather, it was like a grisly maze. Jonathan realized that he had been led to this very place from the beginning. They were not ahead of the thing that stalked them in the woods; it was miles and eons ahead of them. He had suffered under the guilt of killing Thomas Terrywile; his life – all their lives – were tormented with the memory of that night.

But they were not guilty. They had freed Thomas Terrywile from an eternity of hell, from being a plaything for a demon summoned by crazed men with dead faces. He saw it all in the dream, the hallucinogenic vision that left him paralyzed on the rocks. He and the Braddick brothers thought they had come back to Coombs' Gulch to save themselves; instead, their trip was a desperate attempt to cling to the trappings of their lives – an elaborate fate set in motion by a being that could see in and out of time and space. They were here to be tortured and killed. They had taken its plaything away and would suffer for it.

Jonathan sat up quickly, his back frozen and wet from lying on the rocky beach. His face numb with cold. The open case with Thomas Terrywile's remains sat inert and uneven before him, the lid open to the world. He saw the raft where they had left it, stirring slightly in a breeze, snowflakes gathering on its swollen sides. He heard Michael's voice, choking, insane. Jonathan turned and saw him sitting on that lonely shoreline, rocking back and forth, his eyes staring at the box, his lips whispering something Jonathan couldn't make out. Conner stood on the other side of the coffin, still staring down into the darkness. He looked up at Jonathan and then back down at the box. "We have to finish this and leave," Conner said.

The sky was darker now, but not just with cloud cover. Jonathan checked his watch. Four hours had disappeared. The snow fell gently. It would grow worse.

"What happened?" Jonathan said. "What did you see?"

"I don't know. It was just a nightmare. Some kind of reaction...." Conner said.

"None of this is right," Jonathan said. "I don't think we know what we're dealing with here."

Michael sat cross-legged before the case. He whispered and mumbled. Conner walked to him and pulled him up by the collar. Michael's eyes refocused for a second on his brother, and they stood, face-to-face, in a momentary embrace, staring into each other's eyes.

"Pull it together," Conner said softly to him.

"We're not pulling anything together," Jonathan said. "We're just walking into this thing! We're just doing what we're told! It's like being stuck in a film. It's all predetermined."

"I don't believe that," Conner said. "This is reality. This is where we are and this is what we have to do. It doesn't matter what you dreamed up. If it's all fate, then it won't matter what we do anyway. You said it yourself! So we might as well do what's in our best interest." Conner bent down and took a large rock from the shore and dropped it into the case. Thomas Terrywile's former body splashed up and spattered his pants, black droplets that blended in with his hunting fatigues. He grabbed another rock and another. "I'll sink this thing to the bottom, so deep it will be like it never existed."

"You're overloading it," Michael finally said, clear and cogent.

"Are you helping or not?" Conner said.

Jonathan looked at Conner for a moment and then at the mountains around them, dark and wet. He looked out across the lake and up the hill they would have to climb to get home. There was no other place he could be right now. He was here, trapped in an unfolding tragedy of his own making. He waited a moment for the veil to be lifted, but nothing came. He imagined himself transported to another reality where one wrong decision hadn't set his life on such a fatal course, but it was pointless. The true horror of life is that it continues on without miracle, without reprieve, until the end. We are powerless before it. He thought of the creature in his vision: *Do you see?* He picked up a small stone, walked to the box and dropped it inside. He crossed himself and said a prayer he didn't believe, the same as he had done over Gene's casket.

Conner closed the lid and sealed it shut again. Michael kneeled before the case, took out his Bowie knife and plunged the stainless steel through the hard plastic as if he were killing a man. He did it with violence and speed, his features distorted under the strain. The box they had carried across miles of forested mountain was now riddled front and back with thick gashes. It leaked onto the rocks.

Jonathan took one hundred feet of nylon rope from his backpack, tied one end to the raft and left the rest coiled on the shore. The snow fell harder now. The air was wet and heavy, his back numb. He could see the brothers shivering beneath their coveralls. There was no way they could attempt a hike back to the cabin tonight. They would need to set up camp, make a fire and dry their clothes. The temperature was dropping as evening approached. Conner looked frantic to leave, his normally calm demeanor replaced with desperation and fear.

"We will have to set up camp," Jonathan said. "There's no way we'll make it back tonight."

"We'll make it back," Conner said.

"You're freezing," Jonathan said. "And so am I."

"We're dropping all this stuff here," Conner said. "We'll be able to move faster. This will all work out. It'll be fine."

Jonathan saw no use in arguing further.

"Just get in the goddamned raft," Jonathan said.

Jonathan walked to Michael, and together they took up the coffin one last time and clumsily walked it over the rocks and placed it in the center of the raft. It was heavy – much heavier than before, now that it was laden with stones. Jonathan nearly slipped under its weight.

Conner sat down in the rear of the raft so he could paddle, keeping his mass in line with the case, and waited; he looked like a traumatized child waiting on a mother who would never arrive. Jonathan saw the image of Conner's body gutted and strung across the trees of Coombs' Gulch.

Do you see?

He saw. It was the fate of a bullet fired ten years ago that traveled still, never stopping, no matter who or what it struck.

Michael and Jonathan stepped into the water and pulled the raft behind them into the shallows. The water rose quickly up to their thighs and shocked the breath from them. They pulled the raft and together set Conner adrift with the box and then walked back to shore. Conner took out a small paddle and began to row toward the center of the lake. The raft sagged with the weight. Jonathan took up the other end of the nylon rope. His legs felt frozen and stripped to the bone. The rope spooled out, and they watched as Conner floated silently away from them. The lake reflected a glassy gray from the skies; snowflakes kissed the surface. The rope went taut, and the raft stopped and turned slightly as if looking back at them.

Jonathan watched the ghostly scene – Conner alone on an overburdened raft with the body of Thomas Terrywile, drifting with unseen forces. Above there was only a gray expanse of nothingness and below a terrible cold. A deep nausea and dread overtook him.

Do you see?

He didn't want to see, to accept it – few did. He searched himself for some remnant of faith, but found nothing. Why would God be here? They had left the holy far behind.

Conner steadied himself and attempted to get purchase of the sides of the case. His first attempt to lift it nearly sunk him. Water poured in from both sides.

"It's too heavy," Jonathan said.

"He'll get it," Michael said. "He's good at this kind of stuff." Jonathan remembered Conner deftly flipping those plastic cups at the East Side Tavern the night they shared this plan with him – the precision, the concentration, the soft touch. But this was not a parlor trick or a game. He gripped the rope tighter in his hand.

Conner tried again. He lifted one end of the case and attempted to tip it over the side into the water. The raft seemed to hold as he stood the case upright on its side at the bloated edge and began to push it over.

With a final shove, the case splashed down into the lake. The side of the raft collapsed, and the water seemed to leap up and grab Conner by the shoulders. The opposite side of the raft kicked into the air and flipped over. Conner let out a small cry and fell beneath the surface.

The case floated for a brief moment and then sunk like a stone. In its place a dark bilge flowed upward. Bubbles coated in grime shook to the surface. Conner splashed around in the middle of it, his coveralls soaking through with water, overwhelming him. His hands scrambled for the overturned raft, but he was being pulled below the surface, unable to fight against the weight of his clothes, unable to strip them off.

Then Michael was in the water, shedding his clothes till he was bare-skinned. "Pull it back!" he screamed. "Pull it back now!"

The blackness flowed up from the bottom of the lake and spread. It was more than what should have been contained in the case, more than just the decomposed body of Thomas Terrywile. It spread like an oil slick across the surface so the whole lake turned from sky gray to the same deep blackness Jonathan had seen in his unconscious delirium.

"Pull him back!" Michael screamed again.

Jonathan pulled the raft, but Conner couldn't reach it to grab hold. His head dipped below the surface again. He reappeared sputtering and splashing like a child who has fallen in the deep end of a pool, seconds from drowning. The black water poured into his mouth.

Michael dove into the lake and swam hard and fast. Jonathan followed, but the bottom fell off quickly and he was up to his waist in the shocking cold, his coveralls soaked through. He stopped. Michael was halfway to where Conner struggled and gasped, Michael's pale white skin pulled tight and prickled with cold as he cut through the black slick. Jonathan could only stand and watch, the useless nylon rope in his hand.

Conner disappeared beneath the surface and was gone.

Michael dove and followed his brother down.

CHAPTER TWENTY-TWO

Michael could barely walk when Jonathan pulled him shaking and gasping from the shallows. His lips were blue and his jaw trembled and shook; his skin was white as the falling snow. Jonathan slipped and stumbled trying to support him as his legs gave out. Michael's breath was short and rapid; his muscles convulsed as his body tried to warm itself. Jonathan dragged him from the rocky shore into the trees, and Michael fell to the ground in the fetal position, still shaking and wet. Jonathan stripped a sleeping bag from his backpack, unzipped it and covered Michael, enfolding him completely.

Michael tried to speak. "I had him," he said, "but I let go. I had him but I let go."

Jonathan waited until Michael stopped chattering and could take a full breath. He walked back out to the lake. The snow fell harder now, silent and mortal into the pitch-black water. The overturned raft had beached itself on the rocks. Jonathan stared out at the scene for a moment. The lake was still, but somehow he expected to see Conner burst through the surface one last time, gasping for air, for life. But Conner was gone, drowned and dead, and there was no escaping that truth. He waited for something to appear and give purpose to it all – from the bullet to Conner's death. He stared at the mountains and lake, spread out before him like a grand canvas.

Michael groaned and wormed inside his cocoon.

It was nearly dark; the woods grew deep with shadow. There was no way to make for the cabin tonight. Michael was nearly dead with cold and Jonathan's clothes were soaked through. His mind raced. He thought through the possibilities, the stories, the ridiculous lies he would have to tell again and again to explain Conner's disappearance and what happened to him. More lies, more trappings, more of the guilt that had brought him back to Coombs' Gulch in the first place. Jonathan thought of Conner's wife and children, left without a father and husband, crying in the cold as a casket was lowered into the earth. He thought of all those serious executives with their rounds of golf and martini lunches, huddling together in a boardroom to discuss the loss of one of their top men. He thought of Michael, set loose to drift without the comfort of his brother.

The burden of it would fall on Jonathan. The questions would come fast and angry: What were you doing out there? Why were you at the lake? Why was there a raft when you were supposed to be hunting? He pictured helicopters and detectives, state police rescue divers searching the lake for a body and perhaps finding a box with the bones of a boy. He would have to build a castle of lies – one after the other. No explanation would satisfy their curiosity.

Jonathan found himself in the same position as the night they killed Thomas Terrywile. The music changes, but the song remains the same. He desperately wanted Conner to emerge from the lake alive – more than anything right now he wanted that. He wanted Michael to snap out of it and help craft a plan. Only time would determine how this worked out, but he had little patience at this point. Jonathan checked the backpacks. They were down to a couple of sandwiches and some jerky. He found a bottle of whiskey stored in Michael's pack. He unscrewed the top and took a long drink and then another. It burned and warmed and numbed and let him move on for just a moment, like it had for all those years since the boy died.

He waited for his vision of the world to soften and for his mind to rest. He took the bottle to Michael, put it down beside him and went to look for firewood. Jonathan cleared a space in the snow, dug down past the leaves until he reached dirt, where worms wriggled in the exposed air. He gathered rocks from the shore to form a ring. He found kindling and some large fallen wood that had dried. He took the lighter fluid from Conner's backpack. The kindling burned bright and orange for a moment and then began to die. He bent down and blew the flames, watched the small sticks redden and then piled on larger branches until a steady fire consumed the falling snowflakes and sent gray smoke up through the trees. Michael stirred in his sleeping bag.

Jonathan walked back to the lake, coiled the rope from the raft and threw it on the rocks. He took out his knife and stabbed the raft. Each side burst like a gunshot, exhaled and died. He folded the heavy, wet rubber, wrapped a heavy stone in it and threw it as far as he could back into the lake. He took the rope and strung it between two trees near the fire and hung Michael's clothes on the line. Jonathan cleared a patch of flat land and set to staking down the corners of the tent. He leaned his rifle against a tree nearby. At times, he would look up from his work and gaze out through the timber and over the endless lake. The sky deepened and swirled and grew colder still. A wind came down from the mountains, and the trees began to dance, their high branches knocked together so all around was the echo of dead wood.

The fire crackled and threw light and shadow, and suddenly it was as if the whole forest were alive and moving – the shadows ran and jumped like children, the trees groaned like old doorways, ripples from the lake sloshed upon the shore and streamed rivulets through the rocks.

Jonathan sat on the ground and fed the fire. The fire made his wet clothes steam, and the mist rose into the night; it singed and burned his knees, threw smoke into his eyes and lungs. He sat with his rifle at his side and waited and listened to all that moved.

Michael finally emerged from his cocoon and sat naked by the fire, the nylon sleeping bag draped over his shoulders. He stared into the flames.

"I still feel cold," he said. He spoke as if he were the last man on Earth, muttering into a dying darkness. Jonathan fed another piece of deadfall into the fire. "I touched him down there," Michael said. "I felt his hand for a second and then he was gone. I couldn't see him. I couldn't see anything. The water was all black and freezing. I could only feel the cold and then his hand. I tried to grab it, and then it was like he was yanked down deeper. My lungs...they hurt. I couldn't do it. And then I came up. I don't even know why I came up. I didn't want to. It was like my body made me do it. When it really mattered I just came back up."

Jonathan stared at him. "You would have died down there, too. You're lucky you're not dead now."

"No," he said. "That's not why."

"Why then?"

"It was cold and dark," he said. "I couldn't make myself go deeper."

Jonathan watched Michael from across the fire. His face seemed to move and shift in shadow.

"Conner is down there," Michael said, and then he took a long pull from the whiskey.

"Probably shouldn't drink too much out here," Jonathan said.

"I don't care," Michael said. He stood and pulled his clothes from the line and put them on. He took the bottle and the sleeping bag and went into the tent. Jonathan stayed near the fire and tried to eat, but the food made him feel emptier and more desperate. He waited a long time, feeding the fire, unable to think about sleep as his mind raced through possibilities, outcomes, fears and regrets. He had loved Conner. They had all been like brothers – estranged after the incident in Coombs' Gulch – but he still held the memories of his childhood, of Conner and Gene, and he wondered how everything had gone so wrong.

He looked out at the lake, an endless black mass in the night. He allowed himself a brief tear before he tamped it back down. Regret and sadness would change nothing in this place. There was no comfort – only the trees, the lake and whatever it was that awaited them in the dark. He watched the snow fall gently into the dying fire.

Jonathan stood and brushed off the snow that had gathered on his back and shoulders. He took a flashlight and shone the beam through the trees to find more wood. He wanted to keep the fire going throughout the night, if only for comfort. He walked in a growing circle around the tent where Michael slept. He dusted the snow off a few more fallen limbs and placed them gently into the circle, careful to leave room for the flames to breathe. His light reached out into the forest and found only shadows and ghostly trees, which stood so still and quiet he couldn't help but feel they watched him. He wandered far till he was lost in the darkness, and then he turned around to find the firelight of camp.

Behind him, farther back in the trees, a thick limb bent slowly until it snapped and fell to the ground. It was close to him, close enough to see if he turned his flashlight toward it. Jonathan stood still. There was only the sound of his heart beating and his lungs pushing warm, wet breath into the night. The fire and the tent were fifty feet away, the endless dark behind him. But he was paralyzed, unable to take a step toward the camp and unable to shine his flashlight on whatever waited for him out there. He was too scared. He didn't want to look at it. He didn't want to see the truth – he couldn't. In that moment, he prayed for an end he was too cowardly to face.

Now it waited for him just a few yards away. He could feel it staring at him. He could feel its presence, but he didn't want to accept it. It was the ultimate truth – a force that played on all their fears, insecurities and deceptions – and he could not yet face it. He feared it would break his mind. If he didn't look, if he didn't see it in its true form, then he could tell himself it was merely the product of his imagination; he could deny with skepticism and doubt, will himself to believe it was a bear or some other common creature, that it was a vixen or bobcat shrieking those awful cries in the mountains, that it was a mere accident that sucked Conner into the lake. If he did not look, maybe he could just dismiss the story of Thomas Terrywile as impossible; he could shrug off his visions at the cabin and beside the lake as nothing more than stress dreams. He could tell the world that it was all just an accident, another incident of Coombs' Gulch hikers and hunters losing their way.

But if he shone his light out into the darkness and saw it unmasked, in all its strange and impossible reality, he feared he would forever be trapped in its gaze.

He thought of death. He feared it. But more than death he feared living with the vision of this thing that stalked him in the woods, that it would forever stalk him in the recesses of his mind. He thought of Mary and Jacob. He thought of what he would face back home. The lies and tortures would continue unabated for the rest of his life. It was not enough to overcome his fear of glimpsing it in that very moment. At some point there would be a turn – a shift – and this thing would move itself forward into the light, and there he would be – there they would all be. But not now, not here.

In the darkness came the sound of slow, heavy footfalls, soft on the snowy ground. They were not the gentle and precise touches of a deer or the lumbering shuffle of a black bear, but the upright steps of something humanlike, which sounded for a few moments before disappearing completely into the night. Jonathan walked back to the tent with the same slow and steady footfalls until he was once again in the light and warmth of the fire.

He dropped the timber from his hands into the fire and sent a volley of sparks into the air. They swirled about in the night like tiny suns. He moved quickly and quietly, at every moment tense and waiting for something to tear him apart. He took his rifle and checked the chamber. He switched on the safety, took his flashlight and crawled into the tent.

Michael's dark mass lay in the tent, rising and falling with his troubled breath. The bottle of whiskey rolled empty on the ground. Jonathan lay down beside him and felt the comfort of another living person – the last person in the world who truly knew him. Jonathan pushed his body against Michael's. He didn't want to feel so alone and unsafe.

His eyes were wide open but he could not see. His heart pounded, but it was all merely a dream of life. He listened in the night.

CHAPTER TWENTY-THREE

Thoughts came to him during that dark night – thoughts of what could have been, what should have been, and in that deep darkness he wondered if he was capable of love, if the ability to love had survived his guilt and regret. He claimed to love Jacob and Mary more than anything in the world; it was something he told himself but now doubted. He thought of the hunters in the past who'd become lost in the Gulch, and he wondered if he was already listed among the vanished, or the dead. He was lost in himself. His past had stripped away all things like a hunter pulls away the hide. The bullet that killed Thomas Terrywile had killed them all. After that they were strung up and slow cut.

Outside was silence. The snow was gentle, light through the trees. The evening wind died down and the whole world seemed still. There was only the sound of Michael beside him.

He thought of the night he screamed at Jacob for urinating in the closet during one of his trancelike night terrors. Jonathan held back tears thinking of it, wishing he had done something different, wishing that moment was not burned into eternity. The poor boy; he woke from a nightmare to the reality of Jonathan looming large over him, furious and angry about something the boy could not comprehend. It was like a monster from the boy's dream made real. Perhaps it was not that different from the creature that loomed over Thomas Terrywile, the thing that followed the boy as he wandered unknown forests, the thing that stole him away into that dark and cold void.

A child in pain – lost, cold and alone with no one in the world searching for him; it pained Jonathan to think about it. It seemed there could be nothing more tragic and awful.

He remembered when Jacob was three years old. It was a weekend and Jonathan was home from work. Mary had gone for the day; he couldn't remember where she had gone or why. Perhaps it was some kind of social event, those things that normal people do, people adjusted properly to life. But it was just Jonathan and Jacob. The boy played by himself, and Jonathan sat on the couch, a sensation creeping in on him, the feeling of a tiger in a cage. Something wormed in his soul, something trying to break free. The prospect of a long day set in, the sad banality of his quiet little house on this quiet little street in a small town with only one traffic light and a seemingly endless amount of daylight. It stretched over him, oppressed him. He waited for as long as he could. He watched cartoons with Jacob. He fed him peanut butter and jelly like any other normal, cookie-cutter parent. But it was all a lie and a farce. At times, he tried to distract himself by staring into the computer, scrolling through other people's lives – happy, well-adjusted, beautiful lives – and it all melted away until he couldn't stand it anymore.

Jonathan made it until noon that day before he pulled a bottle of vodka down from above the refrigerator and poured his first drink. He drank fast; he always did. It always took too long to set in, and by the time he felt the first effects it was too late. One, two, three…it was never enough to quiet that lonely, aching thing. It was never enough to tamp down the feeling that none of it was right.

He poured his drinks. The sun was bright that day. It was a mild seventy degrees. A day when normal people – the parents who populated this normal town – would have their children outside, playing with them, doing the things magazines and social media posts said you should do. He let things blur and numb. He waited and watched and wondered at what was wrong with him. He sunk, lost in it.

The boy was somewhere. The last he remembered, Jacob had been playing with his toys in the living room. A television program was on, the screen filled with bright, puffy colors and rounded shapes. Jonathan was writing something on his computer. He was unsure now what it had been, but it was something, some effort to reach out and find that other life, the other self, that had escaped so long ago. Escape. He thought of that feeling – the tiger in its cage. The hunter held back, trapped, but always pacing, always watching for that moment when your back is turned. All was hunting, he thought. All was dealing some kind of death, small as a beetle, large as the world. In this life, he played a role. He worked his job, he paid the bills, he came home every night to the same thing, but it was not his. It never was. It belonged to someone or something else. That night in the Gulch took it from him, led him down a path not of his own making. He was carried along by death and brought somewhere deep inside the forests of his soul to be sacrificed.

Even now, the memory of that day came in pieces of a half-remembered dream through the haze. He was suddenly in his home again, suddenly aware of the kitchen table where he sat with his laptop opened, suddenly aware the television no longer played that program with the shiny colors and singsong voices, suddenly aware that something priceless was missing.

The sliding glass door that led to the back porch, the backyard and the woods was half open. Outside air poured through, touched the back of his neck. He turned and looked for Jacob, but he was gone.

Jonathan stumbled to the door that day. The sun was bright. He looked in the yard, but Jacob was not there. He looked toward the darkened trees extending out behind the house, but saw nothing. He saw nothing and heard nothing. It was empty space, a void made of grass and trees and sun and air. His heart began to race, and he tried to think how long it had been. When was the last time he had seen his son? How many hours, minutes, seconds, milliseconds since he had been conscious enough to see his boy and know that he was there in the house with him, safe and present? The panic began to set in – the fear, the guilt. His mind tried to tell him that it would be okay, but his gut knew he had just crossed an unseen line.

He gasped at first. "Jacob?" It came out as nothing more than a question, as if he were hearing the name for the very first time and not comprehending it. No answer came back. No explanation. The universe heard, but held back. Then he said it louder and louder still, but there was no reply. Jonathan ran through the house, checking the bedrooms, the bathrooms, the basement until there was no other logical place his son could be except outside. He ran to the front yard, to the street, and looked up and down the road. There was nothing – no cars, no neighbors, nobody about their business, no Jacob. Then he was screaming like a lunatic in the daylight, trying his best to keep his footing, still under the alcoholic haze, the caged tiger disappeared, replaced with something weak and helpless against the world – a gut-shot fawn, a chick fallen from its nest, a child alone in the woods.

Even then, his skin was being peeled back, his center cut from stem to stern, his arms and legs tied upon the rack. He was opened to the world. His true reality stumbled through the daylight, broken and dumb, lost and guilty – a drunk who'd lost his only child.

Then came a shout – a voice at once familiar and with a tone of assurance and salvation, something he envied. He heard the voice call his name again, and Jonathan looked around dumbly, turning his head, his floating eyes trailing behind. He walked around the house to the backyard, and he saw his son, hand in hand with his neighbor, Rachael. Jacob ran to his father and Jonathan picked him up. Rachael stood back, arms crossed, staring at him. Her children were older, already well beyond the wandering-off phase of their childhood.

"He was in the woods behind our house," she said. Her voice was flat, harsh. "It was lucky I saw him."

"He went out the sliding glass door," Jonathan said. "I don't know. I don't know what happened. Thank you."

"It happens, I suppose," she said and stared at Jonathan a little longer. "Are you okay? Do you want me to watch him for a couple hours until Mary gets home?"

Jonathan's stomach tightened. She knew. Everyone knew. He turned his eyes downward. "No. No. Everything is fine. He just got away while I wasn't looking." He tried his best, but she could see straight through him, all his protections against the world gone. She said nothing, turned, and walked back through the woods toward her house. Jonathan kept Jacob in his arms and brought him inside.

That night he felt a change in Mary. She came home so angry there were tears in her eyes. Rachael had called her – they were friends – and Jonathan expected as much. But she wasn't just angry. She had been angry before, but this was something deeper, more primal. "You could have lost him," she said, trying not to cry. "Something awful could have happened to him, and where were you? What were you doing? You're a fucking mess."

Everything changed after that day – the day Jacob wandered into the woods while Jonathan was lost in drink and guilt. The rest of their marriage unraveled and stagnated and then unraveled some more. They didn't leave each other. He hung on to the idea of family, even though being home with Mary now was like being alone. She grew so distant and cold it was as if she were a million miles away while sitting in the room. Jacob grew up in a chill between his mother and father that would probably hang like a cloud over his adult relationships.

Yes, that had been a turning point in Jonathan's memory. That was when the true descent began, when he couldn't hide the fact there was something wrong anymore – not from his wife, not from the neighbors, not from anyone. From there his desperation, sadness and isolation grew, leading him inexorably back to Coombs' Gulch, to the start of it all.

The Gulch had claimed another of his oldest friends, the second person who knew the truth. Now there was only Michael.

He lay in the silent darkness, in this small cocoon with the night world turning endlessly around him, and wondered why Jacob had wandered into the woods that day. What had prompted his young boy to open the sliding glass door and walk alone into trees dark with shade, instead of staying in the yard with his toys or wandering toward the road, the way so many children seem drawn to the flat, asphalt strips of civilization? The same awful scream echoed across the mountains in the night.

He listened to the scream die off in the trees, and then he heard something else. The water in the lake was moving, sloshing against the rocky shore as if something large disturbed its black surface. The small waves broke on the rocky beach. Then came the sound of dripping, something rising up from water.

Jonathan stayed silent and waited. He could see his breath inside the tent. The disturbance in the water grew closer to shore. In the silent darkness, the sound was like a waterfall, but it was distinctly familiar – the sound of something emerging from the lake. The dripping and sloshing continued, grew closer and louder and faster. He recognized the sound of legs pulling themselves up and then stepping back down, of a living body struggling to walk to shore as the water sloughed off in dripping streams. It grew closer; moving through the shallows, the steps grew quicker. The water poured off onto the rocks of the shore now, and finally he heard it emerge from the lake completely. Rocks moved under its weight; the gravel crunched hard and wet. He heard footsteps moving toward the tent, settling into the snow with a wet, muffled crunch underfoot.

Then it stopped and all was silent again. But the presence remained there, watching, waiting. He could feel it in his gut, the realization he was being watched, eyes staring a hole through the tent. Jonathan took up his rifle and flashlight and moved slowly toward the front of the tent. The presence did not move or make a sound. As far as Jonathan could tell, it stood at the edge of the trees, where the forest met the rocky beach. It stood in silence and waited, and Jonathan waited with it, barely breathing, heart racing.

In the silence he heard a light and innocent voice: *Daddy. Daddy, come find me.*

He felt the same panic as the day Jacob wandered away from the house alone. It was like a hook pulling at his heart, overwhelming and desperate. He tried to tell himself it was not possible, that it was some trick of his imagination, a waking dream, a night terror of his own in the forest. But he felt the clammy cold of his skin; he felt the heft of his rifle and the cold of the air.

Daddy. Daddy, come find me.

Jonathan unzipped the tent. The empty night air blasted his face and he looked out toward the lake. There were four inches of snow on the ground, and it glowed with a soft, deathly light. The trees shot straight up in deep, black lines to the night sky. He looked at the dead fire and then beyond to the lake. It was out there, just beyond the limit of his sight. He heard something shift in the darkness.

Jonathan turned on the flashlight. The sallow circle of light rolled over the trees and the ground, capturing them for a moment in its pale eye and then letting them disappear back into the unknown.

Conner stood at the edge of the tree line, his skin dripping, cold and blue white. He did not seem to support his own weight. Instead, he looked like a marionette held upright by strings from the darkness above. His mouth hung wide open – far too wide – as if he could swallow a human head whole in his mouth. His jaw appeared broken, merely skin and sinews keeping it from falling to the ground. His clothes dripped with water from the lake. His eyes were dead white.

From the black hole of his unmoving mouth came Jacob's voice: *Daddy, do you see me now?*

Jonathan's skin ran with pinpricks, and the blood drained from his limbs like a cut artery.

In that moment, he could think of nothing; he could do nothing. He merely sat staring in wonder, paralyzed by the sight, terrified at what he beheld. As he stared, the skin on Conner's face seemed to slip just a little, threatening to slide off and fall to the ground.

"You aren't real," Jonathan said. "You're only a disguise."

The thing that was Conner moved sudden and fast. It bent toward him and stretched out its arms in a fit of rage, animated and life-like, and from its mouth came that ghastly high-pitched scream, full of all the terror and pain and helplessness of the infinite. The sound overwhelmed him, so loud he felt his eardrums would burst. It seemed nothing on Earth could create such a sound.

With sudden swiftness, it bounded off into the night faster than any deer Jonathan had ever seen. Its strange limbs moved awkwardly, pulled up and down by some unseen force. It disappeared into the trees. Jonathan could hear it bounding – its leaps and footfalls – as it faded into the darkness until all was silent again.

Jonathan sat there in the night, unable to move. He waited and listened in the deep and heavy night with only his breath and heartbeat.

Then something much softer and quieter whispered in his ear.

Daddy. Daddy, come find me.

CHAPTER TWENTY-FOUR

Jonathan sat outside the tent, his eyes felt bloodshot, sinking into hollows, his skin cold and breath weak in the morning light. He still clutched his rifle and flashlight in his arms. As the air brightened and sunlight touched his eyes, he moved his arms slightly, afraid to turn his head and see the corpse of his friend dancing in the trees. The whole night he sat frozen, staring out at the lake, waiting for what came next. During that time, he thought of nothing; it seemed his mind spun, but no conscious thought stepped out from the chaos. It was just a swirling mess of visions of his family and friends, nightmares and questions, warped by the impossible things he saw and heard in the night. It taunted him.

The morning sun lit the top of the mountain, which glowed bright and white in the fresh snow, and slowly the light began to roll down the mountainside to the shadow of the valley in which he sat waiting, watching. The sky was clear now, but the air smelled of snow and burning wood. In the west, clouds rose like floating kingdoms.

Then, like a stone statue suddenly coming to life, he stood. A light covering of frost shook itself free from his coveralls, and he walked down to the water's edge. He stared out across the lake to the tops of the mountains glowing in the sun, and he wondered how different the world looked from the top of the mountain or the bottom of the lake.

Then a voice from behind him: "Whose tracks are these?"

Jonathan turned and saw Michael standing outside the tent, looking sunken and withdrawn. His pale eyes seemed distressed, seemed to look through Jonathan to the lake where his brother had drowned.

"Whose tracks are these?" he asked again, pointing to the footprints left behind by the revenant Jonathan had seen in the night. They trailed off into the maze of forest, longer steps than any man could take. Jonathan followed the tracks with his eyes. He should have known, and wondered to himself how he could have made such a mistake.

"I don't know," Jonathan said. It was all he could think to say. A stiff wind from off the lake pushed up against his back.

"Where did they come from?" Michael's voice was flat and dead, as if he were only speaking and not thinking – a talking doll whose cord was pulled.

Jonathan didn't want to be left alone – he couldn't be left alone. It was more than he would be able to bear. They were out of food and out of time. They needed to get back to the cabin if they were to survive and needed to somehow face the world together. "I said I don't know. They were just here this morning. Maybe they're mine from last night. I had to look for firewood, you know."

Michael stumbled down from the tent and shuffled through the ash of the fire. He stared down at the tracks and then followed them into the distance. His mind worked, picking apart the possibilities, the mechanics of it.

"They start here," he said, pointing at the small ledge between the shore and the forest soil. "And they head in that direction. No other footprints coming or going. They aren't yours. They came from the shore."

"No, Michael. That's not it."

"Do you see any other explanation? There are the tracks, the evidence right in front of you. Where did they come from?"

"I was out looking for firewood..."

"You looked for firewood up there," Michael said, pointing behind the tent, "and over there. I know that because your tracks wander around and then come back to camp. Those tracks just go straight out and never come back, and it looks like they were running."

"Michael, we need to leave and we need to leave now. We have to get back to the cabin today or..."

"Or what?"

"I don't know. We need to get back and tell somebody. Get help. I don't know. Things aren't right out here. You know that."

"I know there are human boot tracks starting here and leading out there. You have no explanation. Want to hear mine?"

"No. No, I don't." Jonathan started walking back up to the tent. "What we need to do is break down this tent and leave. Now."

"My explanation is Conner made it to shore down that way where the lake empties into a stream and then walked up the shoreline here. He was probably freezing, disoriented and walked off into the woods in the middle of the night. He got turned around, lost in the snow." Michael reached into the tent and pulled out his jacket and his rifle. "And now we need to go find him."

"We can't!" Jonathan yelled. "We have no food. We're miles away from anywhere, and more weather is moving in. We won't be able to survive much longer out here!"

"You can go for days without food."

"Listen to me. Even if what you said was true, he'd be frozen to death by now. He couldn't have made it."

"He could make it. We have to look. We have to know we tried."

"He's gone, Michael. You know that. There's no way he could have survived the water, the cold. There's no way he could have made it that far. He would have just come back to the tent."

"Maybe he did," Michael said. "Did you see anything last night? Hear anything?"

Jonathan pursed his lips and looked back out at the lake.

"I thought so."

"We need to leave and get help. That's the best way, even if what you say is true. We could get a search and rescue team, helicopters, anything..."

"And what are we going to tell them we were doing up here?"

"Hunting, fishing. The same thing everybody does up here. We'll tell them we got lost. It doesn't matter; we can think of something, but we need to go get help. If we leave now, we can get to the cabin in time."

"In time for what? If he's dead, what would time matter?"

Jonathan said nothing.

"What did you see last night?"

"I didn't..."

Michael turned his rifle in his hands. Its barrel swayed back and forth, lazily pointing in Jonathan's direction. Michael gripped it tighter and the barrel pointed directly at him. "We've been friends for a long time," he said. "Tell me now what you saw last night. I know you're lying. You're not good at it unless you have three other people doing it for you."

Jonathan stared at him and at the rifle. "Don't do anything you'll regret. You'll have a difficult time explaining a gunshot wound to the authorities."

"I didn't have to explain anything to anyone last time there was a gunshot wound up here," Michael said. "There's no burying this one in a box and hiding it in the ground."

Jonathan waited a moment. He searched for words, an explanation, but nothing came. His mind was at a loss. "I don't know what I saw."

"Was it Conner?"

"It looked like Conner, but it wasn't him. Not like this. It wasn't alive. It made strange sounds out of its mouth. It wasn't Conner. It was something pretending to be Conner."

"Spare me your nonsense and suit up," he said.

"He's dead. It came walking up out of the water. What in God's name do you think could have survived in there for that long?"

"What did he say?"

Jonathan's voice caught in his throat. The words — the sound of the words — came back to him, and he couldn't repeat it. There was no way to tell Michael what he heard. "What did you see when we opened the box, huh? Tell me what you saw."

Michael was quiet for a moment. "I saw a boy being taken to a place in the woods. I saw three men doing things there. I saw that place we found in the Gulch, or something just like it. That's what I saw."

"And what did that boy look like?"

Michael looked away and back out to the lake.

"Do you really think he just happened to be there in Coombs' Gulch that night? That this is all just a big coincidence?"

"I saw other things, too," Michael said. He slowly lowered the rifle. "I saw stars. I saw galaxies. I saw different times and different places."

"And did it hurt?"

"I never felt pain like that in all my life."

Jonathan pointed at the tracks leading into the trees. "Out there is more pain like that. We're being tricked. Led around like dumb, blind animals. You go out there and you're just going to find yourself in that place again, except this time it will be permanent."

"What makes you the expert?"

"Up in the field. You saw something through the scope; what was it?"

"I couldn't be sure…"

"What was it?"

"It looked like a man."

"What man?"

"I can't be sure. It was too far."

"Tell me. Just say it."

"It looked like Gene but…not him at the same time. I could only make out a couple of his features. He looked different, though. He looked like he was smiling. I thought it must be my imagination, with everything going on, and when I looked again he was gone."

"Did that make you think that Gene was still alive?"

"No. Gene's dead."

"And yet you saw him."

"This is different."

"No, it's not! Something out there is playing with us. Trying to trick us into following its plan. The best thing we can do is just get back to the cabin."

Michael looked down and then back out at the tracks. He blinked tears out of his eyes. "I don't know what to do without him," he said.

"I know. But we have to do the right thing, the logical thing. We need to get back to the cabin as quickly as possible and get help."

"What will I tell them? Madison? Brent and Aria?"

"I don't know."

The footprints in the snow led out into the infinite. Michael stared at them and Jonathan could see him calculating the odds, toying with the possibilities, a look of desperate longing in his eyes.

"Fine," he said. "We'll go now."

Michael lowered his rifle and turned back toward camp.

CHAPTER TWENTY-FIVE

Nothing was dry. Their clothes, the sleeping bags and tent were still damp with melted snow. The air was thick with moisture again. They broke down the tent and Jonathan strapped it to his pack. They were hungry and tired. Jonathan's stomach felt as if it were eating itself. He searched for food but there was none. Michael stayed silent and cold as the snow. Jonathan watched him for a moment. He pictured the barrel of Michael's rifle pointed at him. He had the terrifying and lonely sensation of realizing his life was worth far less than another's. All the years together, growing up, he knew he was on the outside looking in on the Braddick brothers. He thought he understood it, but did not. He caught glimpses of Michael standing at the edge of the trees, staring down at the path of footprints in the snow.

And that loneliness made him wish for home even more – for Mary and Jacob. The times throughout the brief history of their small family during which he was absent – numbed with drink or suffused with regret and rage – stung him all the more now. It made him fearful. Time was strange. It faded away but lived forever. Small and vastly important moments were lost to time and yet somehow echoed through lifetimes, like the light of a long-dead star finally reaching a child's eye as he stares through a darkened window to the night sky. He felt it. His life, his words and actions, everything he had done lived on forever, infecting the world. He wanted to be a good man, but he feared the echoes of his past grew too loud.

He strained for hope. He told himself he would return home and make it right. The present could be changed, the future rewritten. He tried to tell himself he was not trapped. All those years of regret and guilt and remorse were unnecessary. He told himself they had saved Thomas Terrywile from an eternity of cold, lonely pain. Through death they saved him, yet sacrificed themselves. There was no nobility in what they did, but perhaps there was forgiveness. Perhaps there was a chance at goodness. He felt he could live with it. He felt he could move on from it. He just needed to get home and hold his wife and son and tell them he truly loved them – that everything had been for them – and then it would be different. Then there would be life where there had only been the specter of death.

This was what he told himself and he tried to believe it.

It was just after 8:00 a.m. They could make it to the cabin by dark. They could get in the truck and go home and, in time, put it all behind them.

He looked over at Michael as he stared into the woods. The snow would come again, and then there would be no trace of them left. The fire, the tracks, everything would vanish beneath a white blanket. Thomas Terrywile's bones rested somewhere at the bottom of the lake.

Jonathan checked his rifle, made sure a cartridge was in the chamber and slung the Remington over his shoulder.

"Are you ready?" he said, but Michael said nothing back. Jonathan wondered how Michael's life would be now, with half of himself missing, dead and wandering through the trees. "Let's keep up a good pace. We will get back and get help."

"There's no help for this," Michael said. It didn't matter where Michael stood, which direction he faced; his eyes looked to the trees.

They left the lake in the woods behind and started up the mountain toward the meadow, at least one thousand vertical feet above, the conduit that would plunge them back into Coombs' Gulch and the cabin. The ghostly gray birch trees stood silent in the pale world, their strange, peeling bark pulled away like old skin. Jonathan thought of Mary – his vision of her dancing upon that lonely stage, peeling away her own skin, crying silently to no one but herself. He thought of the dancer on the first night of his bachelor party, the way he walked hand in hand with her to that small back room, how she removed her scant clothes piece by piece and how he took so much from her that night and lost so much of himself. He thought of all the deer they had killed and flayed over the years, strung up in the air, cores opened to the world, worked over with sharp, curved knives.

It had taken all this time, but Jonathan now knew he was the one being skinned. All the time and effort and pain was merely his skin being removed, leaving him open and exposed. There would be only truth at the end, stripped of all its garments, and the truth was not sane.

A darkness fell over him, a feeling of dread. The things he'd seen in that ghastly vision were of past and present and future – history and prophesy. But he could change it. He knew he could.

The blood seemed to drain from his body, his arms and legs tired and limp. Relieved of the burden of the coffin, he and Michael could make better time, but now even his backpack felt like a paralyzing weight. He breathed the heavy, cold air and it hurt his lungs. The four inches of snow made the slope perilous and slick. His boots slipped off unseen rocks and roots buried under the snow. He fell and stood up again. He pulled himself up the hill on all fours at times. The snow melted on his coveralls, and his clothes soaked through. He grasped trees to pull himself forward, slid downward, fell and pulled himself up. The muscles of his legs burned. Michael persisted forward, farther ahead now. He didn't stop or turn back.

The clear sky disappeared behind low cloud cover. The flat, gray light hid the contours of the slope. Jonathan could no longer discern indentations in the ground, the small bumps of rocks and roots. All he knew was that he trudged uphill, slipping, regaining, straining, wanting to call out for Michael in that gray limbo and wondering if Michael would even turn back to see him.

Jonathan cried out and Michael finally stopped to wait. His legs ached. The peeling birches were everywhere. He leaned against a tree. His lungs hurt.

"There's something out there," Michael said. His voice seemed lost in the impenetrable gray. "It's way out there, pacing us. Hard to see. Just past where you can't see any farther."

Jonathan tried to catch his breath. He looked into the maze of ghostly birch.

"You see it," Michael said.

"I don't," Jonathan said, barely able to talk.

Michael stared. He seemed almost to smile. His mind worked some kind of angle, seeing something in his own way the rest of the world could not comprehend, breaking it down, piece by piece, to find what was broken. Jonathan was no longer there. It was only Michael and whatever he saw in the trees.

"What does it look like?" Jonathan asked. His mind flashed to Conner, dead white and dripping, walking from the bottom of the lake to stare at him in the night and speak in the voice of a seven-year-old boy.

"It doesn't look like anything right now," Michael said. "Maybe in a little bit it will look like something else. But it's there, waiting for us to move. It's like a reflection in the snow, the light hitting it a certain way, the trees bending with it."

Michael raised his rifle and stared through the scope. Jonathan took his Remington and did the same, but saw nothing. Perhaps what Michael saw was no different from what Jonathan experienced the night before while gathering wood – the knowledge that something was there without laying eyes on it.

There were only hints, no real answers.

"It's like when you go to a kindergarten play," Michael said. "Me and Annie went to one last year. It was Brent's first school play. You remember the one? I think Jacob was in it, too."

Jonathan nodded. He remembered the play. Little kids garbling lines, trying to follow teachers' directions from the wings while parents cooed and laughed and snapped pictures.

"Before the play began you could see the stage curtain moving and rustling as the kids took their places. Their little hands and feet pushing against the curtain, trying to find their way out into the light where people could see them. That's what it looks like. The curtain is moving."

Michael stared intently into the trees. He had not moved. His voice was flat, far away. "It's breaking down."

"What's breaking down?"

"All of it," Michael said. "Whatever it is we're in. There's a way in and out. That's where Conner is."

"Conner is dead."

"Maybe. Maybe not. Maybe that's what we're supposed to believe, but you saw him back there on the beach."

Jonathan stood up straight now and stared at Michael. "We need to keep moving. We can't be stuck here. Michael? Do you hear me? We can't stay here. We have to get back to the cabin. I have to get home. I have to."

"We're behind the curtain as well…"

Jonathan grabbed Michael by the shoulders. He was a larger man, but Jonathan turned him like a top. "How many more miles to the cabin?"

Michael stared in silence for a moment, and Jonathan quizzed him again. "Do the numbers in your head. How many more miles to the cabin?"

He blinked and paused for a moment, looking as if he was trying to reach into his memory, retrace the outline on the map. "Six, I think."

"How long will it take us to make that trip? C'mon. Do the goddamn math in your head."

"This terrain? Seven hours probably."

"That would put us at the cabin by five," Jonathan said. "It'll be nearly dark by then. We need to get back before it's dark, before it starts to snow again. We need to get there so we can get help, okay?"

Michael's eyes lost the shine in them and suddenly seemed more familiar, as if he were coming out of a drunken haze, sobering up and recognizing the world around him.

"Just look straight ahead," Jonathan said. "Let's get to the field. There's cell service there, and it will be mostly downhill once we get over the ridgeline."

From the corner of his eye, at the farthest reaches of the trees, a lone branch bounced back and forth as if it had just caught on a piece of clothing, pulled, and let go.

They climbed again. Jonathan led Michael up the mountain. The steep incline leveled off as they approached the meadow. He could see it through breaks in the trees – a seemingly endless expanse of white with brittle and frozen brown straws reaching through the snow, bending in the open wind. The dense trees faded away, the land flattened. Jonathan pushed through the last hundred yards until he stood at the edge of the field and stared up to the top where the snow-covered meadow touched the gray sky, the way an ocean touches the horizon. For a moment he was disheartened. It looked so much farther than he remembered. He fought the urge to just lie down in the snow and let the cold overtake him quietly, silently. The field was an endless expanse of nothingness. Jonathan walked farther into the field until he was completely clear of the trees and stood for a time, listening to Michael's footsteps behind him. The wind fell from the tops of the mountains, pushed cold against his face. The tip of his nose felt numb. The cold set deep into his bones.

He turned to look back. Michael stood among the trees staring at him, his rifle once again leveled at Jonathan's heart.

Michael's voice sounded dead and desperate. "You go on," he said. "Don't follow me."

"No," Jonathan said.

"I see him out there."

Jonathan started to speak. A crack, a sudden explosion, filled the air and rung his ears. Dirt and snow jumped into the air beside Jonathan's feet and smoke rose from the tip of Michael's rifle. Jonathan didn't move. "You go on," Michael said. "You get help. Don't follow me. He's out there and I have to go find him. I don't have a choice. I have to. You don't understand."

"I do," Jonathan said. "But please don't."

"He needs me," Michael said. Then he turned and ran back into the trees, and Jonathan was completely alone in the snow-gray field. The wind came down from the mountain again, and the stalks of straw bowed their heads.

CHAPTER TWENTY-SIX

Michael felt he had finally returned to his right mind. Conner was out there. He knew this because he saw him. They had looked at each other across a distance of trees and snow. Jonathan was the one who had lost it. He had always been the weakest among them, with a strange mind easily given over to fantasy. This was quite simple, really. Conner had fallen in the water, come ashore but was confused and lost due to nearly drowning. There was clearly something wrong. Michael had seen Conner – glimpses of him, really – as he and Jonathan hiked the mountain toward the pass. At first Michael couldn't be sure if his eyes were playing tricks on him, but then, just as they reached the clearing of the meadow, Michael looked and saw his brother clear as day. He stood somewhat crooked, as if bones were broken, among the trees at the farthest range of vision. Conner stood there staring at him, mouth open like he was trying to say something, but couldn't get the words to rise up.

Jonathan was already hiking into that desolate field, trudging his way toward the cabin, trying to ignore the truth so he could continue hiding behind lies and fantasy. Jonathan was spinning out of control – his crazed ideas about the boy they had buried, about Coombs' Gulch and something stalking them in the forest. Things had been tragic and strange, but there was no reason to assign it some kind of supernatural quality. Michael had seen someone who looked like Gene through his scope yesterday, but that was all it was. Someone – probably another hunter – who happened to look like Gene. Gene was dead and gone. Conner was not. Conner was up and walking around, hurt and confused, and Michael had to find him.

Jonathan had grown more paranoid and insane, so the easiest thing to do was force him away, fire a shot so he knew Michael was serious, and let him go. Best case scenario: he makes it to the cabin and gets help. Worst case: he slips further into his own delusional fantasy and ends up lost or dead. Jonathan had been a friend, but Conner was Michael's brother, and there was no real choice in the matter. Blood is thicker.

Michael looked out into the trees. Conner had been there a second ago. He was sure Conner was saying something to him, but he couldn't make it out. A creeping sensation rolled up his spine, as if his body was revolted by this place. But it did not matter. What mattered was moving as quickly as possible, finding Conner's tracks through the snow and getting his brother back.

Michael couldn't help but flash back to the moment he saw Conner fall into the water and sink. At that moment it seemed everything inside him suddenly vacated his body; he was suddenly hollow and numb. That terrifying time Michael spent under the water, in the black, unsure if he would drown in the paralyzing cold, haunted him. He had reached his hand down into the deep – his lungs screaming, his eardrums about to burst – and felt Conner's hand there for a moment. Michael seized on to it, but Conner's fingers slid away like loose strands of seaweed.

It was that moment that drove him now, more than the dead boy, more than all this bullshit about something stalking them. It was the moment when he chose to save himself over his brother. He had been out of air, and his body began to panic, the cold draining the life from him. Michael felt himself slipping. During drowning, the body involuntarily forces you to inhale, and Michael felt his mouth opening, the black water slipping in. It would be only a matter of seconds. Rather than plunging down farther, he kicked to the surface and Conner was gone.

But now Michael had seen him. Now he knew Conner was not gone. He was out there. He was up and moving, and that meant he was alive. Jonathan was full of shit. How can you deny something when you've seen it with your own eyes? He had seen his brother staring at him across that expanse of trees. Now was the time to strike out and make that final plunge.

Michael was as hungry and tired as he had ever been. It was cold, and the clouds rolling over the mountains meant more snow. If the snow came hard, it could cover Conner's tracks, so he had to move fast to get to him and bring him back to the cabin. With any luck, Jonathan would have reached it by then and have gotten help. It was all a simple matter of risk and reward. He risked much tracking his brother through the forest now; he risked much trusting in Jonathan to reach the cabin and find help, but the reward was too great to ignore. It was a calculated risk – statistically, this was the only acceptable course of action.

Michael left Jonathan standing in the endless field, which disappeared into the sky. He turned to his right and began to move quickly, pounding through the snow, keeping his footing as best he could. Through a break in the trees, Michael took one last look over his shoulder and saw Jonathan watching him like a scarecrow in the maize. It didn't matter now. Nothing mattered but getting Conner.

Michael reached the spot where he saw his brother staring at him like a ghost. He could see the tracks. Solid proof. Incontrovertible evidence. The tracks led up from the lake. Conner had followed parallel to them the whole hike up the hill toward the meadow. Now his tracks led south, toward the adjacent mountain, which bordered the pass. The tracks disappeared into the trees. Michael called for Conner as loudly as he could, waited, and then called again. There was no answer, only silence. Looking into the staggered trees rising from the snow, he thought he detected movement, something just behind them, just out of sight. He couldn't see anything definite, as if his eyes saw something whose form his brain could not distinguish. He thought of a child playing hide-and-seek, trying to hide behind a tree not thick enough to completely shield him from view. There was something, but he could not make it out. Michael looked down at the tracks and followed.

He moved quickly at first, trying to run through the snow. His daily regimen of jogging several miles around the block, followed by a workout with free weights in his garage, kept him moving. But the extra gear – the heavy backpack, the rifle, the hunting suit – slowed him down. The previous long days of hiking meant his legs were already sore and burning; the lack of food made him weak, and the thin, cold air hurt his lungs. But he kept his bouncing pace, slipping occasionally on the slope covered with the wet snow.

The tracks continued past the edge of the meadow and then turned and began to climb up the slope of the southern mountain. Fuck. How had Conner gone this far so quickly? Michael stopped, breathing heavily. The tracks seemed to trail on forever and again turned sharply up the mountain, moving straight up the incline. But they were there, and they were real; there was no doubt. Michael caught his breath for a moment. He called for Conner again but there was no answer.

He made a decision then, another calculated risk: drop the backpack here so he could move faster and better navigate the steep mountain. He could make better time, catch up with Conner and then follow his own tracks back to his gear. He kept the rifle, just in case of bear, or to signal rescuers by firing shots in the air. Michael unloaded the backpack and found a strong limb jutting out from a thick yellow birch. He hung the pack and strapped the rifle tight across his back so it wouldn't bounce on his shoulders as he hiked. It seemed a momentous decision, but at times like these certain gambles had to be made. Besides, there wasn't much in the pack that would help anyway. Jonathan had the tent. The food was gone. All he had was a sleeping bag and some tools. He should have reached Conner by now. Michael's pace should have overtaken a weak, confused and injured man. He figured it would not be much longer. Conner would just be a little farther, beyond the trees. He had to push himself a little harder, move a little faster. Conner would be slowed down on the climb. Michael could catch up, get his brother and head for the cabin. They wouldn't be able to make it by nightfall – especially if Conner were injured or in shock – but if they kept moving they wouldn't freeze.

It was Michael's only chance to bring his brother back from the dark depths; to bring him back from the dead was worth anything, even if it meant his own life.

Michael followed his Conner's tracks and wondered for a moment if he had been following his brother's footsteps his whole life. Despite being the younger brother, Conner had always been the one who seemed to lead, to take control of the situation. He had a gift for making people like him, for making conversation when few others could find something worth talking about. Michael, on the other hand, could never be bothered. He had always been confused as to why people insisted on so much pointless talk. Why not just stay silent? Michael remembered a famous quote about that: "Better to say nothing and let the world think you're a fool than to open your mouth and prove them right." Michael was no fool; he just didn't see the point in a lot of conversation. The weather? Could anything be more boring? Take a look outside and recognize there is absolutely nothing you can do about it. Sports? Who could keep up with it all and why bother? He almost pitied those who spent their lives watching ESPN on endless repeat and memorizing stats that would never, ever, at any point in their lives make a single ounce of difference. It was like a homoerotic obsession. Michael appreciated a good football game as much as the next guy, but the men who stood around talking sports stats at parties would probably sneak into Tom Brady's bed given the chance. *Just shut up and drink your beer.*

Michael had no use for useless things, and so many people seemed obsessed with useless things. Michael liked things that worked. He liked making things work. He liked finding and eliminating the errors that stopped things from working. In that way, he had little use for ninety-nine percent of people who more or less threw a wrench in the gears of functioning society – those who did dumb things to make life worse all around, obsessed over inanities or were useless as babies when they reached a challenge. It was one of the reasons he liked hunting and had taken to it so quickly. It was one of the reasons he kept hunting even after the accident ten years ago. Hunting gave him two things: solitude and utility. In the early-morning hours, he was alone with the world. Cold, sitting in a tree stand, watching life unfold all around him as the sun rose and the forest grew progressively lighter. Watching, waiting, listening to the sounds creeping up in the morning light, spotting a buck or doe – perfectly created for dashing among the trees, wandering in from the abyss of night into his vision. On those cold mornings it was just him and his prey, hunter and hunted. It was the true nature of life.

Then, when he took a deer and gutted it there in the middle of a forest, he could see the truth of life. Ancient civilizations sacrificed animals to communicate with the gods. Michael wasn't religious, but, to him, this seemed by far a more effective form of prayer than anything taught in churches with high altars and stained-glass windows. In the blood and guts and organs was the truth of life. And if you're seeking revelation, staring at the stark, cold, animal reality of life was a good place to start. Mammals were all largely the same – same organs, same functions. In one end, out the other, and everything in between is there to absorb and use energy. When you looked at the inside of a newly gutted deer, you essentially saw the same functions inside yourself. This was what people were. This was what everything was. And then you drag the weight of that realization back to your home. You skin it. You age it. You cut it up and you eat it. That was true utility. Supply yourself with the base truth.

Conner had been one of those few people who did not fuck things up or make life more complicated. Conner greased the wheels. He was not much different from Michael. Whereas Michael liked to discover what made things work and rid them of errors, Conner essentially put those functioning things together to form a grander whole. That was why he'd been so good in business – taking a bunch of moving parts and putting them together to make money. Eliminate waste, fire the useless and capitalize on strengths while taking advantage of others' weaknesses. If Michael was the engineer who designed the machine, Conner was the guy who created a pipeline to move that machine into the hands of well-paying customers. They were in vastly different businesses, but their minds were symbiotic. Losing Conner would be losing the only person with whom he felt that kind of connection.

Powering through the snow, legs burning from the strain of pushing uphill, Michael almost felt guilty about his sudden frank realization; Conner meant more to him than anyone else – even his own wife. As he struggled through the snowy terrain, he thought about Annie and the one thing that didn't make sense, the one thing for which he could not envision a fix.

For years they had tried for a baby. Annie wanted a family. Michael was indifferent, really, but he wanted her to be happy – an easy fix for his home life because, as time wore on, Annie became more and more despondent. A child would fix that, would bring her joy and relief and restore his house to something more comfortable. Comfort was one of the drivers of society. It was why there were engineers like him – to ensure maximum effectiveness, ease of use, comfort. Michael worked on helicopters, made them function successfully to keep the discomfort of crashing or even the fear of crashing from encroaching upon passengers. Utility was the ultimate comforter – the maximum benefit with the least expenditure of energy.

But Annie's despondency at their inability to conceive challenged Michael's equation for life. They expended massive amounts of time, money and energy trying to create a life. They saw doctors and ran tests. She took hormone treatments and drugs, and he humiliated himself jerking off into a cup. They talked about it; she cried over it, and he drank over it. All so that this future baby would give Annie some comfort. But then, babies were also difficult, expensive, lifetime commitments. In essence, he was putting in all this energy to create something that would ultimately sap more energy and make his life more difficult instead of more comfortable. True, it would make Annie happy, and a happy home is an easier, more comfortable home, but, he figured, people can get used to anything. Even if there was never a child, eventually her sadness would wane and they would fall back into the same routine and find a form of comfort and contentment.

But still, throughout the past four years, his utilitarian theory of life was upended, and he wasn't sure why. It was a lot of effort in order to expend more effort. He loved Annie, but he could not love a child that was not yet conceived. Annie was different. She loved something that did not yet exist. He couldn't understand it.

Death was much easier to understand than life. Hunting was the perfect expression of the beauty of life's engineering. Even that night in Coombs' Gulch when they had found the boy dead, he understood the tragic simplicity of it, the perfect functioning. It was as simple as the pull of a trigger. He could take life apart much better than put it together.

And now he was here, on this mountain, struggling through the trees, following the tracks of his brother, hunting him down the same as he followed deer tracks throughout his life. This wasn't to end life but to save it, and once again it led to more complications, more gambles, more decisions in which neither option offered a solution. Michael pursued his brother the way his wife pursued a child – with all his physical and mental stamina. The difference, he figured, was that he knew Conner was out there. Conner was a true, living, actualized being who could be found if he just pushed a little harder.

The trees grew thinner as he followed Conner's tracks higher up the mountain. Not only were the trees more spread apart but they were also smaller. The soil was shallow against the rock of the steep incline. It was easier to see here. There were fewer places to hide, fewer places where his brother could be out of sight, but still there was no sign of him other than the tracks. He wondered how it was that Conner could keep this pace at this distance and this incline. The mountain face was steep, and Michael slipped in the snow, risked sliding a thousand feet down the slope and cracking his head on the trees.

The footprints in the snow led up the mountain, seemingly forever. He stared up toward the peak. Clouds swept across, and it disappeared in the gray expanse. Michael wondered where he was for a brief moment. He put his rifle to his shoulder and looked through the scope, tracing the tracks up the slope, but lost them. He dropped the rifle and looked down into the valley where the meadow ran between the mountains and into Coombs' Gulch. It was far, far below. Michael didn't realize how far he'd climbed as his legs burned and mind churned with the machinery of his life. He looked through the scope to see if he could spot Jonathan. He saw a small, dark figure standing at the crest of the meadow. So far away and so high up the mountain, struggling against the slippery snow and rock, Michael suddenly doubted himself. Perhaps Jonathan had been right – not about all his supernatural shit, but about making for the cabin and getting help. Michael suddenly felt stranded, lost and alone on this mountaintop. Somehow, being so high up, he began to feel desperate.

Michael steadied himself, talked himself back into his right mind. This wasn't hard. This was easy. He wasn't lost; he knew exactly where he was. He just needed to reach Conner and then go back down the mountain and back toward the cabin. Simple. Michael tamped down his irrational emotions. The tracks did not continue much farther; he could catch up. There was no place left for Conner to hide up here.

Michael breathed deep, strapped the rifle across his back again and pushed on, stepping into Conner's tracks when he could. He felt dizzy, breathless. He ignored the growing fear in his gut. Did he make the wrong decision? Was he following a ghost? He had seen Conner. Seen his body, his strange, distorted face. He had followed the tracks. The only logical explanation was that he was on the right path to save his brother. Michael looked back down at the meadow one last time and saw a tiny figure moving quickly through the tall, stiff grass toward the tree line of Coombs' Gulch. Jonathan would be back to the cabin by dusk. He would get help. Michael would save Conner.

Michael kept climbing, struggling. Conner's footprints in the snow appeared steady, casual even, as if his trip up the slope were a comfortable walk through a park rather than the harrowing, dangerous struggle Michael faced. It was almost as if Conner had floated up the mountain, just touching down his boots in the snow. Michael dug into the snow with his hands to find rocks to pull himself up. His boots slipped. He crawled on his knees, slid downhill several yards and panicked before grabbing hold of a shrub to stop his fall. He pulled himself back up and pushed farther. Anyone following his tracks would see a near-death struggle up a mountain that shouldn't be climbed without proper gear; they would think he'd lost his mind and his tracks would tell the tale of an insane man. Rescuers would look at each other and shake their heads because they wouldn't understand it; they would deride him with comments about another 'weekend warrior' who had no business being this far out in the wilderness. Someone would say there ought to be a law, but no one would know what that law should be. What could guard against these strange instances of human stupidity?

Would that be it? Would he be another case of sudden and mysterious stupidity in their eyes?

Michael climbed over a ridge, and the rock flattened out so he could stand. He stopped and caught his breath. Sweat clung to his face, burned his eyes and soaked his clothes. At this elevation, he breathed clouds. The gray sky and snow made everything appear flat. He couldn't see the contours of the land; the incline was barely perceptible. He could now see the peak of the mountain. The wind howled, pushing against him. It seemed for a moment he had been transported from the Adirondacks to some massive Alaskan peak, tens of thousands of feet high, treeless and surrounded on all sides by an angry sea of rising rock and snow-blown valleys. He was in a different time and different place – a place no man should be, seen only as a last vision by doomed explorers. Michael looked around the world from this massive height and did not recognize Earth anymore. He was at the top of the world, but he knew, logically, he shouldn't be.

Conner's footprints in the snow ascended, and he followed them with his eyes one hundred yards until he saw a figure standing at the base of the peak, staring into the sky. Conner's back was turned to Michael, but the sight of him after this journey was shocking, almost frightful. The wind kicked up hard and seemed to push Michael back toward the ledge. He called his brother's name, but it was lost in the lonely expanse of wind and sky.

Conner didn't move. He stood motionless as a statue. Michael called to him again but he did not turn. Michael pushed one last time to reach him and struggled up the trail of his easy footsteps. It seemed the entire world was stripped away and there was only Conner standing in this lonely place, staring at something only he could see. As Michael made his way closer, he called for his brother, but still there was no answer, no movement.

Michael's legs gave out when he was only a few yards from him. He couldn't breathe anymore and dropped to his hands and knees. The lack of food, the expenditure of the last ounces of his energy, had pushed him to his final limit. But there was Conner, standing before him, and Michael felt he was on the edge of darkness and had to make one last surge to grasp his brother. Michael stood, reached out and put his hand on Conner's shoulder.

Conner turned and gazed at Michael with dead, whitened eyes, his jaw drooping down below his neck. The skin seemed to fall away from the bone like a carcass left in water. His arms and legs were bent at strange angles. He seemed to float, held up by some invisible force. The wind blew, and as it swept across them, Conner's giant, gaping mouth gave forth a deep, cavernous moan.

Michael stared, disbelieving, and then Conner held up a long arm and touched him. It was real. The evidence was in front of his eyes, defying the logic of life. Michael fell backward in the snow, staring in horror at the thing that was his brother. It moved closer to him.

It all came to him at once: perhaps death was not so simple.

CHAPTER TWENTY-SEVEN

Jonathan stood in the snow with the tall grass rising up and bending in the wind and watched Michael run into the trees until he disappeared, swallowed whole by the mountain. The sound of his heavy footfalls, the mad scramble through the brush and branches faded away, and there was nothing but the soft rustle of the frozen meadow. Jonathan was alone now. He felt the world turn, and the mountains seemed to pass by slowly like the sails of a great ship. He felt dizzy, caught between life and death – the same fate that befell Conner and now, most likely, Michael. He tried to convince himself he was still among the living. He thought of Mary and Jacob. He thought of love, but when he tried to feel it, there seemed an impenetrable wall separating him from any emotion besides fear. It was all that was left in him.

It was an interminable climb up through the meadow – the horizon far above, the grasses pulling against his clothes, the cold reaching into his blood. At the top he would have cell service. He could call for help; he could hear Mary's voice. He could know that he was still alive. The meadow lay out before him like a strange vision of hell, an encroaching doom on the wind, a cold, lonely and eternal place.

He heard the whispers rise up from the land itself. He heard Mary's low and beautiful voice in the darkness, a memory of the night they snuck hand in hand out of a wedding and into the surrounding hills to make love. It was her cousin's wedding, held in the brick remnants of an ancient factory in the wooded farm hills of Pennsylvania. Sparkling white lights hung from brick edifices. Some of the structures lacked roofs, or were merely an empty foundation with four brick walls that looked ready to collapse; former windows were gateways to nothingness. It was all rust-belt hip, beautiful in its decay. The revelers danced and drank deep into the night on the grave of a once-meaningful existence. The converted factory grounds were surrounded by thick forest, patches of forgotten farm fields and hills that rolled like distant thunder through the night. They were slightly drunk – laughing, touching. He brushed his hands against her ass, tender and strong beneath the silk of her black dress, caressed her thighs and ran his hand up into the warmth of her body. She stifled a laugh; he fumbled with his belt and pants. They fell into the grass beside a bush, and she whispered to him in the darkness, "Take me now and forever." It was a marriage proposal of sorts – not official, but enough. He disappeared into her in that moment, and all was lost inside. It was a happy moment, one unburdened by the coming future in which everything would be stripped away. She whispered in his ear throughout the entirety of their lovemaking. She told him things. She said she wanted all of him and he promised. Those whispers followed him as he made the long hike to the crest of the meadow.

He had broken that vow. He had held something back – something dark and dangerous and awful. The lies, the guilt, the remorse ate through what they once had and poisoned the blood, darkened their home, haunted their lives like a specter.

When they finally married after the incident in Coombs' Gulch, he took her not as his wife, but as his victim.

The anguish inside him rose up out of the ground, from rock formed at the beginning of time, when the Earth was young and without love or hate or thought, when it was without time or consequence, when it was merely a tiny stone in a sea of emptiness.

More thoughts and memories came to him – the slow creep of ruin throughout the years. Conversations in hushed tones around their lonely kitchen table when there was no reason to whisper other than to gently conceal the truth from themselves: "What is going on with you?" "I feel like there's something you're not telling me." "You're so far away." "I think there's something wrong."

The tender, foreboding moments that marked his life as a father and husband.

Deep in the night he woke to the sound of Jacob's tiny voice, his tongue mispronouncing words in a hurried and hushed tone: "Daddy, I'm scared." And Jonathan opened his eyes and slowly took in the shape of his head, so perfectly formed and whole, lacking the star-shaped hole in the left eye that haunted Jonathan's dreams. Jacob's face was so close to his they nearly touched, and his eyes seemed to shine in the dark of the room.

"What are you scared of?"

The single word uttered by a boy summed up all the horrors of the world: "Monsters."

And now, walking through the meadow, nearly reaching the crest of the hill, Jonathan shared that fear. Before, he feared the guilt, the prospect of being caught, shamed, convicted, banished to prison, of being alone. Now he feared something more – the monsters that lurk in the spaces between, in unseen dimensions and in his own soul. He was the monster, more than anything else. Jacob had been right to fear – the monster slept in his home.

Jonathan's pace slowed as he neared the horizon, where the meadow rolled over and began its descent into Coombs' Gulch. He turned and looked back toward the lake, but couldn't see it anymore. He looked to the mountain to his right and wondered where Michael might be – if he, too, was chasing a monster that was more a part of himself than anything else. He listened and tried to hear the reeds in the wind, hoping for an answer, or a glimmer of hope, but all that came to him were memories of his past that, pieced together, now seemed to form a tragic and predestined downward spiral.

He reached the top exhausted, sapped of will. It seemed as good a place as any to die. Everything felt wrong, but he wanted to hear their voices. He breathed hard the cold air. Jonathan dug through his pack and found his cell phone to see if it would pick up a signal. He held it aloft in the air until a lifeline appeared and immediately dialed Mary's number.

The phone began to vibrate and ding with incoming messages, voice mails and missed calls. Over and over it shook and rang and dinged – civilization surging back at him, connected through the air.

Mary answered by screaming his name, screaming that Jacob was gone. Someone had taken him.

As Jonathan, Conner and Michael lay on that rocky beach with horrific visions creeping through their brains, as Conner attempted to drop the boy in the box to the bottom of a lake, as Jonathan had stared into the darkest part of the night and felt a horrific presence staring back, Jacob had disappeared. He boarded the bus at 7:30 a.m., attended his classes, played outside during recess under the eye of teachers patrolling the playground, attended more classes and boarded the bus home at 2:30 p.m. The driver let Jacob off at the corner, two doors from his home. Mary normally met him at the bus stop. She had been extra vigilant lately because of the sounds outside the house at night and the scratch marks on the door. But while she stood in the kitchen, putting away the last of the dishes from the dishwasher, she looked out the rear window to the woods behind the house and saw the figure of a man limping through the trees. It was a bright day. The trees were just beginning to shed their leaves and the thick underbrush was wilted and dead. But there in the long shadows cast by the afternoon sun, she had seen a figure moving in and out of the darkness. She was tired. She thought her eyes were playing tricks. It had always been a quiet neighborhood. Everyone knew each other.

But she saw him walking with a strange gait, and she stopped her work and watched, an anxiety growing in her heart that her house and her life were being encroached upon by the unknown. It was like the figure knew she had seen him. It stopped walking, turned and looked and stared right through the window and into her eyes. She could see those eyes in the shadow of the trees. It was like they glowed, she said.

And suddenly it was gone and she snapped out of her daze. The steaming dishes from the washer gone cold, the afternoon just a bit darker, the sun a bit closer to the horizon.

She looked at the clock. It had been fifteen minutes and Jacob should be home. The bus had already come and gone. Dizzy at the sudden time shift and now afraid there was some unknown person stalking through the neighborhood where her seven-year-old son was getting off the bus, she ran out the front door toward the corner bus stop. The neighborhood was bright and empty. She heard the diesel engine of the school bus roaring two streets over, continuing its route. Normally, two other children disembarked at the same corner, but she saw no one at all. She heard no voices. She was completely alone.

The police were interviewing everyone, she said – teachers, the bus driver, parents, neighbors. They retraced his steps throughout the day. Mary sat for hours at the kitchen table as detectives ran through her day, asked where her husband was, debated with her the timing and nature of her absence at the bus stop. She told them she had seen someone in the woods and reminded the officers of the man who had approached Aria less than a week earlier. She told them there had been strange noises outside the house at night. She showed them the scratch marks on the door. They frowned at her answers; skepticism hung on their voices. What did this man in the woods look like? She couldn't give a clear answer. It was impossible to tell, the shadow and light crossing his face, his eyes glowing bright, boring into her. Police and local volunteers combed through the woods, made their way to the wetlands that stretched between two low ridges, the place where small liquor bottles littered the ground and fallen trees served as benches for small gatherings around a fire. Search dogs were brought out, picking up the scent from Jacob's tiny red shirt, pulling their handlers deeper into the places hidden between beacons of homes and neighborhoods and then farther out into the surrounding hills.

They wanted to know where Jonathan was, how long he had been gone. "How is your marriage?" they asked her. "Did you have an argument with your husband before he left?"

"Where are you?" she cried, but he could not answer. He didn't know just then. He just knew he was away – too far gone to make any difference whatsoever.

"I'm lost," he said quietly.

And then Mary screamed. It rose up from her gut, from her heart, from her whole being – summing up the past years and everything with it. It was a familiar sound, an animal-like scream that cried out through the distance and echoed across the mountains. It had been with him all along. That pain-filled shriek that heralded the coming of horrors and the torture of loss.

It was the sound only a mother could make, and the earth shook with its vibration.

CHAPTER TWENTY-EIGHT

He ran, tumbling and tripping through the snow and grass down the slope. He dropped his pack; his rifle remained strapped tight to his back. The long reeds of the meadow whipped across his thighs. Unknown muscles, suddenly shocked to life, tried to balance, push, lift and absorb. His ankles rolled, feet slipped, but it didn't matter – he kept going because he didn't know what else to do. He ran to escape this place and to get home to find his son; he ran to escape the trappings of his past and the presence that stalked him through the trees. He wanted to believe that if he could get home the nightmare would end, but a voice in the back of his mind – one he sought to ignore and deny with all his heart – told him it was already too late and the true nightmare, the kind in which you walk through the darkness, eyes open to a world beyond, was just beginning. Perhaps, if he could get home in time, he could save Jacob. Perhaps he could save Mary from the terror and the loss. He was unsure if he could save himself. All would be revealed in due time. He would be exposed once again, not as a good man but as his true self – weak, destitute and dying. Evil is patient, secure in its timelessness, content to slowly strip away the facade piece by piece until death is a relief.

The dark trees that marked the entryway into Coombs' Gulch bounced and shook and blurred as he stumbled and ran down the hill. Visions from the rocky shore of the lake ran through his head. He pictured the men who took Thomas Terrywile from that small path through the woods as he walked home from school. He remembered the strange, deathly smell of them as they carried the boy to that place deep in the forest. He remembered the bitter cold and loneliness of the void in which he was trapped for decades, the confusion of his random appearances in strange places, his tears and yearning as he tried to reach out to everyone, anyone to rescue him from hell; he remembered the feel of that long, clawed hand gripping the boy's shoulder as it stood looming over him like a demonic father figure. Was that what it wanted? A child it could keep, abuse and terrify at its whim?

It did not accept sacrifices; it accepted offerings brought to it by human puppets.

Jonathan tried to tamp it all down, tried not to think of it, of what it meant for his only son. He focused on this one fact: Jacob was still alive. He could be found, and Jonathan was the only person who could find him, the only person with this awful knowledge.

The meadow fell away and dropped toward the darkness of Coombs' Gulch. The clouds darkened with the setting sun. The clouds were heavy now; the smell of snow suffused the air once again. The trees were black and appeared to shift and move with an unseen presence rippling in the shadows. Before him, the forest seemed to twist itself into a strange and horrifying grimace like a child's Halloween mask – a ghastly pantomime of life. The mouth opened wide for him, swallowed him down into the Gulch.

He reached the point of exhaustion. The terrain was now too steep and rocky to run, the trees and underbrush seemingly impenetrable. He slipped on roots underfoot; branches slashed his face, and rock outcroppings left ten-foot drops that could break his legs, leave him crippled and dying in the wild. He careened off a tree and slid to a stop. The forest turned like a kaleidoscope, silent and fractured into a million pieces. He felt it crawling over his body, like an army of ants roaming beneath his skin. The entire mountain pulsed with an unseen force, which was finally pulling back the veil, making itself known.

Jonathan found his footing and began to move as quickly as he could, sliding, falling down the slopes he and the Braddick brothers had climbed just two days before. He struggled for a grip in the snow. He tried to calculate in his mind the fastest route back to the cabin. He wondered whether Daryl Teague had left Conner's Suburban there as he promised. He feared what would happen when he called the authorities, the story he would have to tell. But most of all, he feared for his son and feared it was already too late.

Snow began to fall, softly floating to the forest floor between the leafless crowns of trees that grabbed at the sky. He caught glimpses of the eastern ridge of mountains; they seemed to dance and sway with the pounding of his heart. He remembered what Daryl Teague told them about the Gulch: the mountains were like mirrors of themselves. People got lost, thought one direction was the other. He wondered for a moment if another man now stumbled and fell toward his doomed destiny in Coombs' Gulch on the opposite mountain.

The trees were a maze. The undergrowth was stripped of its leaves, its remains like fossilized bones against the snow.

He now realized the distance he had yet to cover, and suddenly began to wonder if it was all futile, doubt reaching up and gripping his heart. He could practically kill himself trying to get back home through the Gulch, but what difference would it make at this point? He was like the buck who, startled at the piercing thundercrack of a gunshot, runs and bounds through the forest as his life pours from the hole in his side. Jonathan had so much farther to go, so little light left to find his way. He stared at the eastern mountains and tried to scream the way Mary had screamed with all that pain and loss, but his dry throat cracked and it came out as only a whisper. He had no voice now. The only thing left was a heartbeat, moving arms and legs, and a mind slowly spiraling into the abyss.

He clasped trees to keep from falling on his downward slide. He constantly turned his head to scan the forest behind him like a paranoiac, but there was nothing. He listened to the blood pumping through his veins and secretly hoped some malady would suddenly stop his heart and give him an easy excuse to bow out forever. But it didn't happen. He had a debt to pay and there was no escaping it.

Time stood still. The slope was endless, plunging deeper than he could remember until the mountain peaks disappeared from view. It was like burrowing beneath the Earth's crust. The air grew dark; walls closed in. The trees were everywhere, endless. It seemed like an illusion, but he knew if he reached his hand out, his fingers would find purchase. It was like being led through a hall of mirrors. He thought of his bachelor party night in that strip club nestled in the looming hills, when the doe-eyed girl had taken his hand and led him to the back rooms. He remembered the image of himself walking with her hand in hand to that dark place. He remembered wondering whom he was looking at – a pathetic stranger, more alone in the world for taking this stage girl as a prize. What had she whispered to him in those moments? In the dark, with the flashing lights? Had she changed forms momentarily? His animal prey, splayed open and hollow to the cold, empty world, had whispered in his ear.

Now, in the mirror of the trees, he looked to his side and saw he was not alone. She walked with him. Every step, every movement mimicked his own. She was dressed the same as that night in the strip club – a line of cheap fabric arching over her rounded hips, which seemed to glow faintly in the dusk; her breasts were tanned and rippled slightly with each light step. Her dark hair fell like a deep stream and brushed thin shoulders. He watched her, and she watched him. He continued his downward trek into the Gulch, and she moved with him. He stopped and she stopped. He turned to face her, and they stared into each other's eyes. She seemed so far off, yet, like a fever dream, she was close enough to touch. He could make out every detail of her. Like a mirror she moved perfectly with him; like a mirror, it was not real. There was no soul, no life.

He looked away from her and turned to the narrow slope. Root systems gripped massive stones and held them. He turned to look at her again, but she was gone.

Instead, he saw his wife. Mary's thick brown hair fell heavy down her back. She was clothed, wearing the sweatpants and T-shirt combination he found so sexy on those long, lazy weekend days when they felt cut off from the rest of the world – the early days before the trappings of this life had fully formed and moved in for the kill. The days when they would lounge around and rent a movie, make love in the afternoon and talk about whatever came to mind. She had been his best friend and lover. She had been his whole world. She looked at him now through the trees of Coombs' Gulch – a ghost, a memory, a reflection of the past. He smiled the moment he saw her, and the same smile flashed across her face, too. Everything he hid from her over the years was out here, buried in this purgatory of mountains and trees, burning through his arms and legs and lungs. But all they had been together was gone, and now there was only this ghostly image beside him. They walked together for a long time deeper into the Gulch. She stayed with him through every step. He fought back the urge to take her hand and hold it as he took her to the place he could never take her before – the place where a bullet was fired and killed everything they had not yet created. In this hidden place, with the air dark and swirling, he hoped she would say something – anything – to make it okay again. To tell him that it would be all right, that he was good and she was with him and loved him. He looked over at her with tears in his eyes, and she looked at him. He held back the urge to cry.

Then Mary was gone, and small, innocent Thomas Terrywile stared at him from the snow. He was closer than Mary had been. He tilted his childish head as Jonathan tilted his; he reached to grip the broken limb of a black spruce as Jonathan did, and he shifted his weight to his downward foot to keep from sliding, just as Jonathan did. His eyes were big and brown. Jonathan was not smiling, but the boy smiled wide and long.

Jonathan continued his hike, and Thomas Terrywile hiked with him, every movement a perfect mirror except his face. Even the land itself was reflected – they touched the same trees, stumbled on the same rocks, walked the same land. The pitch leveled off, and the trek became easier. Thomas Terrywile stayed with him. Jonathan tried not to look, but he caught glimpses from the corner of his eye. He wanted to deny it, but the boy was still there, walking with him. The light was nearly gone and Thomas became harder to see. When Jonathan turned and looked, little Thomas Terrywile looked back. But from the periphery of his vision – when he could barely make out the figure beside him – the boy appeared monstrous and huge, a massive shadow filled with awful angles. And in the moments before Jonathan would turn to look upon it, he could feel its horrifying gaze, its size and presence. Then he would turn, and it would just be the image of a boy staring back at him, mimicking his movements like a boy might do with his father.

The slope of the Gulch flattened as he reached the base of the valley. He neared the stream, the vein through the heart of it where he would turn south for the cabin. The massive thing beside him flickered in and out of existence. He turned his head quickly to face it, to see it in its full form.

Thomas Terrywile was gone. Now there was only his son, Jacob, staring at him in the darkness of the wood. A small gasp of desperation left Jonathan's lips. Jacob was missing from home, but now stood directly in front of him. Jonathan tried to tell himself it couldn't be true, that it was a trick, but every ounce of his being told him to run to his son, to take him up and hold him. Jacob's mouth mimicked his own – a silent scream. Jonathan fell to his knees. Jacob did not move but merely watched him, as if he didn't understand his father's pain. Jonathan held his arms open wide to embrace him, and Jacob did the same, his small arms and fragile hands stretched out. "Jacob," he whispered, but the boy's face broke into a wide grin; his eyes wrinkled and sunk into deep black holes. Jacob shook his head slowly back and forth, and from his mouth came a deep, cavernous voice as if from the bottom of a well.

No.

Jonathan scrambled to his feet, turned and ran, the image of his child running steadily beside him in a mirror of mockery. Snow began to fall again, hard and fast. Jonathan saw the stream ahead, still flowing with water not yet frozen over. He fell before it, plunged his hand into the icy water and brought it to his mouth to drink. Debris and dirt crunched in his teeth. He turned to look at Jacob, but he was gone and there was only the dark forest in the night. He looked in the other direction, and there was nothing.

Then he felt it just behind him: something there, looming tall over his shoulder.

There was a breath – a chuffing sound that blew up against the back of his neck. He stayed so still that he did not breathe, did not allow his chest to rise and fall. He waited there for what seemed like hours. There was only the slight trickle of the stream in the vast silence, and he waited to be killed, to be run through by some predator he couldn't fathom. He waited for the end to what began ten years ago, all that time from then till now only a fraction of a second between the bullet leaving the gun and striking home to the heart of its target. All this time, he'd been nothing more than a dead man walking, no different from when Conner's corpse crawled out of the lake and presented itself to the world.

At least the revenant could scream. Jonathan could not summon the strength or courage to cry out. He would die with a whimper in this place, put to rest with only a breath of fear. He thought of Mary then. He thought of Jacob being offered up to this thing, which now stood behind him. He thought about where Jacob might be right now – that infinite, dark and cold place – and then his fear turned to anger, a welling up of animal rage from his gut that overwhelmed him, that felt as big and terrifying as the day his son was born. Life surged within him, forced its way out into the world, even in the face of death.

He felt the metal and wood of his rifle strapped across his back.

It chuffed another breath high above him, like some great African animal, too large to be bothered with a human. Yet it waited for him. He thought of Michael in his tree stand, letting out a birdlike whistle so a deer would lift its head and turn toward him before he punched it through the chest with a shotgun slug. Jonathan breathed in through his nose. He felt every part of his body; he felt the rifle, the way the strap slid slightly to the right so he could slip it off quickly, the way the stock touched the side of his leg. He tried to remember if there was still a round in the chamber.

Jonathan's movement was not as smooth as he would have liked. He turned quickly, slid the strap from his shoulder, hefted the Remington in his hand, fumbled the safety for a moment and raised the barrel to fire. He didn't know if it could be killed, but his rage urged him on to try.

And there, just a few feet away, he saw his own image staring back at him. He saw his own horrified face, his same camouflage coveralls, worn, wet and dirty; he saw his facial hair rubbing against the flesh of his neck, his eyes staring wide in wonder. Jonathan paused for a moment. He could not think, and his mind spun and snapped, unsure of who or what he was – whether he was the reality or the reflection, whether he was truly in control of his actions or merely the puppet for this thing, its desires and motivations. Jonathan slowly began to lower his rifle.

But he could not let it go.

Jonathan raised his rifle to shoot, and his mirror image, in turn, turned the barrel of its rifle upward, lodged it beneath his chin and fired.

Jonathan watched his head erupt outward with blood and bits of gore; teeth blasted out like buckshot from the explosion of gas and fire; flesh shook and limbs quivered and Jonathan watched as his mirror image dropped to the ground and slumped forward, reddening the snow and pouring blood into the rotten soil.

Jonathan screamed, fell to his knees and clawed at his own face.

CHAPTER TWENTY-NINE

Jonathan wandered through the forest in the dark. He could not tell if he was man or ghost. He still felt the ground underfoot, felt the frozen air chafing his cheeks, felt the fear and desire to return to his wife and find his lost boy. But something lay dead in the Gulch. He followed the stream because it was the only thing he could think to do, as if his body were on autopilot to return to the cabin, get home and face...he didn't know what anymore. The future was nothing more than a gray fog drifting toward him. It brought nothing but more pain, yet all he could do was continue onward. He stumbled. His legs weren't working correctly anymore, tired and dead from three days of heavy hiking through the mountainous terrain. His gait was awkward; only the last remnants of his willpower dragged his body through the trees. Anyone who saw him would think a corpse had risen from the grave and stalked through the trees. He turned to see if his body still lay dead and faceless on the ground. He could see it – a black stain in the pale snow.

He did not know what time it was anymore. Time had lost all meaning. Time didn't matter for Jacob – if indeed he were trapped in that terrible, lonely limbo like Thomas Terrywile – and time no longer mattered for Jonathan. He was dead. Whether it was spiritually or physically, it no longer mattered. All blended together, all was the same. The curtain had been pulled back momentarily, and he saw himself dancing on the stage, his own movements controlled by an unseen puppeteer. It was almost laughable, except he was the lone audience.

The snow ceased momentarily and the moon shone full and bright in a break between the passing clouds. The mountain ridges glowed, each a reflection of the other. He followed the stream but couldn't be sure he was headed in the right direction. All he could do was keep on moving – keep living, if that was what it could be called. He saw identical places a thousand times over. He saw the stars turn. He heard branches move and break in the darkness, first on one side of the stream and then the other. The sounds and movements were too quick to be just one person or animal; it had to be many, all of them closing in. For what, he did not know, but he moved forward anyway. From behind came the sound of heavy timber being uprooted and thrown to the ground, heavy crashing sounds of thick, splitting wood. He looked to the moon, but it was half-hidden behind the canopy of black spruce trees. There was another sound – something on the cold air that moved like ghosts through the bracken.

He left the thick timber behind and walked among the tall grasses, the flatland that lined the stream, the place where it had all begun with that single gunshot. Everything was dead under the snow. The moonlight poured down, and everything glowed bright and ghastly and cold. He heard whispering again. It came stronger now, heavier, carried on the air; the voices became more human, but still he could not make out the words. It sounded like a small group of men talking, plotting, just out of listening range, the way voices mingled together in a crowded pool hall or downtrodden dive bar. He thought about the night at the East Side Tavern when Michael and Conner approached him with this plan. The strange bar patrons who somehow looked familiar, how they watched him even though he did not know them. It was like the entire world was in on some kind of joke and he was the mark, left to spin and cry in his ignorance.

Perhaps the voices were just a ghostly recording, the sound of men standing over the bloody body of a boy with a star-shaped hole in his eye, plotting how to bury him in a box. It played over and over again, like songs from the past on endless radio repeat. The past and present blended seamlessly into a new reality – a nightmare into which he was waking. The Gulch was an eternal recurrence and his life nothing but a minor detail, twists on the truth, a ruffling of the veil.

Jonathan stood at the edge of a hole. A deep hole, square shaped, a couple of yards long and about one yard wide. There was a pickaxe and shovels on the ground, partially covered in snow. It looked strange now, this hole near a stream in the middle of the Gulch. It seemed to be drawing him closer. He wanted to lie down in it. He was tired, so very tired. Clouds rolled overhead. The moon disappeared, and snow began to drift silent and steady across the land.

He could feel many things watching him. They were just over his shoulder, just hidden in the darkness of the tree line, just out of sight. He could not see them, but they were there.

He looked again into that hole and saw his own body lying there, head broken open, limbs at strange angles, eyes wide and partially set free from his skull – straining to see something in the sky, just before the bullet tore through.

Jonathan looked out into the distance, where the tall grass of the wetlands met the trees. A pair of yellow eyes shone in the darkness, high off the ground, bright as the moon, glossy and sinister. Someone spoke to him from the trees.

"Where is Jacob?"

He turned to look, but no one was there. The tree line was dark and impenetrable. He looked back to where he had seen the eyes shining in the night. They were gone. He walked to where they had been and stared up into the spiraling spikes of a dying black spruce tree. They seemed like a staircase or ladder climbing up into the darkness of space. Or perhaps he was at the top and they led downward into the earth. He was too tired and dizzy to know the difference anymore.

He walked to the southern edge of the valley and stood before the blackened trees as the land sloped gently upward toward the cabin. It wasn't much farther now. He could hear the sound of the electric generator turning, a horrendous sound rendered soft by distance.

The broken spikes of tree limbs plunged into him like knives and scraped his numb face and bruised his hollow chest. He lumbered up the hill like it was a mountain, dragging his body along. There was whispering again in the trees, the sound of men's feet running through the forest like a pack of unseen wolves closing in on an injured buck. He heard the padding and crunching of the snow, breaking branches, cursing and giggling, like children with low, gruff voices. They were everywhere in the darkness. Jonathan stared straight ahead. Through the trees, he could make out the faint glow of electric light from the rear of the cabin.

He pushed on farther. The light grew steadily brighter, reached into the trees and cast shadows across the snow. Large flakes of snow fell from the sky, drifting lazily through the pine canopy.

A face appeared from behind a tree, poking out into the light. A beefy man with a round face and fire-shocked beard. He laughed like he was playing a game, his smile ruddy, red and giddy. For a moment, Jonathan recognized him – the man from the bar in Pasternak, who had mumbled those strange words to Michael before the fight broke out.

"Where is Jacob?" he said and then disappeared from view back behind the tree.

Then another face appeared from behind a different tree. He was tall and gaunt, half-hidden in shadow. He smiled like death, his voice deep and cavernous. "Where is Jacob?"

Then another and another and another, all appearing momentarily from behind tree trunks, their faces suddenly visible like apparitions, giddily asking, "Where is Jacob?" and laughing to themselves before disappearing into the darkness as if they were playing a game of hide-and-seek. They moved around him, shifting places, breaking branches, but he could not see them until they popped a head out from behind a tree and whispered that same, awful taunt: "Where is Jacob?"

He recognized them all from that night in Pasternak, their elbows on the wooden bar of The Forge, half-finished beers falling over, faces bloated and heavy, secretive smiles and calculating eyes, sizing up the world for a fight. They looked different now in the winter night, cast in shadow and dull light. Their skin was gray and pockmarked, their eyes like beads on the face of a doll, their movements jerky and broken, like his own. He saw Daryl Teague among the pines. His massive body and head reached high into the tree limbs. He whispered, "Where is Jacob?" and raised his clawlike hand with only three fingers to his mouth to stifle a laugh. His strange eyes stared right through Jonathan as if he were sleepwalking, like Jacob during his night terrors – eyes open to the world, but trapped in his mind, simultaneously existing in two different worlds. Perhaps they were all trapped, animals who constructed their own prisons over time and suddenly realized what they've done. Their laughter sounded strange – an animal-like cackling of anger, pain and insanity.

Jonathan felt it somewhere out there – true reality. He had been half asleep for so long, trapped within his guilt and terror. His body moved, but he fell deeper and deeper. Something tried to wake him. He could feel it now.

Daryl Teague's face pulled from both sides into a grin, and he stepped back into the darkness.

Jonathan could see the firepit and oakwood bench where they found Bill Flood's body. He could see the doorway of the shed where they'd hung the deer and stripped it of skin and meat ten years ago. He could smell something gentle on the wind that moved softly through the trees and caused the snow to dance.

Where is Jacob?

He was out of the Gulch now and stood beneath the electric floodlight, facing the wooden wall of the cabin. He could see the driveway from here. He saw Conner's Suburban parked in the driveway, large and heavy, the light glinting off the body, the tires new and polished. He turned and looked again into the doorway of the shed, its entrance black and beckoning. The snow fell silent through the shadow and light. He still heard them in the trees; he heard their rustling feet, their whispers and taunts. He waited and breathed and then turned to look.

In the light of the overhead lamp his own footprints leading from the trees to the cabin were the only ones he could see. The tracks curved slightly with the small incline, showing a line of indentations and slash marks where his right foot dragged like an animal with a broken leg. The wind pushed the snow sideways for a moment but then ceased, and the snow fell dead and straight again. He waited there in the night for what seemed like hours, and they waited in the trees, watching.

He heard a tree snap somewhere in the darkness. He unslung his rifle and waited. All went silent, and he could hear only the beating of his heart – it sounded a million miles away.

A face appeared from behind a tree like a mannequin pushed slowly into his range of vision. It showed no movement or life – a wooden mask painted by a disturbed child who saw the world in flashes of carnival terror. It stared with unblinking black eyes. Atop its head was a crown of antlers. Its impossibly tall body was clothed in a Druid robe. It floated farther out from behind the tree and faced him directly. Then it began to float toward him over the snow.

Jonathan chambered a round in his rifle and raised it to his shoulder, aimed and fired. The sound echoed off the mountains and disappeared.

The figure did not flinch or move, as though the bullet hadn't touched the cloth of its robe. It simply continued to float silent and unmoving toward him. It didn't look real, but it was there, in front of his eyes. He could see it – the light landed on its wooden mask, which grew larger and larger with its approach. It existed, and yet it did not because it could not be killed.

Jonathan chambered another round and fired again. The figure continued toward him. It grew large in Jonathan's eyes, coming so near now it seemed he could reach out and touch it.

It was what hid behind the veil of this dream world. It was where Jacob, his little boy, would be taken to suffer with this unspeakable thing keeping watch over him like a monstrous father figure, reveling in the terror of a child woken from a dream, plunged into a cold, empty hell.

He chambered another round and fired again and again till the rifle was empty and there was nothing but the hollow click of the firing pin.

The figure stood before him now, face-to-face. An arm like the broken branch of a tree rose up from beneath its robe. A long, bony finger reached up to the wooden mask and pushed it aside. A deep, croaking and guttural voice rose up from the darkness, as if the land itself had cracked open and, from a great crevasse, its words filled Coombs' Gulch and poured down into him.

"Do you see?"

Jonathan stared into its true form. He could see. It was all he would ever see.

He could not look away.

CHAPTER THIRTY

The lights flashed on bright, making Mary's eyes water. A small microphone nestled in her lapel. The Channel 8 news reporter – Sonya Martinez – sat across from her in a chair, pleasantly pretty and covered in makeup.

"What would you like to say to whoever took your son?" Sonya said.

Despite the rehearsals, the words she had memorized and the coaching from detectives and experts, Mary could only bring herself to say, "Please, bring him home."

And even that was choked and dead on arrival.

It had been three weeks since Jacob disappeared and her husband, Jonathan, had returned home, crazed and alone, talking nonstop about something in the woods, some kind of ritual, demons and children lost in space. The police immediately hauled him away. He put up a fight in the middle of the police station and tried to escape, injuring a couple of officers with strength she did not know he possessed. They placed him in a locked psychiatric hospital and charged him with assault.

The New York State Police began their search of the mountains where Jonathan and Michael and Conner Braddick had taken their last hunting trip. They found no trace of Conner and only found Michael's backpack and gear high on a mountaintop – a place where few people would tread on their own – but no other trace of either man. They had disappeared as well.

Jonathan would ramble nonstop when she was allowed to visit him, his eyes wide, desperate and insistent as he tried to convince her of something incomprehensible. It was all gibberish. *Something* had happened, of that she was sure, and his already fragile mind had snapped. Mary still had that horrible sense of alienation from him – of seeing him completely lost and yet standing right in front of her. He looked like a madman, his hair matted to his scalp, his pale face gaunt and soured with desperation, sweat and grime. His eyes, once blue, now looked nearly white. She had needed him so badly in that moment, needed him to hold her so they could find a moment of strength together and gird themselves against the horror of what had happened to their son. But he was untouchable. It was like watching a dead and broken branch finally fall to the ground.

The police questioned him extensively. They suspected him of murdering his two friends. They tried to connect him with Jacob's disappearance. It was all too strange – too coincidental to just be coincidence, and the detectives looked for any connection between Jacob's disappearance and the disappearance of Michael and Conner.

The newspapers and television had a field day. It was on the evening news; even some national publications picked it up. The multiple disappearances fueled all sorts of insane theories spread over the internet, television and newspapers, which twisted in her head and caused her to feel dizzy. Everyone had 'facts', and yet there were zero facts at all. Those 'facts' were woven into a tapestry – multiple tapestries – and hung like a veil before the stage of the world. She was so desperate sometimes she almost felt herself succumb to Jonathan's story; it made as much sense as anything else at this point. He kept telling police to search the forests surrounding their town, to find a place with markings on trees and a ritualistic design in the ground. A place where trapped and possessed men offered gifts of children to a demon-god. They laughed and shook their heads. Mary kept her arms across her stomach, trying to keep her insides from spilling out.

Then they found it. Three miles up Route 4 – a long scenic road that rose and fell with the hills – and deep in the woods off old hiking trails no one used anymore, police dogs picked up Jacob's scent and followed it to a strange clearing in the woods with a ring of stones laid in the ground and a pattern of intersecting lines. Symbols were carved in the surrounding trees, just as Jonathan had said there would be. The cops came down on him ten times harder. Now he wasn't just some unlucky sap with bad timing – now he was an honest-to-god suspect.

So far they hadn't been able to fit the pieces together, though. The timelines didn't work. They triangulated his cell phone to a remote meadow in the Adirondacks that bordered Coombs' Gulch – exactly where Jonathan said he had been the entire time. The detectives had to drop it after a while, but still, she could see it in their eyes – they were constantly thinking about it – how he did it and managed to baffle them all. They would never let it go.

"What do you think happened to your son?" Sonya Martinez said with a built-in sympathetic voice Mary recognized from every other female reporter who interviewed the family of a missing child, a voice sweet enough to convince you she cared, easily digestible for the masses, but with a slight edge of skepticism to let the viewer know she was on the case, determined to solve the mystery.

The camera lights left a halo over everything and everyone in her range of vision, as if angels had descended from heaven to question her and dredge the pain. Maybe if she told them the right things, the angels would find her son.

"He was only a boy. A little boy," Mary said. The tears were coming now. She couldn't help it. She cried automatically these days. Anything set her off. The lights and the questions were overwhelming; the loss and the fear ran rampant inside her. "I don't know. I just don't know, and that's the worst part."

She lied to the angels. She had heard it said that not knowing what happened to a missing child was the worst part. Maybe that was true after years of searching and heartache. Right now what she feared more than anything was the phone call that a body had been discovered, that detectives and forensic technicians were descending on some lonesome wooded area to piece together some horrid and lurid story of what a monster had done to her only child. Waiting to hear confirmation of what she, deep down, knew was the worst part. She felt the dead emptiness of true loss, like she had been killed and gutted like one of Jonathan's dead deer.

Maybe that was all she was now – a doe strung up, hollowed out, with everyone taking their pound of flesh. The media questioned her parenting: Where was she when Jacob got off the bus? What was Jonathan doing in the mountains? How was their marriage? Remember JonBenét Ramsey? They painted the portrait that fit their notions, stripped the meat from her bones and dined on the six o'clock news.

And yet here she was offering herself up as further sacrifice. It was what the detectives and the experts told her to do, so she did it. Her life was not her own anymore – it too had been taken. Now she only did what she was told to by her handlers, her puppeteers, and she walked to and fro in a daze. When she spoke, there was nothing but breath behind the words. She had lost her son and her husband. At this point, it was a miracle she could get out of bed in the morning.

Mary looked at Sonya's pretty-but-not-too-pretty face across from her. Sonya was probably Mary's age, hair highlighted with blonde and cut at a sharp angle to make her look sharp – a real go-getter. Her vacant eyes dampened on cue, her face well conditioned in front of a dressing room mirror to look deeply concerned but skeptical, caring but not without reservation. Mary couldn't help but wonder where this woman would go and what she would do after the interview. This was just another workday for her. For Mary it was the culmination of the end of her life.

"You told the police that you had seen someone – a man – in the woods behind your house? That Jacob had told you he'd seen a man back there at night, watching the house?"

How do you describe something like that? She saw something back there. It looked like a man…but the eyes – they were larger than the world. She had lost herself in them, in their crazed look, and all her memory seemed erased. She didn't know how to describe him. She didn't know how to explain the way his eyes seemed like swirling pools of yellow, and his open mouth like a cavern. She tried to rationalize it to herself, tell herself she was upset and making a monster out of a man, but she could never quite convince herself. Man or monster – what was the difference? Weren't we all just awful, godforsaken creatures anyway? She looked at her audience of cameramen and audio technicians and Sonya. Perhaps the halos and bright lights hid something darker. Demons were just fallen angels.

Of course, when Jacob told her of a man out at the edge of the woods walking back and forth like a zombie, she had dismissed it. How do you tell the world that sometimes, as a parent, you don't have the time or energy to entertain every thought or story a child blurts at you throughout the day?

"I thought it was a dream. Just imagination," Mary said. "I didn't think he was real."

"Do you mean when Jacob told you about him, or when you saw him yourself?"

Mary paused for a moment. "Maybe both."

"Do you think Jacob's disappearance is in any way connected with what happened to your husband on that hunting trip? With the disappearance of his friends, Michael and Conner Braddick?"

Mary shook her head slowly. "I don't see how Jonathan could have anything to do with it. He was gone. I don't know what happened up there, but he didn't take Jacob."

"What about the suspicious site found near the Aspetuck River Valley just this week? Police dogs traced your son to that location – what looks like a ritualistic site. A place your husband told them they would find. The body of his recently deceased friend was dug up just days before your husband's hunting trip and your son's disappearance. Doesn't all that seem a bit strange or suspicious to you?"

"I don't see how…"

"Is it possible your husband had something to do with the disappearance of Jacob?"

That fake little bitch was pushing hard now. Her questions came fast and with a twinge of anger. Or perhaps it was condescension. What did this reporter want her to say, anyway? That her husband had gone insane? That he was somehow responsible? Mary didn't know what happened in those mountains other than Jonathan's ravings. Perhaps that was what the audience wanted. They wanted her to fuel these strange conspiracy theories, the internet stories that talked about some strange cult and ritual human sacrifice, bloggers who posited Jonathan was a murderer of children. That Jonathan, Gene, Michael and Conner were all part of some satanic pact, that they had arranged it so that Jacob would be taken by others while they were in Coombs' Gulch, thereby removing all suspicion, that something had gone wrong between them and Jonathan had killed them both. The world thought he was mentally ill at best or a monster at worst.

But none of that was true. She knew that. She knew Jonathan. He had his faults, and things had been bad between them at the end. His drinking had grown out of hand. He was like a shadow that somehow crowded the house. He was angry over something. He seemed to harbor some kind of deep, dark sadness, which he never revealed – but she *knew* him. He was incapable of the things the world suggested. He could never hurt a child, much less his own. He loved Jacob as much as any decent father, maybe more. And he had loved her, too. She remembered their times together – dating, the wedding, their honeymoon, Jacob's birth. They were once happy and very much in love.

The image of the last time she saw Jonathan flashed through her mind: head down, woozy with drugs, dressed in a hospital gown and escorted by orderlies the size of linebackers. Something happened in those mountains. Perhaps she didn't know him anymore, and, in these last weeks as she faced the cold, lonely terror alone, she wondered if, perhaps, she had ever truly known him at all.

But that was not yet an admission she was willing to make.

Mary refused to sacrifice her history, everything she knew, by admitting on national television that she had no idea who her husband was, that he could very well be a killer and a monster. She would not let that pound of flesh be taken – not right now, and not by Sonya Martinez.

"No. There's no way. Jonathan was…" – Mary paused for a moment, her throat suddenly tightening – "…is…a good man."

★　　★　　★

The lights went off. The halos were gone. The angels disappeared and were replaced by mere mortal men and women. The crew started moving their gear, and the world went back to its dull colors, the facade of life. The pretty-but-not-too-pretty Sonya hugged her, but Mary could barely bring her arms around for an embrace before the reporter said a few hollow words and walked off into the darkness of the studio. Crewmen stripped Mary of the recording gear and led her out to the front offices and the glass doors that opened to the parking lot in front of the network branch office.

Detective Rick Gerrano met her at the doors and walked her to her car.

"How did it go?"

"Hard."

"I know," he said. "It'll air tonight, and we'll see what kind of response we get. This kind of publicity can bring people out of the woodwork. Get people talking. We just need to find a thread to follow."

"Like finding your way out of a labyrinth," she said.

"Kind of like that, yeah."

But the labyrinth was a trap; it was stalked by a monster.

Detective Gerrano shook her hand. His hands were cold from standing outside, and his grip was viselike, practiced with condemning the guilty. "We'll see what comes of it, and I'll be in touch," he said and then left.

Mary was alone again. She could hear the sound of the highway droning in the distance, beneath the gray, wintering sky, and in that moment she felt she was stuck in some kind of eternity, condemned to this lifelessness forever.

It was a forty-five-minute drive back to her house. She didn't want to go there. She dreaded it, in fact. But for now there was nowhere else to be, and she was told she should stay there on the off chance that Jacob returned or a phone call was placed by a witness or the person who took him.

The silence of being alone was awful, and she played the radio as she drove, occasional news reports buffering songs of love, life and loss that musicians tend to capture with two-line rhymes.

She stopped at the intersection where the bus had let Jacob off. She could see her house and driveway just through the small copse of trees, which were bare and gray in the cold. She wondered if this was all just some kind of dream from which she would wake, that it was an alternate reality to which she'd been transported in that moment when she stared into the woods behind her home and saw into the eyes of a stranger. If one thing – just one second – had been different that day, her life would be different; Jacob would be home. It wasn't fair that such horrid weight should hinge on one split second, one coincidence, one decision. That was an unfair burden of life, and it made her think that life was not what it seemed, that it was, in fact, some kind of false light, a holograph meant to tease, test and eventually destroy. But for what purpose, she did not know. *This can't be it. This can't be reality.* She wanted to tear through it as if it were a movie screen, but that was impossible. Everything was just too real – empty, hollow and real.

She was trapped here in this world, in this ungodly version of reality, this tragedy played out on a stage she could not leave.

She opened the door to the house, the culmination of her and Jonathan's life together, a place they had worked and saved for to raise a family and live a quiet life tucked into an average neighborhood. The scratches were still on the door, the five-finger grooves that sliced across the barrier between the outside world and what they had created inside. She stared at them for a minute. Something had tried to get inside, to get at her and Jacob. What was it? No one had an answer.

The silence overwhelmed her. Mary went inside, put her bag down and looked around the empty living room, the kitchen, the stairway to Jacob's bedroom. The afternoon seemed to stretch out long and terrible before her, and she realized she had nothing to do – nothing she could do – but sit in the awful silence.

The guilt and rage and regret built up inside – a ball in her gut that seemed to expand with every moment, with every second, in which her child was gone and her husband locked up and her life no longer her own. She didn't know what to do, and perhaps that was the worst thing of all.

Mary walked to the kitchen sink and peered out through the small window that looked on the sloping backyard and the trees beyond, the place where she had seen that stranger on the day Jacob disappeared.

She stared into those dead trees with their branches intersecting at angles, forming fractal patterns, one on top of the other, mesmerizing her as they reached farther and farther into the depths, beyond what she could see with her eyes. What was out there? Beyond what anyone could see? What hid just out of sight, behind the trees and in all the unknown dark spaces?

The woods seemed to rush up to her. The yard disappeared beneath it, until it swallowed the whole house. The neighborhood disappeared. The world grew dark, and she found herself alone in a cabin in the woods at night – the trees innumerable, the possibilities endless, the horror overwhelming. It was a dreamscape, as if she had suddenly plunged into a dream within a dream, or, perhaps, a nightmare. She wondered if in that moment she understood what Jonathan had seen on that trip, if the madness she saw out there had found its way inside, into their lives. She wondered if that was where Jacob was hidden, in that dark maze of forest and frozen ground and silence.

She thought she could see, at the edge of her vision, a small figure standing among the trees. She strained her eyes to see if it was him. She heard a whisper follow through the branches, carried on the wind, like the voice of a frightened child standing over his mother's bed in the night, whispering about monsters.

She reached out into the abyss, and something awful reached back.

EPILOGUE

I am being watched. I think, perhaps, since the first day of my life, but certainly since we buried Thomas Terrywile in Coombs' Gulch. And I am being watched by others. For a long time I was locked in a hospital where I was on 'suicide watch', and nurses, accompanied by big orderlies, would come to me with needles when I tried to tell them the truth. The injections made me dizzy and tired. I would sleep for days, drifting in and out of this world and finding myself back in the Gulch, seeing visions of Jacob trapped in the dark nothingness. In those long hours of unconsciousness, I relived my previous life, over and over again. I made different decisions; I walked various paths. But each time, I ended in the same place. Our lives are preordained nightmares. Our strings are attached to the puppeteers and cannot be cut. I would wake and try to tell them, tell them about Jacob, tell them about me, and each time it was another needle and a return to the darkness. I drifted in and out of alternate realities that all ended the same, and behind it I sensed the horrid truth.

I was watched by them for a long time until I finally learned to shut up and keep the truth to myself so they finally let me out.

Mary was gone by then. I tried to reach her, but she was gone from me, from everything, I suppose. I went to the house. The locks were changed, and it was empty. There was a For Sale sign in the front yard.

The police watched me for a long time. I would spot an inconspicuously dressed man or a dark-colored sedan behind me at various intervals, keeping track of where I went and what I did. They followed me when I drove out to that place in the forest where they had followed Jacob's scent to the very end. The design of rocks had been removed to discourage the curious public, but I found the spot and knew that I was in the right place. I could feel it. Standing there, I closed my eyes and felt close to it – to that place where my boy was trapped, to the demon-god that kept him there. I could practically see it, and in that moment I heard a distant whispering. Something in the trees urging me to action, to do something terrible.

Do you see?

I saw.

The police tail didn't last long. Jacob's case went cold for everyone but me. I think even Mary gave up after a couple of years. I would occasionally call her, but her voice was dead and distant. There was nothing between us anymore. Perhaps Jacob was all that really held us together – our tether – and once he was gone, Mary and I were connected by nothing more than an absence. Once, I tried to tell her what I knew, but she immediately launched into histrionics. She didn't want to hear it. It was insane, a product of a broken mind. "What were you doing out there in those mountains?" she asked once, but I did not have an answer that anyone wanted to hear or believe, so I said nothing.

But I understood what she was asking in that question: How was I connected to Jacob's disappearance? Did I do what everyone suspected, but could not prove? She once told a television reporter that I was a good man, that I had nothing to do with Jacob's disappearance. She had steeled herself, set her jaw and told the world that I could never do something like that. But the answer to Mary's question wasn't so simple. I *was* responsible. Looking back over all the difficulty I put my family through leading up to that awful day, I was responsible for so much. Sometimes, I felt I was partly responsible for every damn horrible thing that happened in the world. And maybe I was. Maybe we all are. Maybe that's why I can't look at anyone with a straight face.

Mary still does interviews every now and then, typically on the anniversary of Jacob's disappearance, which has some imaginary importance media outlets can make a headline out of – two years, five years, ten years.

A few years after I was released from the hospital, I found Rich, the old hunter I had once asked about the most dangerous animal to hunt. He lived in the same place and was very familiar with the circumstances and stories surrounding what had happened to me and Jacob. I looked ragged. I was practically homeless, sleeping in some no-name motel on my earnings as a line cook for a wedding hall, a place where young men and women start their lives together like gears being milled for work in an unknowable machine. Those days were filled with regret, the constant reminder of all I had lost. I looked on those couples and wondered what secrets they hid from each other that could eventually rise up and swallow them whole.

Rich answered the door and looked at me like he might kill me. I told him I wanted to hear more about the polar bears, about the white tundra of the North Pole, about what made him so uneasy hunting them.

"I didn't hunt them," he said, his voice insistent and animated. "I was a contractor for an oil company working in the Arctic Circle. My job was to keep the workers safe, keep the executives with their two-thousand-dollar parkas from being eaten by the wolves or the bears, or kicked to death by an angry mama moose. Even back then, white men couldn't hunt them. The Inuits had special laws that allowed polar bear hunting in particular seasons. But I was there to defend the bigwigs and employees from threats when they had to go on expeditionary excursions. Frankly, I didn't do much. I think they kept me around because it looked good, made a good story, made them feel like they were doing something to keep themselves safe up there. We lost more men to them getting drunk, wandering out into the tundra and freezing to death, than anything else. The six months of light and the six months of darkness threw a lot of them off, made them crazy, in a way. I was used to it. I had done military training stints up there. It's a different kind of place. It's like a world that functions according to a different set of rules – physics, maybe. Anyway, I didn't have any trouble. Didn't even get to shoot anything, just basically kept an eye on things from a distance. The animals didn't come close, really. But there was one time.

"We were going out to scout a new pipeline route. A real desolate area. Nothing but snow and hillocks and frozen tundra. We took a helicopter in. It was bright that day. The snow blinds you, so I had on goggles. They make everything look flat. You can't see the contours of the land. It's hard to distinguish what's alive and what isn't. I wasn't too concerned at first because nearly everything up there is cold and dead.

"But I could feel it almost as soon as we stepped off that helicopter. Something out there, something watching. The thing with polar bears is they rarely come across humans. They don't know to stay away. They don't distinguish between food sources up there. A human might as well be a seal who can't swim, and there we were, six fat seals all lined up like a buffet.

"You ever seen how polar bears hunt? They're patient. They wait and stalk for hours. And you can't see them out there in all that white. They'll sit dead motionless watching. They'll wait till the wind is kicking up snow like a blizzard so their movement is hidden. They'll be staring straight at you with those triangular heads just a few yards off, and you can't see them. But you can feel it sometimes. Maybe it's those leftover instincts from our caveman days. Anyway, we were no sooner on the ground than I could feel it. It was just us out there. Not another human soul for hundreds of miles, but I could feel something watching us. I glassed every bit of that tundra, couldn't see nothing. I kept the executives and engineers in a tight group and separated myself to draw whatever it was out toward me. I was carrying a .45-70. A close-up gun. A hundred yards at best. I knew anything out there would be up close, fast and personal.

"I was a few hundred yards from the group. I looked back and could see them in their little huddle against the wind, so many layers of clothing and gear they looked like a poor man's astronaut, that big whirlybird sitting on the snow with its blades bending toward the ground. Then I turned back, and in a rock outcropping I could make something out – an outline of white on white with a little black triangle of a nose, still as rock, pointing right at me. I put the binoculars up and looked. I knew what I was looking for, but he was still impossible to see. I didn't want to backtrack. I didn't want to turn my back. They run so fast. Fast enough to run up on a seal before it slips into the sea. I just stared at him, and he stared back at me. I was pretty sure I could make out those beady little eyes.

"I put that Remington up to my shoulder and sighted that black nose in as best I could. It was then I heard something on the wind. My name. Someone was screaming my name. I broke concentration for a second and turned to look over my left shoulder back toward the group, and it was then that I saw this massive white mass pounding across the snow toward me, flanking me. This big male was coming at me like a freight train. It was so fast. There was so much force behind it. For a moment I was completely stunned – literally immobile with fear and surprise. He was ten yards away when I got off my first shot. I didn't have time for a second. But I was lucky. A head shot. All fifteen hundred pounds of him came sliding up to my feet."

"They were hunting in pairs? I didn't think polar bears did that."

"They don't. There was no other bear. I was staring at the rock outcropping, thinking I saw something that wasn't there. I imagined it, made a bear out of some random rocks and snow, and the whole time that big bear was moving up on me from my left. It was like a trap. The glamour of the snow tricked me, lured me in with an illusion before he made his killing strike. The guys back at the helicopter saw him running me down, screamed my name. If the wind hadn't carried their voices, I probably would've never heard. It was a split-second shot. Pure luck, nothing else. Their heads are small, sleek. It was an impossible shot. Frankly, to this day, I wonder if that bear actually got me and everything else is just a dying dream. You know how they say your life flashes before your eyes just as you die? Everyone assumes it's the memories of the life you've lived that flashes in your mind. But what if your whole life flashes before your eyes? Not just the life we lived but the life we were going to live? Sometimes I wonder about that," he said. "What if all this" – he gestured around to the small, dilapidated house, his random collection of belongings, the world – "is just my life flashing before my eyes while that bear is tearing me apart?"

★   ★   ★

The following years, I wandered the deep forests, searching. I combed through hunting grounds during off season. I thought of those moments, those images of lost children captured on hunting cameras, glowing eerie and strange in the night, appearing out of nowhere in the middle of nowhere. I thought back to the visions I'd had of Thomas Terrywile, the moments he was given form and shape again to wander in the wilderness, the moments when he would see campers or a vacationing family and try to reach out to them. It was like he had no voice to speak. Or maybe it was the people who had no ears to hear or eyes to see. Maybe everyone was looking at something else.

But I knew what I was searching for. I knew I could see them, because I knew where to look. I knew how to look, because I had been there. I had seen that evil presence. I had seen the beyond. I had glimpsed the horror underlying it all.

I wandered the hills, the mountains, everywhere for years, and I came to understand Rich's experience in the tundra as much as I understood my own experience in the mountains. I was being watched, followed, tricked into looking at one thing while being savaged by another. The police were long gone. They could never be bothered to follow me out so deep into the wilderness, so far away. But there were others watching me in those deep forests, when I would spend days and nights surrounded by nothing but mountains and the maze of trees.

I would see them every once in a while, looking at me from a distance. Or their faces might appear from behind a tree. Michael, Conner and Gene waited for me out there, their faces distorted, their bodies moved by some unseen force. They were both dead and alive. Perhaps they were dead in this life but alive in another. Perhaps their corporeal forms were possessed with that cold blackness of the netherworld, forced to wander the world and do its bidding. I could feel that darkness in myself, as well. A core of cold that spread through my veins and grew like a cancer, changing me, influencing me, corrupting my thoughts. As I camped in the wilderness at night Michael, Conner and Gene would whisper to me, sitting just outside my tent, their strange voices penetrating the thin fabric and boring into my mind. Four friends brought together again. They told me what I must do. How I could win back my boy, my Jacob, and somehow make everything right again. Perhaps I had flashed forward, like Rich said. Perhaps this was all just a dying dream and I needed to wake.

I could hear them walk through the trees around my campsite. They would move things and sometimes take them in the middle of the night. They gave offerings at times, dead animals, whose carcasses would lie at the entrance to my tent. Offerings, trades; I knew what they wanted.

I found the perfect spot in the Appalachians, just beyond a small hunting town in Maine. It was a clearing in a sycamore forest, where the trees seemed to part in a natural circle and left the ground bare. I knew it was the right place because I saw, just for a moment, Jacob standing there in the center of it, staring at me with a quiet, pleading fear on his face, dressed in little boy clothes – the same outfit he wore when Mary sent him to school that day. He hadn't aged a day. I looked like a crazed and ragged vagrant who'd been sleeping in the woods for weeks, but he recognized me. Then he was gone like a ghost or hallucination. I vomited right then out of shock and longing. I wished I could switch places with him. I would happily give my life for his. I walked into the center of that clearing, fell to my knees and felt his presence, as if he were standing just over my shoulder where I could not see him. I turned around and around, but he was always just out of sight.

I snatched six-year-old Ryan Temple from the edge of a soccer field while his family watched his older brother play a heated match against a rival town. I hadn't made much of a plan, but everything just fell into place. I knew from the whispers outside my tent that I should be there, hidden in the bushes at the far edge of the field, which fell toward a brook and a small wood, a tentacle from the large forest beyond where my stone altar waited amid the sycamores. Ryan was a good-looking boy, skinny with a mop of hair, which seems to be the style for children these days. He was dressed well and had big brown eyes that sparkled with curiosity as he wandered along the wooded edge of the sports field.

He just disappeared from the world and into my arms. His parents were distracted. Everyone was looking away at just the perfect moment. Maybe they were watching the game. Maybe they were lost in the eyes of the strange-looking figure stalking near the parking lot on the opposite side of the field from me. Maybe they were wondering what such a horrid man was doing near their children, near a place where wholesome families gathered to reaffirm their lives were worth living, trying to create purpose in small, meaningless games. Ryan was drawn over to the far edge of the field by a moment of curiosity, sparked by something he perhaps saw or heard. I don't know. But there he was, and I took him; no one knew better until we were far, far away.

It wasn't easy. In fact, it was the hardest thing I've done in my entire life. The burgeoning horror of my actions was second only to the moment years ago when I knew my son was lost. The boy struggled against me, squirmed and cried. I felt sorry for him, but then all I could think of was Jacob's horror at being taken that day, of Jacob's cold terror, trapped in the eternal darkness, a plaything for this demon-god that now awaited my offering.

Do you see?

Yes, I saw. I saw what needed to be done. There was little that could possibly make my life worse but maybe one thing that could make Jacob's better – even if it meant damning myself forever.

It was dark when I reached the clearing with my offering in tow, but the white stones I dug from the surrounding hills glowed in their occult pattern. At the edge of their soft light, I could see Conner, Michael and Gene and make out the strange symbols they had carved into the trees. They stood in a perfect triangular formation at the outer ring, their ghoulish countenances looking on. They seemed completely devoid of life, but there was some kind of eagerness emanating from their broken forms.

The child struggled and screamed. I clamped my dirty hand over his mouth. I stepped across the threshold of the circle and brought the poor, trembling boy to the center. Conner, Michael and Gene, my oldest friends, began to give up some awful chant; their mouths did not move, but the sound came – a summoning in half-formed words that I did not understand.

The rocks, the trees, the stars and the earth seemed to swirl around us in that moment. The glow of the stones grew more intense. The disembodied chants grew louder till they filled the air with their vibrations.

I put the boy on his feet in front of me and stood over him, holding him in place with my hands on his shoulders.

And I, in turn, could suddenly feel something standing over me, something familiar breathing down my neck with a sickening chuff.

The boy cried, but I held him there, waiting to see Jacob, waiting for him to suddenly appear and come back to me, and for this poor child to be relegated to that cold, dark place. It was an even trade. Sometimes we have to do awful things. I knew in my mind this was wrong, perhaps the most wrong thing I'd ever done. But there was Jacob. There was my boy trapped in that world, tortured and alone. I made my choice long ago when we buried Thomas Terrywile in Coombs' Gulch and kept it secret to save my own skin.

A heavy, clawed hand clasped my shoulder. A shiver of knives traced down my spine. That terrified little boy looked up at me. His wide eyes glowed in the moonlight.

I am not a good man.

ACKNOWLEDGMENTS

I would first like to thank Don D'Auria and the whole team at Flame Tree Press for seeing the potential in this novel and for all their hard work, making it the best it could be. It was an honor to be able to work with them and I'm grateful for the opportunity.

I wrote this novel during a very difficult time of my life and I'd like to thank the people who helped see me through those very tough times, starting with my parents, who have always supported me even if they wished I wrote in a different genre. Thank you to Laura for giving me a place to live and being a great friend; thank you to Stephen, who helped keep me on the right path; thank you to Carla and Kim for your friendship and support; to J.B. and Stephanie for helping me during some low times; to all my work colleagues who kept pushing me (and paying me, thank God) and to S.H. for helping me believe in myself again.

Lastly, I want to thank my four beautiful children without whom I would surely be lost.

FLAME TREE PRESS
FICTION WITHOUT FRONTIERS
Award-Winning Authors & Original Voices

Flame Tree Press is the trade fiction imprint of Flame Tree Publishing, focusing on excellent writing in horror and the supernatural, crime and mystery, science fiction and fantasy. Our aim is to explore beyond the boundaries of the everyday, with tales from both award-winning authors and original voices.

*

Other horror titles available include:
Snowball by Gregory Bastianelli
Thirteen Days by Sunset Beach by Ramsey Campbell
Think Yourself Lucky by Ramsey Campbell
The Hungry Moon by Ramsey Campbell
The Influence by Ramsey Campbell
The Wise Friend by Ramsey Campbell
The Haunting of Henderson Close by Catherine Cavendish
The Garden of Bewitchment by Catherine Cavendish
The House by the Cemetery by John Everson
The Devil's Equinox by John Everson
Hellrider by JG Faherty
The Toy Thief by D.W. Gillespie
One By One by D.W. Gillespie
Black Wings by Megan Hart
The Playing Card Killer by Russell James
The Siren and the Specter by Jonathan Janz
The Sorrows by Jonathan Janz
Castle of Sorrows by Jonathan Janz
The Dark Game by Jonathan Janz
Will Haunt You by Brian Kirk
We Are Monsters by Brian Kirk
Hearthstone Cottage by Frazer Lee
Those Who Came Before by J.H. Moncrieff
Stoker's Wilde by Steven Hopstaken & Melissa Prusi
Creature by Hunter Shea
Ghost Mine by Hunter Shea
Slash by Hunter Shea
The Mouth of the Dark by Tim Waggoner
They Kill by Tim Waggoner
The Forever House by Tim Waggoner

*

Join our mailing list for free short stories, new release details, news about our authors and special promotions:

flametreepress.com